He'd tried to prepare her for this emergency

During one emotionally charged afternoon in her kitchen, he'd taught her exactly what to do. But that afternoon was more like a dream, and now she was faced with the reality. Nothing had prepared her for this.

She looked around wildly for help, knowing there was none, knowing there was no one but her.

She didn't know she was crying until her nose began to run, and then she sniffed and whispered tensely, "Cam—don't you die. Don't you dare die." She drew a shaky hand across her eyes and wiped her cheeks on the sleeve of her T-shirt. Except for the labored contractions of his chest, Cam didn't move.

ABOUT THE AUTHOR

Kathleen Carrol has always written—poems when she was nine, short stories in her adolescence. It wasn't until twenty years later, though, after an injury, that she began to read romance novels, and it was an immediate love affair. Kathleen likes to write about people with a touch of the wild and untamed in them, the spirit of the pioneers and adventurers—people like Suzanna and Cam of *Angel's Walk*. Also writing under the name of Kathleen Creighton, she makes her home in California with her husband and family.

Angel's Walk

KATHLEEN CARROL

Harlequin Books

TORONTO • NEW YORK • LONDON
AMSTERDAM • PARIS • SYDNEY • HAMBURG
STOCKHOLM • ATHENS • TOKYO • MILAN

For those who loved the big old house...
In memory it's always summer.

Published May 1986

First printing March 1986

ISBN 0-373-16151-4

Chapter One

The ring of the little brass bell hanging on the door ought to have warned Suzanna Day that the Kern River Valley Historical Society museum had an early visitor. The sound might have alerted her if she had been within light-years of the museum. But she was at that moment far, far away— in the nineteenth century, to be exact.

Suzanna was reading a love letter. It was from a slender, ribbon-tied packet that was part of a trunkful of memorabilia bequeathed to the society by a distant cousin of Suzanna's. The letter was from one Herbert W. Potter, written to his young wife Isabelle not long before he succumbed to malaria in the Philippines, during the Spanish-American War. It began sedately: "Dear Mrs. Potter." And then, as if the emotions that were filling his heart had burst the bonds of propriety, the author continued:

My dearest, beloved Isabelle, how I do long to see your face again. There is not much to be found here in the way of tenderness and beauty, though I will not offend your gentle sensibilities or would wish to cause you concern by describing the day-to-day existence of so many men so far from home and in such a state. The very air oppresses. Not a night passes but that I

dream of you and of lying with you in the garden
when the air is cool and smells of lilacs....

Suzanna was weeping unashamedly, taking care not to
drip on the faded brown ink. She gave a loud sniffle that
was only partly stifled by the damp tissue ball she held
pressed to her nose and started violently when a deep
masculine voice immediately responded, "Hello, is anyone here?"

Thus rudely returned to the present, Suzanna hurriedly
dried her face and began to reassemble the pages scattered
across her lap. With a voice only slightly huskier than
normal, she replied, "I'll be right with you. Please feel free
to look around."

She was quite invisible to the visitor. She wasn't entirely
sure how she had come to be sitting on the floor behind her
desk—half under it, in fact. It was just that she found it
impossible to sit in a chair for any length of time and
sooner or later always seemed to find herself in a more
comfortable position cross-legged on the floor. While engrossed in Isabelle Potter's letter, she had naturally gravi-
tated toward seclusion. Now she was mildly surprised to
find herself sharing the knee space under her big, old oak
desk with a wastebasket and an old pair of shoes.

Suzanna was even more startled to look up and find a
sun-bronzed face inverted just a few inches from her own.
Eyes of a rather ambiguous color stared into hers. It was
difficult to tell very much about the upside-down face except that it was deeply tanned—even weathered—and there
were paler lines radiating from the corners of the eyes. The
eyebrows were golden against that dark skin. And oh, the
hair! Now that she had torn her gaze away from those eyes,
she could see that the hair was an astonishing red-gold, the
color of firelight on polished copper.

The upside-down mouth opened to reveal strong, even teeth. "Hello there," the deep voice said softly. "Is there some reason why you're hiding under your desk, or are you just naturally shy?"

"I'm not hiding," Suzanna said, a little affronted.

"Shy, then." The smile softened, deepening the eye creases. "You can come on out—I don't bite."

"I'm not shy."

The burnished eyebrows shot up. Or was it down? A hand appeared, hovered a moment, and then a finger brushed moisture from her cheek. "I'm truly sorry." The smile had completely disappeared. "I see I've come at a bad time."

Suzanna opened her mouth, wondering why her voice had temporarily deserted her. In its absence all she could do was stare into those puzzling eyes and swallow hard. And then, suddenly conscious of her ridiculous position, she gave herself a little shake and said quickly, "Oh, no. It's all right, really. I'm sorry—is it ten o'clock already?" She glanced unseeingly at her watch and would have scrambled out of her hole except that the visitor's face was still filling part of it. He seemed to be sprawled across her desk and was showing no inclination to move.

The hand that had touched her face moved, turning to display a large, serviceable-looking watch in front of her eyes. "Ten minutes past," the voice informed her. The fingers hovered again, this time touching the tip of her nose and then each still-damp crescent of eyelashes.

"Why were you crying?"

It was a presumptuous question for a stranger to ask, made even more intimate by his nearness and the almost caressing tone in which he asked it. It seemed almost as if he were sharing her cozy cubbyhole, and she was surprised to hear herself answer in the same kind of throaty murmur, "I was reading a letter...."

"Letter?"

"A love letter."

"Yours?"

Suzanna smiled for the first time, wistfully. "No one writes letters anymore, do they? No, this was from another time, another century."

"I'm glad."

Suzanna blinked. "I beg your pardon?"

"I'm glad it wasn't your letter." The eyes were crinkling again, and the softness had gone from both voice and smile. The face disappeared momentarily and then reappeared, attached to a broad-shouldered, deep-chested male body. The stranger now squatted before her, one arm resting across his knee, the other braced against the desktop just above her head.

And now that she was seeing him right side up and all in one piece, Suzanna did feel shy. She saw a face that was devastatingly attractive without being especially handsome: a high, sculptured forehead, deep-set eyes of still-undetermined color and a straight, high-bridged nose like those found on certain old coins. The mouth was sensuous but firm and masculine. It was a nice mouth with a smile that was both assured and irresistible. The body was hard and brawny, with flexed thigh muscles straining the fabric of faded jeans and a soft nest of golden brown curls showing in the open neck of a khaki shirt. He was, in fact, just the kind of brash, charming, overwhelmingly masculine man that had always made Suzanna feel intimidated. She was completely out of her depth with this man, and she knew it. She could feel her natural poise evaporate, leaving her embarrassed and flustered.

"Hey, I thought you said you weren't shy," the man said, touching her cheek with the backs of the fingers of one hand.

"I'm not," Suzanna asserted, refusing to drop her eyes. "Just embarrassed to death. This is a very silly position to be caught in. I think I'm entitled to blush."

"Oh, I don't know. I don't think I've ever held a conversation with a beautiful woman under a desk before, but it's not silly. A novelty, maybe, but hey, you can come out if it's making you uncomfortable."

"No, I can't," Suzanna pointed out rather breathlessly. "You're in my way."

"Oh, I guess I am at that. Here—" He took her firmly by the elbows and drew her to her feet, then held her steady while she brushed and shook the long skirt of her yellow calico pinafore down around her ankles. His hands fit warmly over the rounds of her shoulders.

"Thank you," she murmured, the breathlessness even more evident. She shook back the thick, taffy-colored hair that had fallen forward over her shoulders, and lifted her chin, forcing herself to meet the man's admiring gaze with one that was cool and businesslike. "Is there something I can help you find? Did you come with a specific question or just to learn some of our local history? We have several rather good books on local history if you—"

"Actually," the man said with an odd tinge of regret, "I'm looking for a Miss Suzanna Day. Is she in today?" He reached into the pocket of his shirt and took out a piece of paper, consulted it unnecessarily and held it out to her. She ignored it, too surprised to even take a look.

"I'm Suzanna Day," she said, puzzled.

It was the stranger's turn to look startled. He shook his head and asked incredulously, "*You're* Tony O'Brian's wife's cousin? The one with the big old house? Lives with an old—a schoolteacher? Rents rooms?"

"Well," Suzanna said with an uncharacteristic touch of asperity, "you seem to know quite a lot about me." It was upsetting to think that this strange man had been discussing her with members of her own family and even more unsettling to realize that for Tony to have mentioned her name to a stranger at all, he would have to trust him. Keeping that thought firmly in mind, she curbed her irritation and asked politely, "How may I help you?"

The man was still staring at her in a way that was making her very uncomfortable. A thought struck her. Could Tony and Meg possibly be matchmaking again? It wouldn't be the first time a well-meaning member of her large and loving family had tried to set her up with someone. But no, surely not. They all knew her much too well to ever imagine she could be interested in someone like this supermacho jock!

The stranger seemed to collect himself, though he didn't abandon his embarrassingly thorough appraisal. "I'm sorry," he said, shaking his head again. "I just didn't expect you."

"Well, you asked for Suzanna Day. *I'm* Suzanna Day. Is there something I can do for you?"

The man's lips curved in a slow smile, and he murmured, "I sure hope so. Oh, I do hope so."

"I beg your pardon?"

He laughed out loud, a sound of such lighthearted good humor that Suzanna had to struggle to reinforce her defenses. He seemed almost like two people; just when she was developing a good solid distrust of all the high-voltage charisma, he'd hit some kind of dimmer switch. Now his smile was soft, not suggestive, and his voice was as gentle as it had been when he'd asked about her tears.

"I'm sorry. I came expecting an old schoolmarm smelling of lavender, and instead I've found Alice in Wonderland."

There was a little silence. And then, as he seemed about to touch her again, Suzanna retreated behind a counter and became very busy straightening piles of brochures. The stranger followed, leaning his elbows on the counter.

"I think I'd better explain," he said gently, still smiling. "Your cousin Tony O'Brian sent me. He said you might have rooms for rent."

The last was a question. "I'm sorry," Suzanna said without stopping what she was doing. "You've been misinformed. I have no rooms for rent."

"Oh, come on," the man said with an engaging smile. "Tony said you had half a dozen empties. All I need is one."

Suzanna fixed him with a cold stare. "Contrary to what you may have been told, my *home*," she said with deliberate emphasis, "is not a rooming house."

"Ah, but you do sometimes rent rooms. Tony told me so. In fact, you have an old schoolteacher living there now, haven't you?"

"Mrs. Hopewell," Suzanna informed him frigidly, "is retired, not old. And yes, I do sometimes rent rooms. And no, I do not have any available at this time."

"I see." There was a pause. "Look, Sue." She stiffened at the unauthorized use of her first name, a nickname no one ever used. His hand moved unhurriedly, closing over hers and pinning it on top of a pile of pamphlets describing a nature walk through a wildlife preserve. "Sue, have you ever lived in a motel for any length of time? I'm going to be here awhile. I don't know how long, but it's too damn long to stay in a motel."

His smile had vanished, and his eyes had an unexpected appeal. She shook her head slowly, transfixed against her will.

"Look, my credentials are good. I even have references. Your cousin Tony'll vouch for me. I'm with the Corps of Engineers. I'll be working with Tony at the dam." The smile was back, radiating charm that could be measured in megawatts. "I'm just a harmless civil servant, swear to God!"

Suzanna opened her mouth and looked down at the hand that covered hers. It was warm and brown and dusted with golden hairs. A small white scar angled across one knuckle. Her heart, she suddenly realized, was pounding inside her chest.

"I'm sorry, but I just don't—" she began with determination, and was interrupted by the sound of the entrance bell. She cleared her throat, murmured, "Excuse me," and gratefully withdrew her hand, hurrying to greet the newcomers, a middle-aged couple in Bermuda shorts.

While she guided the couple around the museum with what was probably a little more than her customary enthusiasm, her eyes kept straying to the golden-haired man as he wandered among the displays, his thumbs hooked in his back pockets. She stayed with the tourists as long as she possibly could, fully aware that she was using them for protection against him. She never had been equipped to deal with his type of man and never would be.

His type. In high school that would have meant the campus big shot—the football star, the escort of cheerleaders and prom queens, the type girls like Suzanna got terrible, unrequited crushes on. The type who never noticed that she was alive, which was probably just as well, because if one of them *had* noticed she was alive, she would probably have expired from shyness. She'd have been tongue-tied, red faced and sweaty palmed, just as she was right now.

Suzanna really wasn't shy. She'd grown up in this valley in the southern Sierra Nevadas a member of one of the first families to settle permanently in the valley, turning to cattle and hay raising after the gold fever had cooled. It was a large, loving and well-respected family. She had been taught from infancy to walk tall, speak clearly and look people in the eye. She had sung solos in church since the age of five and could, if called upon to do so, speak with poise and grace in front of any group of people. She enjoyed and got along well with people, especially the very old and the very young. But there was an element of natural reserve in Suzanna that made it hard for her to form deep friendships. She had always received all the love and emotional support she needed from her family.

In a quiet way, Suzanna had been popular in school. She'd managed to get good grades consistently without making an issue of it and always took part in a wide variety of extracurricular activities. She had never dated much, though she had been comfortable enough with boys she could call friends—the class clowns, the brains, the ones people now seemed to call "nerds." Some of her best friends, she recalled wryly, had been nerds.

Just as long as they touched no chord of excitement in her, as long as there was no trace at all of that pulse-quickening awareness of boy-girl differences, she was fine. But there was that particular kind of boy whose glance was too knowing, whose stance was too suggestive, whose whole being radiated sexual awareness. Sometimes they were sullen and smoldering, with an aura of wildness and danger; sometimes they were brash and outgoing and full of effortless charm. The effect they had on Suzanna was always the same: they made her cruelly aware of her inadequacies.

Oh, she knew very well that she would never be beautiful. She supposed she might be called attractive, but she was so hopelessly average. She had medium-brown hair and quite ordinary blue eyes, unremarkable features and complexion. Her body was average, too, both in size and structure—completely unspectacular. She wasn't, and never would be, the kind of woman "his type" was interested in. She had a reasonably healthy sense of humor but lacked the capacity for the kind of light, frivolous verbal games "his type" seemed to initiate. She was no good at parties or small talk or casual flirtation. She wasn't, she acknowledged with a sigh, *sexy*.

Now, watching the bright-haired stranger prowl her quiet world with that slightly rolling gait very physical men so often seem to have, she was reminded that everything she hadn't been at seventeen she still wasn't at twenty-seven.

So why in the world was this man wasting his charm on her?

The door closed behind her tourists. Suzanna retreated once more behind the counter and watched with a curious mixture of apprehension and amusement as he strolled toward her. It struck her suddenly that with his bright hair he looked like a male bird displaying plumage. And that, she realized, was probably the answer to her question. He was male; she was female. Flirting was just an automatic, instinctive action on his part. He probably would have behaved the same way even if she'd turned out to be the old schoolteacher he'd expected to find.

That knowledge was unexpectedly depressing, but it did help to restore her poise. She felt quite calm now. Politely, even kindly, she said, "I'm sorry. I mustn't keep you waiting any longer. I don't envy you, living in a motel, but I'm afraid I can't rent you a room. I'm truly sorry; it's just not possible." She gave him a courteous smile.

He cocked his head and made a disappointed clicking sound with his tongue. "Your final word?"

"I'm afraid so. I do hope you enjoy your stay here in the valley, Mr., um... Please feel free to look around. I really must get back to work."

Frowning, he patted the pockets of his shirt, then took his wallet out of a hip pocket and extracted a business card, which he extended toward Suzanna. "Me, too," he said with a rueful smile. "It was nice meeting you, Suzanna Day." His eyes held hers for a moment, and she could almost believe he meant it. He seemed about to offer her his hand but changed his mind and touched his temple in a kind of salute instead. "Very nice." He turned and strode quickly to the door.

"Uh, nice meeting you, too, Mr.—" She glanced down at the card in her hand and hastily added, "Harris." But the door had already closed, the tinkling of the bell concluding the whole unsettling episode.

JOHN CAMPBELL HARRIS, known to most people as Cam, leaned on the steering wheel of the green four by four he'd requisitioned from corps headquarters. He looked at the long, low, multidoored wing of his motel, fingering the plastic rectangle attached to his door key. They all looked alike, these motels in out-of-the-way places.

He sighed and got out of the pickup. The initial thrill of excitement he'd felt facing this newest challenge had receded. Now he was merely hot and tired and looking forward to a shower. Flinging his denim jacket over one shoulder, he stepped over the log that separated his parking spot from his door and fitted the key into the lock. He opened the door cautiously a few inches, then stuck his head through and peered into the dimness. "Hey, Cat?" he called softly.

There was a small purr in reply, and a lumpy shadow on the foot of the bed stirred, one front paw shooting out in a brief stretch. A slender gray cat uncoiled itself and jumped to the floor with a faint thud. Cam slipped into the room and closed the door behind him, tossing the key onto the dresser and the jacket onto a chair. The cat was now arching ecstatically across his pant leg, and he stopped to fondle the dainty triangular head. The cat pushed against his hand, touching his palm with her cold wet nose, and then leaped back up onto the bed, posing gracefully and blinking at him, her expression one of extreme patience.

"All right, don't nag," Cam said aloud, unzipping the large canvas tote bag he'd used to smuggle her into this room the night before. He took out a small can of cat food and an opener and kicked the bag back behind a chair. He performed the necessary maneuvers required to open the can under the cat's critical gaze, then stirred the contents with a forefinger and set it on the floor. The cat looked unimpressed, dropped daintily to the floor and approached the can with unhurried dignity, pausing to rub perfunctorily against Cam's shins before settling herself down to dinner.

Cam hauled his shirt up his back and over his head on the way into the bathroom and in a few seconds was cooling himself thankfully under a stinging, tepid spray. When Cam came out of the bathroom, the cat was sitting on the dresser in front of the mirror, washing. Cam paused in the act of vigorously towel drying his hair and said aloud, "Now, who are *you* primping for? You got plans for the evening I don't know about?" The cat replied with one of her interrogative chirrups, and Cam crossed to the bed, piled both pillows against the headboard and lay down naked on the spread. He gave a massive sigh and closed his eyes, lacing his fingers behind his head. Silence settled over the room, broken only by the soft sounds of the cat's grooming.

"Cat," he said softly, "this is going to be a bad one. There's only one way to solve this mess, and people are going to get hurt." The cat didn't reply, and after a moment he went on, his voice a dry murmur. "You know, I think—" He stopped suddenly. "I'm going nuts, talking to a *cat*." He stretched out an arm to touch the button on his tape deck and then relaxed, listening to Bruce Springsteen sing about fast cars, lonely roads and dusty blue-collar towns.

I think I've spent too many nights in too many hotel rooms in too many Podunk towns looking for solutions to other people's screwups, hurting people I've never met and will never see again.

Lord, he was tired of motel rooms! With his eyes closed, he tried to remember the subject of the pictures on the wall, the color of the curtains, the bedspread. Burnt orange, with bullfighters? He opened his eyes. Wrong. Brown plaid, with bucking broncos.

Empty rooms, standard fixtures, sanitized toilets, hard, empty beds. Not that his bed had to stay empty any longer than he wanted it to, he acknowledged somewhat smugly. There seemed to be plenty of action in town, judging from the noise he'd heard coming from that honky-tonk just down the road last night. And this was Friday. In a few hours the local clientele would be augmented by the weekend horde of tourists from L.A., including lots of tanned and tawny ladies ripe for the illusory freedom of a weekend fling. They'd be wearing short cutoff jeans and tank tops with no bras. They'd be eager, attractive and *very* energetic. Their flesh would be firm and sun-warm and taste of salt. He closed his eyes and tried to imagine one in the curve of each arm, pressed hard against his body, and when the fantasy failed to produce even the faintest tingle in his loins, he made a disgusted noise and swung his feet to the floor. He stabbed at his tape player, cutting off the too-lonely wail of a saxophone, and reached for his clothes.

When he was dressed, he reached for the telephone and dialed the corps headquarters number.

"Get me Tony," he said tersely to the girl who answered. "This is Harris." After a brief wait he responded, "Yeah, Tony—Cam here. Listen, I've been going over those stress-test figures. I'll need to take a look at some core samples, but I believe that spillway can come up a good six feet." He listened, tightening his jaw against the entreaty in the park manager's voice. "Yeah, well, somebody usually does get hurt in a situation like this. But you tell me how I can balance a few marinas and some farmland against a whole city! Most of the land we'd flood is designated parkland, anyway. Those people knew the risk when they built there.... Yeah, I'll have the final plans ready by Monday. I know it's moving fast. The fact is, we haven't got a lot of time here, Tony. At the rate that snowpack is melting, I figure Memorial Day is probably our deadline. And if we should get a worst-case scenario—that's right. The worst thing that could happen would be for a tropical storm to hunker down off Baja California and dump a warm rain on top of that snow. Yeah, in the millions, at least. Okay, see you Monday. Oh, hold on a minute." He reached into his pocket for a pencil and drew a piece of motel stationery toward him.

"Listen, can you give me directions to your cousin's place? Yeah, that's right—I missed her at the museum. Okay, got it. Thanks. Yes, I hope so, too. I've had all I want of this damned motel!"

Chapter Two

Suzanna spent a terrible day replaying scenes of her encounter with the man from the Corps of Engineers. John Harris—that was his name.

John. She found it unexpectedly difficult to think of him as John; the name seemed too familiar, too intimate, at least when applied to such an unabashedly sexy man. Why hadn't she ever noticed the way that name issued from the mouth like a sigh? It seemed safer, somehow, just to keep thinking of him as Mr. Harris.

Though why she should keep thinking of him at all was beyond her! The episode was over and done with. Unless her cousins were doing this deliberately, she was unlikely ever to see the man again. And although Meg and Tony had been known to meddle in her love life, for them to send a man like John Harris to her for a room was so unthinkable it was almost funny! Imagine having him living under the same roof, day in and day out, sharing bathrooms, meals... No, it was quite out of the question, even if it were not impossible at the moment, anyway. Suzanna smiled wryly to herself and shook her head. The way things were at Angel's Walk right now, she couldn't rent a room to Mother Teresa!

The front doorbell rang again. It had been doing so with regularity all afternoon; with the weather so fine and the lake so high, the tourist season was off to an early start. Ordinarily, Suzanna would have been delighted. There was nothing she enjoyed any more than helping acquaint people with the Kern River Valley's colorful history, from the peaceful days of the Tubatulabul Indians through the uproarious gold rush era, when the town had been known as Whiskey Flat. Suzanna had grown up listening to tales of the pioneers and settlers, the outlaws and ranchers, who had left their marks on the valley. But today she was preoccupied, and the eager tourists were just so many unwelcome distractions. And now here was someone new, and it was almost three o'clock. Oh, she hoped it wouldn't be someone wanting to linger and chat.

But as she looked up to greet the newcomer, her pleasantly interrogative expression relaxed into a warm smile. "Oh, Ron. Thank goodness it's only you. We've been so busy today."

"So have we, and I love it. And what d'ya mean—it's only me!" He bent to kiss her cheek and then settled himself on the corner of her desk, restlessly jingling things in his pockets and looking at her in that proprietary way Suzanna was beginning to find so irritating.

Ron Weed was a local businessman and took great care to look the part. His crisp brown hair, though thinning on top, was cut short and brushed until it gleamed. His slightly puffy jaws were always smooth shaven and redolent of expensive after-shave. Suzanna had known him most of her life and couldn't recall ever having seen him without a long-sleeved Western shirt, Western dress slacks and a hand-tooled belt and matching cowboy boots. He had been honorary mayor of Whiskey Flat during the annual Gold Rush Days celebration and was currently president of the chamber of commerce. He owned several businesses around the valley, all of them dependent on the tourist trade. He played golf on Tuesdays with the pastor of the Methodist church, who had never quite given up hope of getting him to church on Sundays. On Fridays he went to Rotary. And on Saturday evenings he took Suzanna out to dinner.

Ron was just enough older than Suzanna that she hadn't been really aware of him in high school. She hadn't ever had any reason to be aware of him; in some ways he had been her own counterpart. But he had gone into his father's boat dealership upon graduation and had revealed a latent business sense, expanding the business over the years to include several marinas and a sporting goods store/gas station/coffee shop complex—sort of a sportsman's one-stop—at a key valley crossroads. Ron Weed had a talent for knowing just where and when to move, and more important, whom to move on.

Suzanna had suspected for some time now that he intended to make his next move on *her*. It didn't particularly worry her. She knew Ron wasn't motivated by any overwhelming passion for her; she knew how his mind worked. He had reached the age of thirty; he was wealthy and respected, a solid citizen of his community. It was time to get married and produce someone to pass it all on to. And who was more deserving of the honor of becoming Mrs. Weed than a rather drab but very respectable member of one of the community's oldest families?

In spite of all this, Suzanna rather enjoyed Ron's attentions. It was comfortable being with someone so completely predictable. She had no illusions about his feelings for her, and so she always knew exactly where she stood. And of course, being linked with him protected her from other local suitors. It wasn't that she had any objection to marriage, or to men in general. But not counting the tourists, newcomers to the valley tended to fall into three categories: family men looking for a wholesome atmosphere in which to raise their families; retired couples looking for cheap land on which to raise a few vegetables and perhaps an animal or two; and people looking for an out-of-the-way place in which to hide. And the local men, those still unattached, were like Ron—dull, predictable, nice but unexciting. They would probably make good reliable husbands and fathers, but Suzanna couldn't help but feel that there ought to be something more.

"I'm always glad to see you, Ron; you know that," Suzanna said now, and meant it. She watched him pick up the bundle of Isabelle Potter's love letters, glance at it without interest and toss it back onto her desk.

"Just stopped by to see about tonight," he said briskly. "Pick you up at seven?"

"That will be fine," she murmured, hiding a smile. As if he ever picked her up at any other time.

"Good, good." Ron slapped his thigh once and stood up, but Suzanna noticed that he seemed uncharacteristically preoccupied. A tiny frown made a sharp crease between his eyes.

"You look very somber tonight," she observed. "Is something wrong? We can make it another night, Ron, if there's a problem; you know I don't mind."

"Ah, hell no, Suzanna. I wouldn't miss our Saturday nights for the world. No, I was just down looking at the water going over the dam, and I don't mind telling you, it's got me a little bit concerned. Have you seen it yet?"

Suzanna shook her head, swallowing the brassy taste of dread that always rose in her throat whenever she allowed herself to think about the water level in the lake. Ron went blithely on. "You ought to see it; you really should. Quite a show. Probably the only chance any of us'll ever have to see it. A once-in-a-lifetime thing, for sure. You know, it's got to be a good ten or twenty inches over the spillway. And just lookin' at the water coming down the north fork alone, I'd say it's still got a long way to go before it peaks. They say Bakersfield is in real danger of being flooded. Did you know that?'' Again, Suzanna shook her head. It wasn't necessary to do much talking with Ron. ''Yeah, I heard they were bringing in the Corps of Engineers— they're the ones that built the dam in the first place—to figure out what to do about it. Sure hope they come up with something pretty quick. You know, my marina over in Paradise Cove is almost out of room. Hey, tell you what. Tomorrow after church what do you say I pick you up and we'll drive down to the dam? You should see it, Suzanna; you really should.''

Suzanna looked at him with mild surprise. It was the first time he'd suggested an outing beyond their regular Saturday nights. She wondered if this meant a shift in gears in their relationship. She didn't know whether she was really ready for that.

After Ron had gone, Suzanna moved through the museum, closing up shop, her mind only marginally on her task. She was conscious of vague feelings of restlessness and unease, feelings so unfamiliar to her she hardly recognized them. What was the matter with her today? She'd been like this ever since that visit from the man from the Corps of Engineers. John—no, Mr. Harris.

She picked up the sad little bundle of yellowed love letters and held them for a moment before dropping them back in the cardboard box in which they had arrived. Sweet, poignant—a love story from another time. A time when a young man far from home could write without reservation of his longings and his dreams, a time when

strong men weren't afraid to be sensitive and romantic...

She pursed her lips in a little grimace of regret. She'd
been born into the wrong century—romance was dead. She
could do worse than Ron Weed, all things considered. He
was likable, respectable, wealthy. She felt comfortable with
him. He was solid and dependable. If she had to marry,
why not Ron?

*But why do I have to marry at all? Why can't I just go
on as I am, living in Angel's Walk?*

Angel's Walk. As she drove the winding road that circled high above the northeast shore of the lake, she felt the
familiar dread clutch at her stomach. The water was higher
than she'd ever seen it. But Ron's news about the spillway
was encouraging. If the water was going over the spillway,
the lake couldn't rise much more. It wouldn't come as far
as Angel's Walk.

Suzanna had always hated the lake. Even though it had
been there since before she was born, she never looked at
its choppy gray or mirror-blue surface without seeing the
cottonwood trees and ranch houses, the green meadows
and meandering country roads and peaceful towns, that
had once filled the valley. And she felt a deep sense of
nostalgia for a time she had never known, a longing for
places that would never be again.

And yet she didn't resent the dam—not really. She
understood the need for it. It was only one of many flood-
control and irrigation-project dams in the foothills of
California's mountains, where rivers are born in perpet-
ual snows and expire gently in the arid plains and desert
valleys. Where men, lulled by dry seasons into false security, build cities in lake beds and cultivate the river chan-
nels and build homes on floodplains. Sooner or later, to
protect themselves, men must build dams to control and

manage the unpredictable watershed. Whole towns are re-located, farms and fields and pastures are sacrificed and lakes are born.

Dropping down from the dry, dun-colored hills onto the eastern floor of the valley, she crossed the south fork of the river, ordinarily only a placid trickle in a sandy bed bor-dered by cottonwood scrub. Now a muddy brown torrent foamed under the bridge and on down to the lake. And as Suzanna turned onto the long lane that led to Angel's Walk, she saw the golden gleam of the lake water under a late-afternoon sun. It was chillingly close.

Suzanna had cause to be worried. Her home, her be-loved Angel's Walk, actually sat on designated lake bot-tom.

When the towns of Kernsville and Isabella had been re-located, all of the structures in the area to be inundated had been sold at auction. The smaller ones had been moved to new locations on higher ground, while those considered too large or structurally unsound to be moved were demolished and the usable materials salvaged. Su-zanna's grandfather, in a fit of romantic extravagance, had purchased Angel's Walk, and ignoring the advice of al-most everyone, had steadfastly refused to tear it down. Although he and his wife, Suzanna's grandmother, had never lived there, several of his children had grown up in the beautiful old Victorian house. For thirty years his grandchildren had slid down its polished banisters and climbed its fruit trees and played on its wide green lawns. He'd always intended to move it—experts had told him it was feasible—but the house sat on the outermost fringes of parkland, and in Suzanna's lifetime the lake waters had never once come close to threatening it. When her grand-father died, he bequeathed the house to Suzanna, who had almost forgotten that the ground it sat on belonged to the lake.

Now she could see the green shingled roof and white gables of Angel's Walk through the huge black walnut trees that surrounded it. As always, the sight heartened her. How she loved that house! How could she ever bear to lose it?

As she drew nearer to the two-story white frame house, she was smiling the way a parent smiles at a physically imperfect but beloved child. Angel's Walk was the kind of house children were afraid to go trick-or-treating to, a place where small boys dared one another to trespass on a dark night. It needed paint and a new roof, and the attic window was broken. But it was still a lovely, gracious old house. It was hers, and she loved it.

Even, she thought with a sudden spurt of laughter, *in springtime.*

An ancient white Mercedes was parked at the front gate, its motor running, exhaust puffing out wisps of blue diesel smoke. A tall, thin lady with dark auburn hair drawn back into a bun was struggling through the white picket gate with two large suitcases.

Suzanna scrambled out of her car and ran to help.

"I'm so glad I got here before you left, Mrs. Hopewell—" The suitcases were astonishingly heavy—with books, she supposed. Mrs. Hopewell was stronger than she looked. "Is this all? Is there anything else I can help you with?"

"No, thank you, Suzanna. I believe I've left everything in order. You will find my sister's address and telephone number on the table in the kitchen. I trust you will let me know when it's safe for me to return."

Suzanna hadn't told Mr. Harris the truth. No one really knew how old Mrs. Hopewell was, but the rich chestnut hair had been getting help from a bottle since at least one generation before Suzanna had entered her third-grade class. She and Suzanna had been close friends for years, but Suzanna could no more call her by her first name, Amelia, than she could fly. Her name, as far as Suzanna was concerned, would always be Mrs. Hopewell.

Right now her former teacher, straight backed and thin lipped, was giving her the classic classroom glare. Suzanna wasn't impressed; she knew the amused twinkle in those clear, intelligent gray eyes. She put her arms around the stiff body in a quick, impulsive hug. "Oh, Mrs. Hopewell, I'm sorry. I wish—"

"Now my dear, don't worry. You know I do look forward to visiting my sister each spring. Skunks, being God's creatures, too, are entitled to their fling, though how you can continue on here during the worst of it, I cannot understand." Mrs. Hopewell patted her hair and looked around her. "You have a visitor," she announced crisply. "I won't linger for the pleasantries. Goodbye, Suzanna. I shall return in due course."

She got into her car and drove away without further ceremony, leaving Suzanna to squint curiously at the cloud of dust that was just crossing the wide dirt clearing in front of the house. When a light green pickup with a stylized castle logo on the door jerked to an abrupt halt in the spot just vacated by the white Mercedes, Suzanna's mouth suddenly went dry.

"Mr. Harris," she said faintly as the door opened and he swung himself out of the cab in one fluid motion.

"The schoolteacher?" he asked without preamble, jerking a thumb over his shoulder at Mrs. Hopewell's retreating dust. "I saw suitcases in her car. Does that mean you now have a vacancy?"

He was strolling toward her with that rolling masculine walk. She realized that her gaze was riveted on the thigh muscles bunching beneath his Levi's and jerked her eyes upward. This morning he had worn a khaki work shirt; now he had on a white T-shirt that molded itself to every muscle—and there were a great many of them. He was grinning, his head thrown back in an attitude of easy assurance, the wind lifting the bright hair away from his forehead. He seemed to radiate heat and energy, as if he were a power cell that had somehow captured and stored the sun's radiance.

Suzanna blinked, quelling an urge to shade her eyes with her hand. "No! No, it doesn't mean that at all. Mrs. Hopewell has gone to visit her sister in San Francisco. She always goes in the—at this time of year. I meant what I said, Mr. Harris. I'm not renting rooms just now. I'm very sorry you had to come all this way for nothing."

She was edging toward the fence in a dismissive sort of way, but to her dismay he leaned down to unlatch the gate, then swung it open and held it for her. She had no choice but to go through it, with him close behind. He latched the gate carefully after them and strolled with her up the long cement walk.

"So this is your big old house," he said, tilting back his head to look up at it with open admiration. "Nice. I like a Victorian without all the gimcrackery. It's a little rundown, but I'll bet it's as sound underneath as the day it was built."

Suzanna glanced at him in surprise and chose to ignore the middle part of his assessment. It was nothing, after all, but the truth. "It's very astute of you to see that," she murmured. "Most people think it's about to fall down. But Papa, my grandfather, always said that it was as sound as the day it was built."

"Your grandfather—is he the one who built it?"

"Oh, no—it was built even before his time. But he left me Angel's Walk. You see he—"

"Angel's Walk?" He grinned at her. "Now *that's* Victorian!"

"There's a story behind the name, actually," Suzanna said, smiling back at him. "A local legend." He seemed so genuinely interested that she didn't feel nervous at all. She was never ill at ease talking about Angel's Walk. "It was built by a man named William Neal, for his fiancée. Her name was Angela."

"Ah, I see."

"No, but that's not quite it. She died, you see, very tragically, before they could be married. Mr. Neal never could bring himself to live in the house. He always claimed that his beloved Angela—now, presumably, an 'angel' for real—came there to walk in the gardens."

Mr. Harris was looking down at her, his eyes crinkling with the same undisguised delight he'd shown when she'd told him about Isabelle Potter's love letters. She felt a surge of completely uncharacteristic resentment. She didn't know why she minded him laughing at her eccentricities, but she did.

"A haunted house?" He chuckled. "Is that why you won't rent me a room? Mrs. Hopewell doesn't seem to mind the ghosts."

"It isn't haunted," Suzanna snapped, continuing on up the walk. "No one but poor Mr. Neal ever thought it was. That has nothing to do with it. Why are you being so persistent? I've told you I—"

They were nearing the steps to the front porch. The engineer stopped abruptly, a peculiar look crossing his face. Suzanna waited, watching him with grim anticipation.

"Good *Lord*!" he exclaimed after a moment's shocked silence. "What did you do—trap a whole family of skunks?"

"Certainly not," Suzanna said calmly. "They live here. Under the house," she added as he turned an incredulous gaze on her. "They're actually quite well behaved most of the time. You'd never even know they were there unless you happened to catch them feeding during the night."

"Feeding? You actually feed them?"

"Dog food," Suzanna affirmed blithely. "But right now it happens to be springtime." She lifted her shoulders and let them drop, unwilling to elaborate further. "It will pass. Mrs. Hopewell always chooses this particular time to visit her sister." She paused, her lips twitching. "So now you see, Mr. Harris, why I simply can't rent you a room."

"Cam," he murmured, frowning.

"I beg your pardon?"

"Call me Cam. 'Mr. Harris' makes *me* sound like a Victorian schoolteacher."

"Cam?" Suzanna faltered, hurrying after him as he went ahead of her through the heavy mahogany door, pausing to reverently touch its panes of etched and frosted glass.

"Short for Campbell, my middle name," he muttered absently, opening the door to the left of the front hallway and poking his head inside. "Aha, Mrs. Hopewell's—no doubt about it." He turned to grin irrepressibly at her. "Smells of lavender."

"How can you possibly tell?" Suzanna retorted. Then, as he had already bounded back across the hall to poke his head through yet another door, she said, "What do you think you're doing? You can't just—"

"Living room," he announced triumphantly. "That's a beautiful fireplace. Do you have any idea what it would

take to duplicate that woodwork now?'' He gave a dry
whistle and charged off down the hall past the wide,
sweeping staircase, with Suzanna sputtering ineffectively
in his wake. ''The dining room—ah, I see it's a double
fireplace!''

''Mr. Harris, really, I—''

He glanced at her, looking pained. ''Please, no more
Mr. Harris. I'm not your sixth-grade teacher.'' And he
reached for the doorknob of the room behind the stairs.

Suzanna gave a panic-stricken gulp. ''Oh, no—please.
Don't open that one!'' She flattened herself against it, her
arms spread protectively across the door.

He laughed softly and placed a large work-roughened
hand flat on the panel beside her head. ''Did you forget to
make your bed? Don't worry. I've seen unmade beds before, as well as anything else you might have left lying
around.''

Suzanna closed her eyes in exasperation. She was beginning to feel like the little Dutch boy trying to hold back
the sea with a finger. ''It's nothing at all like that. Mr.
Harris—''

She heard the soft hiss of exhaled breath and opened her
eyes to find him looking down at her with a curious, wry
expression on his face. His eyes, she noticed, were deep set,
and because the hallway was shadowed, she still couldn't
tell what color they were. It occurred to her to wonder why
she should care.

He shook his head and murmured, ''Mr. Harris . . . All
right, Miss Day, what terrible secret are you so melodra-
matically defending?''

''Hummingbirds,'' Suzanna said, her voice emerging
with an unanticipated huskiness. She cleared her throat
and found that she was not quite able to bring her eyes up
to the level of his face. His throat fascinated her; the few

stray hairs that grew there were lighter than his skin. "I'm weaning them."

"*Weaning* them?"

"I raised them. Now I'm teaching them to take nectar from a feeder and catch their own insects. They're almost ready to go out the window, and I don't want them to get loose in the house."

"All right," Cam said, removing his hand from the door panel and holding it up as if in surrender. "I won't disturb the hummingbirds."

"Oh, thank you," Suzanna said dryly, but irony was lost on this human whirlwind.

He hesitated a moment, rubbing his chin thoughtfully, and then turned briskly to the door at the end of the hall. "I don't think it will be a problem as long as that door stays shut. What's in here? Oh—kitchen."

"*What* won't be a problem?" Suzanna gasped, trying to keep up with him.

"Birds," he said absently, without looking at her. "I have a cat. Now this is really nice." He walked slowly into the big, old-fashioned kitchen, now full of soft golden light from the setting sun filtered through Virginia creeper. A stray shaft of sunlight caught his hair, setting it ablaze.

Suzanna caught her breath. "Look here—What do you mean, you have a cat? What are you doing, taking inventory? Can't you get it through your head? I'm not renting rooms!" And especially not to a rude, arrogant bulldozer of a man like this! He'd turn her house, and her life, upside down!

He didn't even hear her angry retort; he'd already gone back into the hallway. Suzanna followed just in time to see him bound up the stairs two at a time.

"What's up here? Ah, bedrooms. Now we're getting someplace!" His voice sounded hollowly down from the landing, and Suzanna, beside herself with helpless anger and frustration, raced after him up the stairs. She found him standing in her bedroom doorway.

"How dare you—"

"Your room," he said with quiet triumph, looking down at her with that soft, eye-crinkling smile. "I'd know it anywhere. It's just like you. Pretty, practical, romantic and—" he touched the tip of her nose with his finger "just a little bit flaky."

"Flaky!" Suzanna cried, incensed, ignoring for the moment the fact that in a roundabout way he'd said she was pretty.

His eyebrows went shooting up. "You don't think a woman who feeds skunks dog food and hand raises hummingbirds is flaky?" He looked over her head into the room, taking in the old-fashioned flowered wallpaper, white priscilla curtains, paper-cluttered desk and worn linoleum in a leisurely way. His eyes seemed to Suzanna to linger unnecessarily on the double brass bed, the patchwork quilt she'd hastily thrown into place this morning—thank goodness—and the white cotton nightgown that still lay starkly across the foot of it.

I'm going to die of embarrassment, Suzanna thought. *But first I am going to kill him.*

"What's that opening?"

She let out her suspended breath in a rush and opened her eyes to follow his interested gaze. "That goes to the attic."

"No door? You just leave it open like that?" His eyes came back to hers crinkled with amusement. "Doesn't it make you nervous, having that black hole right beside your bed?"

Suzanna was beginning to be fed up with providing this man with comic relief. "Anything likely to make me nervous wouldn't be coming from the attic," she said pointedly. "Anyway," she added with a shrug, "the door is missing. I didn't think it was necessary to replace it. Besides—" She stopped. He already thought she was crazy enough, so she wouldn't mention the real reason she didn't board up the attic door.

"Flaky," Cam reiterated softly. The expression on his face was unreadable. *Gray,* Suzanna thought suddenly. *His eyes are gray!*

He was touching her again. What was it about her face that he seemed to want to keep touching it? Not that his touch was unpleasant; it was just the lightest, gentlest of touches, a smoothing of his fingertips along the edge of her jaw, a slight pressure under the point of her chin. Amazing, really, that such a rough, brash man should have so gentle a touch.

"Nothing wrong with being a little flaky. Makes you interesting. But don't get *too* eccentric. Eccentrics scare people, especially eccentrics who live in haunted houses. Before you know it, you could wind up all alone, like Eleanor Rigby." His voice was a mesmerizing murmur; his thumb moved in an oddly soothing pattern across her jaw. "That would be a real waste."

What incredible, absolutely unshakable self-assurance! The man *knew* he had her absolutely transfixed. She knew she should be furious—damn it, she *was* furious!—but somehow all she could do was stare back at him with her mouth open, like a child meeting Superman in the flesh. When at last he released her and moved on down the landing, she almost sagged against the door frame, too drained to summon strength of purpose to pursue him again. Instead, she crossed her arms over her chest and watched him poke his head into every door on the landing.

"Hmm, these two have a connecting door," he observed, his voice coming back to her as he prowled through the rooms directly across the landing. After a moment, he came back out to lean on the stairwell railing, facing her across the chasm. "What's that smaller one? An office? Dressing room?"

"It's always been a nursery," Suzanna said, clearing her throat and straightening up. "The big one is the master bedroom." She shrugged, striving for indifference. "In Victorian times, more probably it was a dressing room."

"Well, it would sure make me a nice little office." He cocked a curious eyebrow at her. "Why aren't you in the master bedroom? It's your house."

"And I was beginning to think that fact had escaped you," Suzanna retorted acidly. "I prefer my own room, thank you."

"Just as well," Cam said cheerfully. "Because these two will do me very nicely. How much?"

"Mr. Harris," Suzanna said evenly, "*please* pay attention: I can't rent you a room in my house!"

"Of course you can. What you mean is, you *won't*. Why not?"

"I should think that would be obvious."

"You mean the skunks? I've smelled worse things, believe me. If you can stand it, why can't I?"

"Mrs. Hopewell—"

"Either Mrs. Hopewell has a more sensitive nose than I do, or she just wants an excuse to go see her sister."

"There is nothing the slightest bit sensitive about any part of you or you'd understand that Mrs. Hopewell's going to visit her sister is the whole problem!" Suzanna shouted, absolutely at her wit's end. She pressed her hand to her forehead and found that she was actually sweating as if she'd been working very hard. What an exhausting man he was—a bulldozer! "I can't have you living here with me, all alone! It wouldn't be—It just isn't—"

As she fumbled for a word that wouldn't sound too archaic, she watched the expression on Cam's face change from amusement to amazement. When he pushed himself away from the railing and came slowly around to where she was standing, she found that her heart was pounding, both from the exertion of dealing with him and from a strange, unfamiliar apprehension.

"Miss Suzanna Day," he said, stretching the syllables in a kind of wondering drawl. "Tell me, what century are you living in?" His hand came out to touch the shoulder ruffle of her yellow pinafore. "Sue, I've got news for you. This isn't 1880; it's the twentieth century. Men and women call each other by their first names. They can walk out together—and even share living quarters—without having to be engaged first. Come on, catch up with this world. You might find out you like it." For one heart-stopping moment she thought he was going to touch her again, but then he reached in his hip pocket for his wallet and said briskly, "Now, how much? For the two rooms?"

Suzanna murmured, "Uh...two rooms," and then mentally shook herself and lifted her hands in frustration and defeat. "I'll have to charge you double the single-room rate, of course...."

"Name it."

She told him and watched him take bills of dizzying denominations out of his wallet. "Here's a month's rent in advance. I may not be here that long, but if I'm not, consider the balance a nonrefundable cleaning deposit. I'm not a neat person."

Suzanna stared helplessly at the money, conscious of rising panic. "I can't . . ." she whispered. "What will people—"

"Come on, Sue," he said, chuckling. "Don't tell me it's ever mattered to you what people think! Here—" When she still couldn't bring herself to take the money from his hand, he reached out and tucked it into the pocket of her pinafore. She gave a startled little gasp as he turned away with a rumble of laughter and descended the stairs, leaving her gulping like a netted fish. His voice drifted up the stairwell. "I have to pick up a few things and settle my motel bill, but I'll be back this evening. Please have my bed ready. It's been a long day."

"This is crazy," Suzanna remarked to no one in particular. "A strange man is moving into my house, and I don't seem to be able to do a thing about it!"

"By the way—"

His voice came to her from the front porch, and she went to lean over the stair railing, muttering under her breath, "There's *more*?"

"Besides ghosts, skunks and hummingbirds, are there any other tenants of this establishment I should know about?"

Suzanna smiled suddenly, with relish. She still had an ace or two in her hand, and darned if she was going to reveal them now! He was entirely too sure of himself. "Mr. Harris!" she cried with wounded innocence. "I may indeed be 'a bit flaky,' but I do *not* run a zoo!"

She heard his low chuckle and walked slowly to the big arched windows that looked out across the front lawn. She threw open the window and called urgently, "Mr. Harris, wait—" But it was too late. As she watched her new tenant leap into his pickup and drive away in a cloud of dust, she was thinking of a dozen things she could have said, things she should have asked him. References. She should have insisted on seeing references. And it occurred to her to wonder just exactly what it was that he did for the Corps of Engineers. And there were his meals and the bathroom schedule to think about. She'd have to call Tony and ask him just how well he really knew this man—this John Campbell Harris. *Cam.*

She stood a while longer, chewing her lower lip and rubbing her arms, and then, when her breathing had returned to normal, she went to find clean sheets and towels for the master bedroom. She was thinking, *Cam. I suppose I really ought to call him that. I really don't think I could ever have called him John.*

Chapter Three

Cam thought his timing was pretty wonderful. Somehow he managed to be arriving at the front door of Angel's Walk with his suitcase, Cat's tote bag and a roll of blueprints under his arm just as Suzanna, obviously dressed for a night on the town, was coming out. She was on the arm of a prosperously paunchy man in cowboy boots. Cam stopped short, affecting surprise and savoring the look of consternation on the fellow's rather fleshy face.

"Oh!" he said after allowing the silence to become awkward. "You must be...?" He shifted his load and thrust his hand forward in an excess of joviality.

"Weed...Ron Weed," the man muttered automatically.

"Glad to know you! Glad to know you! Sue's told me a lot about you! Well, don't let me hold you up. I'll get myself all settled in." He beamed at Suzanna, noting with satisfaction the way anger touched her cheeks with pink. She had the quickest blush he'd ever seen.

"Hey, listen, don't worry about me. We'll have time to pick up where we left off this afternoon...later," he said, managing to put all sorts of possibilities into that sentence, and added heartily, "You just go on and have a real nice evening now, y'hear? Shall I wait up for you?"

Suzanna's voice could have given frostbite to anyone within a radius of several miles. *"Please* don't. Ron and I will be quite late, won't we, Ron?" She edged closer to her date, smiling brilliantly up at him.

The poor guy seemed slightly stunned. Cam heard him muttering, "Who *is* that guy?" as Suzanna was dragging him off the front porch and down the walk.

Cam plastered a toothy, used-car-salesman's smile on his face and waved goodbye, then kicked the door shut behind him with glass-rattling force and uttered one short but satisfying expletive. He didn't stop to analyze the feelings that had him awash with slowly ebbing adrenaline but expended some of the excess energy running up the stairs two at a time. He tossed his suitcase and the roll of plans onto the neatly made bed and set the tote bag carefully beside it.

"Come on out, Cat," he said softly, unzipping it. "Don't mind the smell; it's the neighbors downstairs. Stay away from them. Definitely low-class types."

Cat uttered a soft chirp and stepped daintily from the tote bag. She walked a few paces, sniffed the bedspread twice and settled down to wash.

Cam sat down beside her and rubbed the spot under her chin. "Yeah... good old Cat. Never complain, do you? I guess you've smelled worse in your time, too, huh?" He snorted disgustedly and slapped his knees. "And here I am, still with nobody to talk to but a cat!" He said that word again, more forcefully, and stood up. "Come on, Cat, I'll show you around. And then let's see what there is to eat."

A few minutes later, he was peering into the refrigerator while Cat watched placidly from the middle of the kitchen table. Cam was feeling more depressed by the minute. *These women must be vegetarians!* He sighed and reached for the carton of eggs and a pitcher of milk. He found a small square of yellow cheese, a bunch of green onions and a green pepper and added them to the pile on the counter. He glanced over his shoulder at the cat.

"I'm afraid it's cans again for you unless you've got a better idea. There might be a mouse or two around, I suppose."

Cat stalked to the edge of the table and jumped off. She padded without haste to the door and disappeared into the dark hallway.

"Happy hunting," Cam called after her, and set about finding the utensils necessary to convert his accumulated groceries into an omelet.

Cooking lifted his spirits somewhat. The kitchen was a homey, peaceful place, full of good smells and friendly sounds—the hum of the refrigerator, the rattle of pots, the hiss of melting butter. It was better than listening to the sound of his own breathing. Around him the old house was beginning to make nighttime settling-down noises, and that gave him a comfortable feeling, too. It really was a great old house. Beat hell out of a motel room, even if *she* wasn't around to fill up the silence with that soft, sexy voice of hers.

He ate quickly, staring into space, his forehead tensed in a frown. And then all at once he relaxed and pushed back his empty plate. He shook his head, amused at himself. That's all it was—he'd just been looking forward to company, to getting out of that damned motel and having somebody real to talk to. He'd just been disappointed, that's all....

He stood up and carried his dishes to the sink, frowning again as he turned on the water and watched it flood the congealed bits of egg and cheese on his plate.

"Cam, you jerk," he said softly to himself, "you're lonely. Admit it. Cam Harris, career globetrotter. Breeze into town, fix the screwup and breeze back out again. Keep it casual: first names and small talk and easy laughter and light lovin'—that's the way to go. And never, ever get involved, because it's just one more town, one more dam, one more levee, one more harbor. Tomorrow it'll be another one someplace else."

It had had its moments—the challenges, the excitement—but it was getting old. Or maybe he was. Wasn't loneliness supposed to be something that happened to you when you got old?

He rinsed the plate and reached for the frying pan, studying the eclectic assortment of items on the windowsill above the sink as he scrubbed at it. What a strange girl she was. He'd never run into anyone like her before. Sometimes she seemed as corny and romantic as a Victorian valentine, and at other times... What kind of girl lived all alone in a big old barn of a place like this with nothing but an old lady and a bunch of skunks for company? Why wasn't somebody as good-looking as her married? She wasn't a kid; he'd put her age in the mid-twenties, at least. Although there was something about her that made him think of her as "girl" rather than "woman." Maybe, he thought with a reminiscent smile, it was that old-fashioned costume she'd been wearing this afternoon. Or the way she wore her hair, with the sides pulled up and back like that, and the rest of it hanging down her back. She had pretty hair. Nice skin, too, with that sprinkle of freckles across her nose and that quick blush. And then there were her eyes. All she'd need is a great big hair ribbon and she'd look about thirteen years old!

He gave a soft snort of self-disgust. Cam, he thought, you dirty old man—that's called innocence. Don't you recognize it anymore? If you've got any scruples left at all, you'll lay off her. She'd be too easy to hurt....

But it wouldn't hurt anything just to talk to her. She was different, unpredictable, interesting. He had a feeling it was going to be fun getting to know her.

He turned the water off, dried his hands and rubbed them together briskly, smiling again. "She'll be back," he said to Cat, who was returning from her obviously fruitless patrol. "And we'll see about tomorrow!"

THERE WAS A LIGHT in the dormer window in the master bedroom when Ron brought Suzanna home around eleven o'clock. Suzanna's eyes kept lifting to that light, the single yellow eye in the dark and brooding face of the old house, on the way up the long front walk, and she was uncomfortably conscious of Ron's hand at her waist, as if someone were watching.

In the shadows of the front porch she tensed her body against Ron's embrace. She'd never felt less like being kissed. What a shock it had been to have Ron suddenly start talking about marriage like that. Seeing Cam here this evening must really have shaken his complacency. He hadn't *asked* her to marry him, of course; that wasn't Ron's way. He'd just begun referring to their future together as though it were a foregone conclusion. It would have been better if he had asked her formally; she could at least have had the opportunity to voice an opinion. As it was, she just felt crowded. Railroaded. But then, this whole day had been like that.

When Ron had gone, she let herself in the front door and stood for a moment tapping her fingers on the banister and frowning. She was remembering that she hadn't ever gotten around to discussing meal schedules with her new tenant, and since tomorrow was Sunday she'd have to leave for church by nine-thirty. It appeared that he was still awake; she probably should find out what his breakfast preferences were right now. Belatedly but without a shred of guilt, she wondered how he had fared for supper this evening. She hadn't been grocery shopping in more than a week. She and Mrs. Hopewell ate so little and so simply; it was going to be an adjustment, cooking for a man.

Suzanna took a deep, fortifying breath and stomped up the stairs, taking care to make enough noise to warn him she was coming. It was a very warm night, and he seemed the kind of man who wouldn't bother with pajamas. She didn't want to risk catching him by surprise.

A deep voice rumbled, "Come in," in answer to her sharp knock.

She hesitated a moment and pushed the door open, then mumbled "Damn!" under her breath and pulled it shut again.

"I said come in," Cam said on a low ripple of amusement. "I'm decent."

Technically, maybe. Suzanna opened the door again and cautiously stuck her head in. "I, um," she said, clearing her throat. "I need to talk about breakfast."

"As good a subject as any," Cam said agreeably. "Come on in—sit down."

She eased into the room but stayed where she was by the door. He was sitting up in bed, his back cushioned by pillows against the high, carved cherry-wood headboard. He was naked to the waist. At least. A sheet was drawn up over his lap, only far enough for her to surmise that under it he was naked to the waist from either direction.

He'd been studying some papers filled with complicated-looking figures and diagrams, and he held a pencil in his left hand. He had put the papers down when she entered; now he tossed the pencil on top of them and folded

his arms behind his head, waiting with laughter in his eyes
for her to speak. She could see that his tan was uneven, his
arms and neck darker than his torso, in the pattern of a
man who spends most of his time working outdoors. It was
a familiar enough pattern to Suzanna. She'd spent a lifetime watching cousins and uncles work shirtless in the
fields under the blazing California sun. She couldn't explain why this particular chest should unnerve her so.

In the jumble of pushed-back blankets and bedspread at
his feet, a smoky gray shape made a round puddle of
shadow. It stirred a little, and Suzanna's eyes flew to it,
grateful for a target other than that expanse of coppery
chest with its dusting of golden hair.

"I see you've managed all right, settling in," she said,
staring at the shadow. "Your cat doesn't seem to mind
being in a strange place, does she? I thought cats were
supposed to be very hard to relocate."

"Oh, Cat goes wherever I go," Cam said, prodding her
gently with his foot. She yawned and extended a paw, then
turned her head upside down and went back to sleep. "She
knows where her meal ticket is, don't you, Cat?"

"Speaking of meals, did you get along all right this
evening? I'm sorry—I wasn't prepared for guests, and I did
have a date. I tried to tell you—"

"It's all right; we made out. I had an omelet and Cat
had something disgusting out of a can. They both tasted
like skunk, so it didn't make much difference. You don't
have any mice," he added in a mildly affronted tone.

"Does that surprise you?" Suzanna retorted. "Considering the skunks and the, uh—" She stopped herself in the
nick of time and gave a dry little cough. "And you can't
say you weren't warned about them. I tried—"

"Quite all right, quite all right," Cam hastened to as-
sure her, raising a hand. "I'm terribly fond of skunk, ac-

tually. So is Cat. Now, then, you wanted to discuss breakfast?"

"Oh, yes." Suzanna put a hand over her mouth to stifle the laughter that had erupted unannounced. The whole idea of being in a naked man's bedroom at midnight seemed to be making her lose her head. "Umm... tomorrow is Sunday."

"You're right, it is. Did you have a good time?"

"I beg your pardon?"

"Tonight. Your date with ... what's his name. Have a good time?"

"Yes. No—I mean, it's none of your business! What's that got to do with breakfast?"

"You're home early. You said you were going to be late."

"I have to be in church early tomorrow," Suzanna said, no longer in any danger of breaking into laughter. She forgot about keeping her eyes on the cat. "And that's none of your business, either!"

"Sure it is," Cam said, looking innocently surprised. "We were talking about breakfast, weren't we? If you go to church early, that affects breakfast, doesn't it? And isn't that what you wanted to talk about?"

"Don't *do* that!" Suzanna shouted, repressing a childish urge to stamp her foot.

"Do what?" He looked genuinely puzzled.

"Steamroll me, damn it! I've had enough of that for one day!"

Cam clicked his tongue, laughing at her with his eyes. "I'm sorry," he said softly. "Don't get mad."

"I am not mad," Suzanna said with tenuous self-control. "I just lost my temper. Breakfast will be at eight o'clock sharp. Daily. If you've used up all the eggs, it will have to be cold cereal until I have an opportunity to go

shopping. If you have any dietary restrictions or preferences, I would appreciate a list of them by tomorrow
morning. Do you drink coffee or tea?''

Cam's chest shook with silent laughter. With careful
solemnity he murmured, ''Coffee, please, ma'am.''

''Fine. If there's nothing else—'' She yanked at the
doorknob and backed out of the room. ''Good night, *Mr.
Harris*!''

Safely on the other side of the mahogany panels, she
heard the masculine voice, rich with laughter, answer,
''Night, Sue.''

SUZANNA AWOKE at seven, as she always did, instantly and
without the help of an alarm. She lay for a few minutes
listening to birds' songs outside her open windows and
watching the play of shadows on the wall where morning
sunlight filtered through walnut trees. Inside the house, it
was quiet. She could almost believe she had the house all
to herself. At least the new tenant was neither an early nor
a noisy riser.

Throwing back the light blanket that was all the covering she needed on such a warm spring night, Suzanna
swung her feet to the cool linoleum and stretched. She then
swallowed a yawn with a gulp as a thought struck her. Her
robe, which she rarely bothered with in the summertime,
was hanging on a hook in the bathroom. The bathroom
was several doors down the landing. Unless she wanted to
dress without showering first, she was going to have to
cross the landing in her thin white cotton nightie.

That was something else she should have taken care of
last night. She didn't have any idea what time Cam would
be getting up or whether he liked to bathe in the morning
or evening, or both. One thing Victorian houses lacked was
private bathrooms, though in its day the big bathroom at

the head of the stairs must have seemed the most won-drous and modern indoor facility around.

But what a pain it was going to be, having to worry about privacy and modesty and bathroom schedules. Was there even a lock on the bathroom door? She'd never needed one before. Though she'd had other tenants be-sides Mrs. Hopewell, they had always been female and for the most part had taken rooms on the ground floor. She tried to picture the inside of the door. Was there or wasn't there a hook-and-eye latch there? She couldn't remember. Damn!

She sat frowning at the door, perplexed. It was very quiet. No sound of running water. She stood up and pad-ded to the door barefoot, opened it and cautiously peered out. Cam's door was closed. He was probably still asleep. Good—if she hurried, she should be able to get her bath out of the way before he got up. Biting her lips and keep-ing her eyes glued to the master-bedroom door, Suzanna began to tiptoe down the landing toward the bathroom.

She was nearly there when a voice very close at hand said, "Morning, Sue," startling her so badly she nearly vaulted over the stair rail.

She steadied herself with a hand on the rail and slumped against it, her heart fluttering in her chest. In a flat, hor-rified voice she said, "Oh, *Lord*." She'd been concentrat-ing so hard on his bedroom door she hadn't even glanced toward the bathroom. Now she saw that the door was wide open and that Cam was standing just inside it at the sink, shaving. He wore a towel precariously knotted around narrow hips. In the oval mirror above the sink, his eyes crinkled at her over white lather.

"You're looking very fetching this morning, ma'am," he said cheerfully, pausing to swish his razor in the sink. "Don't think I've ever had a landlady—" he drew the razor along his jaw "—who looked so pretty so early in the morning." He stopped, razor poised, and lifted his eyebrows at her. "I left the door open, since there doesn't seem to be a lock on it. Did you need something?"

"Bathrobe," Suzanna croaked.

"Ah—" He had spotted it in the mirror, hanging on its hook beside the door, and turned to extend one muscular arm and take it in his hand. He held it, moving his fingers in the baby-blue velour, and said softly, "Here it is. Sorry if I'm in your way. Bathroom protocol is something we didn't get around to last night." His face was still half hidden by lather, but above it the greenish-gray eyes were gentle, for once not laughing at her. He hesitated for a moment and then held the robe out to her.

Suzanna couldn't have moved if the house had caught fire. She knew exactly what she looked like in her nightgown, knew all too well what it did and did not conceal. And at the same time she realized that if she turned and ran for her room or tried to cover herself with her arms, she would look absolutely ridiculous. How could she have allowed such an impossible situation? It was crazy. It was exactly the sort of thing she'd feared would happen. It was embarrassing, to say the least, and probably dangerous. After all, she didn't *know* this man! Being a civil servant and even knowing her cousin, Tony, was no guarantee of sainthood. She hadn't known him twenty-four hours, and here she was in her flimsiest nightgown, not two yards away from his soapy, unclothed body. What next?

Oddly, Cam seemed to be wondering the same thing. For a long moment he just stood there, holding her robe, and then he stepped out onto the landing and gently draped it over her shoulders. He arranged it around her stiff body and tugged it together in front in a gesture that was curiously awkward for a man usually so self-assured.

Suzanna stared up at him, confused by the look in his eyes, at once fierce and penetrating—and almost tender. And she was disconcerted by the way it felt to be so near his body she could feel its heat, see the texture of his skin, smell the clean, soapy, wet-hair smell of him. She couldn't even begin to evaluate the sensations; there were just too many of them. She suddenly felt weak and dizzy, and the rail at her back seemed far too flimsy to support her. She wanted to hold on to something much more substantial, like the big, hard body in front of her.

"There . . ." Cam said, and stood back, absently reaching up to wipe a bit of lather from his nose. He made a gesture toward the stairs as he turned abruptly back to the bathroom. "There's coffee downstairs. I'll be out of here in a minute."

The bathroom door clicked shut, and Suzanna stared at it for a long time before drawing a shaky breath and distractedly poking her arms into the sleeves of her robe.

ON THE OTHER SIDE of the bathroom door, Cam glared at his reflection in the mirror and made a noise of self-disgust. "You *ass*," he muttered, patting fresh lather on his jaws. "I suppose you get a charge out of tying tin cans to puppy dogs' tails and pulling the wings off of flies, too, right? She's a baby—a kid! You're scaring her to death!"

But the trouble was that she wasn't a baby. And if he'd had any doubts about that before, he didn't anymore. He could still feel the residual effects of the impression she'd made on him, clad in that virginal nightgown. Hell, *he* was the one who was scared! The unexpected surge of desire had hit him like a solid left to the midsection. If he'd ever felt anything like that before, it was so long ago he'd forgotten what it felt like. He'd had to back off; he didn't even trust himself to touch her. What was it about her,

anyway? She wasn't overwhelmingly gorgeous or bla-
tantly sexy except for her voice. And the damn gown
hadn't even shown that much—just the tips of her breasts,
darker circles under the white, and that faint suggestion of
a darker triangle. But with her hair all tumbled and her
cheeks pink and still showing the marks of her pillow, her
mouth relaxed and unguarded, her eyes . . . *Lord!*

He'd cut himself shaving. He *never* cut himself shaving. Angrily, he applied toilet paper to stem the blood flow
and threw on his clothes, muttering vile oaths to himself
under his breath.

She hadn't been kidding about the cold cereal. There
were several brightly colored boxes sitting on the table beside a carton of milk. But there was also a dish of fresh
strawberries, a huge stack of buttered toast, a little earth-
enware pot of homemade apricot jam, and in a little china
pitcher covered with a fine tracing of hairline cracks that
hinted at great age, there was thick, fresh cream.

There was no sign of Suzanna except for a lingering essence that might have been subliminal rather than olfac-
tory. Cam suspected she had slipped out the back in order
to avoid him. That knowledge sobered him even more. She
wasn't equipped to cope with him, and he knew it. To keep
teasing her would be unforgivable.

She came downstairs half an hour later, while Cam was
on his third cup of coffee. She seemed to have recovered
her composure; at least she didn't try to avoid his glance
and even had a smile for him when she noted the empty
dishes he'd stacked neatly in the sink.

"I'll do it up," he said, jerking his head in their direction. "Are you off to Sunday school already? Do you always go so early?" She was wearing a crisp blue-and-white
seersucker skirt and a white blouse with a sailor collar.

Even without the hair ribbon she looked about twelve years old.

"Choir practice," she said, smiling again. "We're doing Randall Thompson's 'Alleluia,' which is presumptuous of us, but at least the words are easy." She looked around as if not quite sure what to do next. "Where is your cat this morning?"

Cam shrugged. "Haven't seen her. Don't worry about your birds; I've explained that the room is off-limits. Didn't bother to tell her why, though—no sense tempting her."

"Oh, well, I don't suppose she could open the door, anyway," Suzanna pointed out, laughing.

Cam snorted. "Wouldn't put it past her."

She gave him an odd look; he felt as if she were trying very hard to read him and finding it tough going. "She's an unusual cat, isn't she?" Suzanna said, but Cam had a feeling what she really meant was "*You* are an unusual man to have such a cat." The inference made him uncomfortable.

He shrugged. "I don't know. She's the only cat I've ever been on speaking terms with."

"Have you had her a long time?"

"I don't *have* her. But we've been traveling together for quite a while, yeah. She found me in an alley in San Pedro."

"She found *you*?"

"Oh, yeah—if there's one thing that cat has, it's good instincts. She was in a bit of trouble and knew a pushover when she saw one. We've been traveling together ever since."

"But you've never named her?"

"Look, she's just a mangy old cat," he said, not intending to sound as sharp as he did. He was beginning to feel very fraudulent. She was trying to make the damn cat into some kind of virtue, and it made him squirm. But as soon as the words were out of his mouth, he regretted them. Her smile vanished as if he'd hit a light switch.

Crisply, all business, she said, "Well, I'll be off, then. Is there anything you need before I go? What about those lists I mentioned last night?"

"Lists?"

"Your food preferences," she said patiently.

"I'm completely omnivorous. Not voraciously carnivorous, but I do enjoy meat now and then."

Again, he was ashamed of himself. It was just the kind of petty little dig he particularly detested. And he knew by the quick surge of color to her cheeks that she hadn't missed the reference to his two spartan meals. She opened her mouth as if she meant to say something about it and then thought better of it and instead mumbled a farewell and left.

Cam sat where he was, staring after her, then made an impatient noise and stood up to add his coffee cup to the pile in the sink.

Leave her alone, Cam. You can't offer her anything but grief. Again, the thought came to him: *she'd be too easy to hurt.*

"Come on, Cat," he said as the lean gray body came from nowhere to wind around his ankles. "Let's go buy the lady some groceries."

THE HOUSE WAS VERY QUIET. Suzanna kicked off her shoes at the bottom of the stairs as she always did and went to check on the hummingbirds. They pipped hungrily at her and ruffled their feathers and fluttered their wings, begging piteously. She glared sternly at them and slapped the big tin can that covered a plateful of overripe fruit. A cloud of fruit gnats emerged from the nail holes in the top of the can, and instantly the air was filled with the hum of tiny wings as the babies darted about after the insects. Suzanna watched them poke clumsily at the nectar feeder that hung in the open window, then unlatched the screen, lifted it off and lowered it carefully to the ground. She unhooked the feeder and leaned as far out the window as she could to hang it on a branch of flowering quince. Then she stood back, brushed her hands and took a deep breath.

"Goodbye, babies," she said softly, and went out and closed the door.

The house seemed very empty. Funny, it had never seemed empty to her before.

Before Cam.

She snorted. He was like a very loud noise. When you turn it off, it seems abnormally quiet by comparison.

She wandered into the kitchen and took an apple out of the refrigerator. He had done the breakfast dishes, just as he'd said he would. He'd also said he wasn't neat. She wondered if he'd made his bed. She decided not to go and see.

She ate the apple, frowning at nothing. It had been a frustrating morning. The sopranos had massacred the high As in the "Alleluia," and the basses, as usual, had not held tempo in the *sostenuto* section. She had tried to get more information about her boarder from Meg and Tony, but Meg had wanted to chatter about plans for the family's Memorial Day picnic. She had been quite delighted to hear that Suzanna was actually living with a man. But Meg had steadfastly proclaimed herself innocent of having anything to do with arranging that state of affairs. She had not, she pointed out, even met the man.

Tony, on the other hand, had been evasive. If anything, he had looked acutely unhappy when reminding his beaming wife that Cam Harris would, in any case, be leaving in a couple of weeks. His long, worried look had left Suzanna with a vague feeling of unease. She attributed Tony's manner to preoccupation with his job; he had a lot on his mind these days, with the water rising so fast. The latest news at church was that the airport was closed to all but emergency and top-priority flights. One of the two runways was under water. The local business people were becoming irate, claiming the Corps of Engineers should have anticipated the above-normal runoff better and made arrangements to handle it.

Suzanna finished her apple and went to add it to the fruit-fly feeder. Then she slipped her shoes back on and went off to buy groceries.

THE SMELL OF BROILING MEAT reached her clear out on the front porch, even over the lingering odor of skunk. She had a big, heavy grocery bag in each arm and her purse clutched between her teeth, and she had to open the screen door with her foot. At the end of the long hallway, the kitchen door stood open. She made her way toward it in that quickstep people use when they are in imminent danger of dropping something. In the doorway she halted and did drop something. Her mouth fell open, and her purse fell to the linoleum at her feet.

The kitchen table was covered with food—fresh, canned and frozen—in an abundance and variety Suzanna usually encountered only at family gatherings and church socials. At least six brown bags sat empty on the floor. Something that looked and smelled a lot like steak was sizzling under the broiler, and Cam stared at her over the head of lettuce he was tearing apart over a large stainless-steel bowl.

"I, uh, picked up a few groceries," he said defensively.

"So did I." Suzanna sighed. "There are three more bags out in the car." Her voice cracked, and the bags began to slip. Cam dropped the lettuce and lurched toward her. By the time he reached her, she was laughing so hard she could hardly stand, and he rescued the groceries in the nick of time.

"Oh, Cam," she quavered, wiping her eyes and surveying the table, "what are we going to do with all this food?"

He gave the array his narrow-eyed consideration and then looked sideways at Suzanna. "Eat it, m'dear," he intoned in an effortless imitation of W. C. Fields. "And what we can't eat, we sell. Could turn a tidy profit."

By the time he had enunciated the final emphatic consonant, Suzanna was bent over double with laughter. Cam grinned, executed a bow and muttered, still in character, "Thank you, m'dear." In an aside to Cat, who was watching the show with sleepy disdain, he added, "Chick's got a weird sense a'yumah."

HOW INCREDIBLE, Suzanna thought later as she and Cam were working to stash the unexpected glut of provisions in her medium-size refrigerator. *He can turn that magnetism off and on whenever he wants to, I guess.*

It took them most of the afternoon to clear the kitchen, and that included the time it took to fix and eat lunch and convert several things that wouldn't fit in the freezer into something that could be warmed over later. In all that time, Suzanna never once felt ill at ease with Cam. In fact, he made her laugh—a lot. They chatted and teased with the ease of old school chums and with as much seriousness and sense. There was only one time when Cam dropped the lighthearted banter.

It was while they were eating lunch, if you could call a feast of T-bone steaks and a crisp green salad with everything imaginable in it lunch. Cam suddenly interrupted himself in mid-sentence and jabbed his fork in the direction of his gaze.

"You have bees," he said in mild surprise, "going in and out of your wall."

Suzanna glanced over her shoulder. Beyond the creeper-shrouded windows she could see the dark stain on the white clapboard wall of the hummingbirds' room, the small jagged crack that was the hive's opening. "Yes," she said with a smile, "I know."

He gave her a reproachful look. "I thought you said you had no other cohabitants."

"I never said that," Suzanna said primly. "I only said I didn't run a zoo."

"Uh-oh," Cam said darkly. "Why do I have a feeling there's something more you're not telling me?" Chewing in thoughtful silence, he looked back at the bees.

Uncomfortable with the silence, Suzanna cleared her throat and asked conversationally, "Just what is your job? I know you work for the Corps of Engineers and that you're a civil servant. And I know you have something to do with the problems with the excess runoff. But just what exactly do you do?"

A shutter came down across his eyes. He was silent for a long time, frowning darkly at his plate, and Suzanna squirmed inwardly, wondering if he resented her prying. Finally, he took a deep breath and said carefully, "I'm an engineer. Sort of a consultant, really. I go where there are problems—usually in emergency situations—and try to find solutions."

"I see," Suzanna said just as carefully. "And do you find solutions?"

"Usually. Yes, I do."

"Then that must be very rewarding."

His eyes met hers, a cold, bleak look that stirred in her vague, unidentifiable fears. "Sometimes," he said in a voice so low she could barely hear him. "More often it's . . . just painful."

He seemed willing to say more, but all at once Suzanna felt an odd reluctance to continue. "Do you have a family?" she asked, quickly changing the subject.

He seemed half relieved, half annoyed. "I have a family. My parents are both lawyers—Beverly Hills. And I have a sister."

"No wife?"

He smiled. "No wife. My life-style isn't conducive to lasting relationships."

The darkness had gone from his eyes; now they carried a warning that was about as subtle as a rainy-day sky. Suzanna met his gaze with one that was steady and direct, a warning of her own. *Don't worry, Mr. Cam Harris. I have no desire to get involved with a wayfarin' stranger.* Her voice was cold and casual as she continued the polite conversation; there was nothing to betray, and no way to explain, the sudden acceleration of her heartbeat.

"Is your sister older or younger?"

"Younger," Cam said readily, "but not by much. Just a year."

"You must be very close."

"Oh, we were."

"Were? She's not—"

"Oh, no, no—I just haven't seen her in a while. She was in the Sudan, last I heard. She works for the UN—WHO. She spends all her time in third world countries. And the last time she was home I was in Israel.

"My goodness," Suzanna remarked. "What was it that produced two world travelers in the same family?"

Cam snorted and looked uncomfortable. "I don't know. I guess maybe I grew up on the notion of the responsibilities of privilege. My parents were both Kennedy liberals—they call themselves that, but I hate labels. Anyway, they were always into causes. I remember the night they came home from the Ambassador Hotel to tell us that R.F.K. had been killed. Something like that makes a lasting impression. I studied engineering in college. I'd always liked building things, designing them myself, and engineering seemed to be the closest I could come to that in college. After college I went into the Peace Corps—both Tracy and I did. I wound up in Peru building hydroelectric projects. And after that it seemed a natural step to civil service. Because I spoke Spanish, my first job was a bridge in Panama. It had developed stability problems, and well, I designed a system that solved the problem. One thing just led to another." He shrugged and pushed back his plate. "I've been moving around ever since."

His eyes rested for a moment on her mouth, and then he gave a wry little smile and looked out the window at the bees. "I guess it's a good thing I'm not allergic to travel."

When the last of the groceries had been put away and the dishes done, Cam went up to his "office" to work. He had brought in a folding table and a portable fan to help dissipate the second-story heat, and was soon poring over his diagrams and figures.

Suzanna took a big cardboard box filled with notes and old photographs into the living room and settled herself cross-legged in the middle of the floor. The rest of the afternoon passed in extraordinary and wholly unexpected peace and productivity. The house was as silent as it had been earlier, but it was no longer empty.

THE LIGHT WAS FADING when Cam came downstairs. Suzanna, apparently too absorbed to get up and turn on the lights, was sitting on the threadbare carpet, surrounded by piles of yellowed photographs and scribbled notes. She looked up to catch him leaning against the door frame, watching her.

"I didn't realize it was so late." She smiled. "No wonder I can't see anything."

Her voice shivered across his nerve endings like fur. He came on into the darkening room, ignoring the light switch.

"What have you got there?" he asked softly, balancing on his heels beside her. "More old love letters?"

"Oh, no. It's just something I've been working on," she mumbled, trying to gather the jumble closer to herself like a mother hen corralling her chicks. "Nothing important." In the dim light Cam couldn't see her cheeks turn pink with that quick blush, but her voice sounded breathless and embarrassed.

He watched her for a minute and then stood up. All her defenses were back in place. It was a shame; this afternoon had been great. He couldn't remember when he'd had a more enjoyable time. But now it was getting dark; she was facing the evening, alone with him....

A thought as unfamiliar as it was unheralded struck him. He wanted her to trust him. He wanted to reassure her, to somehow recapture the warm and easy mood of the afternoon. He wanted something from her he'd never asked of any woman—her *friendship*.

He stood up, and instead of turning on the bright overhead light, went to the upright piano against the wall and turned on the small lamp up above. It made a pool of golden light and left the rest of the room softly shadowed. "May I?" he asked, gesturing toward the piano bench.

"Oh, yes, of course; please do!" Her voice was breath-less with surprise and expectation. As he cracked his knuckles and flexed his fingers, he smiled wryly to him-self; her image of him, whatever it was, obviously hadn't included musical ability of any kind.

He played a few random notes, testing the action of the keys, and then launched impulsively into the "Maple Leaf Rag." But it didn't feel right, somehow; it didn't fit his mood, and he ended it with crashing discord after the first section.

She said softly, "Wow," and he threw a smile of apol-ogy at her over his shoulder. He'd been showing off, something he rarely felt compelled to do. He gave a soft snort and shook his head. Tom Sawyer walking the fence for Becky Thatcher? Incredible....

"Sorry," he muttered, playing chords. "Don't want to wake the skunks." After a moment, he gave a little rag-time intro and began to sing:

I came from Alabama, with my banjo on my knee,
I'm goin' to Lou-siana, My true love for to see.
It rained all night the day I left, the weather it was dry;
The sun so hot I froze to death; Suzanna, don't you
cry.

He lifted his head to smile at her. "How about a little help?"

She got to her feet and came to join him in the light, and he saw that her eyes were shining with pleasure. The glow in them started a corresponding incandescence inside his chest. She stood behind him, close enough so that he could feel the warmth of her body. Her scent filled his head, an intoxicant as subtle and insidious as fine old brandy.

Suzanna's voice was a rich, husky alto. Together they sang:

Oh! Suzanna, Oh don't you cry for me.
I've come from Alabama with my banjo on my knee....

There was silence when the note had died away, a silence suddenly alive with a mutual awareness that was almost audible. Cam suddenly felt as fraudulent as he'd felt when she'd praised him for owning Cat. He wanted her trust and her friendship, but he was kidding himself if he thought that was *all* he wanted.

He cleared his throat and picked up a small dog-eared songbook. "What's this?" he asked, idly turning pages.

"It's my grandmother's. Just some old, old songs." Did her voice seem even huskier than usual? He was afraid to turn around, afraid to look at her, lest he scare her away. He didn't want her to go; he wanted her right there, close to him. So he put the book down on the piano and began to play and sing, "Just a song at twilight, when the lights are low..." and as he'd hoped she would, she sat down on the bench beside him and picked up the harmony.

They sang "Oh My Darling Clementine" and "Long, Long Ago" and "The Voice in the Old Village Choir." They laughed their way through "Captain Jinks of the Horse Marines." And then, at some point, they both stopped singing. Her arm brushed his, and she didn't move away. He kept turning pages, his fingers rambling over the keyboard, making sad and wistful harmonies. Darkness had closed in on the old house, leaving them and the piano in an island of light. The scent of lilacs drifted in through an open window, dissipating the last traces of skunk.

Cam turned another page and began to sing softly:

Just when the day is over,
Just when the lights are low;
Back to the heart returns
Life's golden long ago.
Far, far away we wander,
Watching the firelight gleams;
Far, far away from the world's shadows gray,
Into the land of dreams....

He stopped playing and turned to look at Suzanna. The light caught the soft curve of her cheek and glistened in her eyes.

"That's one of my grandmother's favorites," she said with a reminiscent smile.

"It reminds me of you." His voice was gruff; she looked questioningly at him, searching his face, and he half turned, lifting his hand from the keys to touch her cheek. "I think you like to go there sometimes. Far away, to a golden long ago." Her eyes gazed at him almost as if she were in a trance. When he lightly brushed her lips with his thumb, they parted unconsciously. He no longer felt guilty; instead, he felt like a teenager on a moonlit doorstep, about to gamble his fragile ego on his first kiss.

His fingers fanned across her cheek, finding the edge of her jaw, the convolutions of her ear. She didn't move; even her breathing seemed to have stopped. He slid his fingers under the heavy fall of hair and found the nape of her neck moist with sweat. The curve of her skull fit into the palm of his hand, and he exerted the gentlest pressure and slowly lowered his mouth to hers. She didn't flinch or pull away. Her eyelids dropped, and he felt the faintest whisper of indrawn breath just as his lips touched hers. His other hand left the cold keyboard and curved over her shoulder, around to her back, and he felt a tremor run through her body.

Oh God, he thought, *she's so soft. She's so vulnerable. She's too easy to hurt....* He felt guilty again, but her lips were so firm and pliant under his, her breath as sweet and fresh as a child's. And the first tentative touching seemed to have generated its own energy, its own magnetic force. Neither of them could pull away or stop what was happening.

Their mouths brushed, touched, melded and withdrew, then touched again—vibrant little forays filled with the excitement of the unknown. In a daring exploration, he touched the moist insides of her lips with his tongue. When they parted readily to let him in, he ran his tongue along the cutting edge of her teeth. Her tongue touched his shyly, tentatively. And he felt a twisting, wrenching sensation deep in his belly that forced a wave of heat to his groin and a low moan from his throat.

He felt her hand low on his side, just at his waist. When it slid around to his back, he put his arms around her, releasing her head but not her mouth. The pressure of his kiss drove her head back against the muscles of his arm. There was no more searching, no more tentative exploration; he owned her mouth, all of it, and he wanted the rest of her, as well. His hand caressed her throat, her jaw, her collarbone, then brushed down across the swell of her breast to her waist, pulling her closer. He wanted her close to his body, wanted her all against him. Their side-by-side position frustrated him.

You're moving too fast! his mind warned, even as his hand was smoothing over her hip and sliding under her, lifting her more fully into the curve of his body. She came unresisting, putting her hand on his shoulder and then hooking it around his neck.

"Are you . . . sure this house isn't haunted? Something is in here with us. It just flew past my neck."

Her eyes slid past him to a far corner of the high ceiling and then closed. A quiver vibrated through her. He realized that it was laughter laced with nervous tension. "Oh, dear," she murmured. "It's Maggie."

"Maggie?"

She cleared her throat and looked into his eyes, struggling to keep her face under control.

"My bat," she said.

Chapter Four

"She lives in the attic," Suzanna said in a small voice.

Cam just stared at her, a fierce, smoky look from beneath lowered brows. "What I can't understand," he muttered after a minute, his voice gravelly, "is why you ever worried about a chaperone."

Suzanna was suddenly, shockingly aware of the position they were in—her head lying back on his arm and her hair cascading down, his hand under her, ready to lift her into his lap. And most shocking of all, her own hands, one pressed against resilient muscle at the small of his back, the other on the back of his neck, her fingers even now stroking absentmindedly through the soft-crisp feathers of his hair.

She swallowed, a difficult, convulsive reflex because of the position of her head. Cam's eyes jerked downward to follow the movement and then lingered on the deep neckline slash of her blouse. She wondered if the wild beating of her heart could be noticeable.

When his gaze finally returned to her face, it was still dark, still smoky, and something else she couldn't read. He muttered under his breath, and when she said, "What?" he shook his head and slowly eased her back to an upright position.

"This has sure been a week for surprises," he murmured cryptically. Then he swung his legs around the bench until his back was toward her and put his hands on his knees, lifting his head to stare up at the corner of the room. A small brownish-gray bat hung there, its head turned, apparently watching them. "How do you know it's a 'she'?" he asked after a moment.

Suzanna, who had been staring at her hands, rubbed her palms down her thighs, smoothing her skirt. She took a deep breath and said evenly, "I don't. It just seemed better, if someone was going to be flying around my room at night, watching every move I made, to think of it as female."

It was sensitive of him to give her a chance to recover. Only she couldn't help wishing he was sensitive enough to realize that she didn't *want* to recover. She felt shaken but not ashamed. She hadn't wanted him to stop kissing her; she wanted very much for him to kiss her again. Of all the emotions quivering around inside her at this moment, the most easily identifiable of them was disappointment.

And then it occurred to her that *he* might be having regrets. Maybe he hadn't meant to kiss her at all. Maybe he'd tried it as an experiment and it had been a letdown. A cold knot of rejection lodged just under her sternum. Maybe, she thought wretchedly, he's relieved. . . .

"I thought bats couldn't see," Cam said thoughtfully. "You know, 'blind as a bat'?"

Suzanna lifted one shoulder. "I don't know about that," she said in a low voice. "She sure *seems* to be watching."

He turned the rest of the way around then so that they were facing each other on the bench. His eyes were clear, and once more that ambiguous shade of greenish gray. He smiled at her, and her chest contracted. *Now,* she thought. *If he wanted to kiss me again, he would....*

But he just looked at her, shaking his head in wonder. "And she lives in your attic. Let me guess. That door in your bedroom—you leave it open on purpose?"

Suzanna cleared her throat and said protectively, "Well, I like her. She can go out the broken window in the attic, of course, and I'm sure that's how she eats. But every once in a while she comes in here to say hello."

"Doesn't Mrs. Hopewell object?"

"Oh, of course not! Mrs. Hopewell would like to catch her. She says it would be a thrill to hold a live bat in her hand." Cam was staring at her as if both she and Mrs. Hopewell were weird alien beings, and she quickly explained. "Before she taught elementary school, Mrs. Hopewell was a biology teacher, years ago, when it wasn't considered a very proper field for young ladies to be in."

"You're kidding. Just how old *is* she?"

Suzanna shrugged her shoulders. "I don't know. I've never asked. She doesn't seem old to me."

He regarded her for several more seconds as if he couldn't quite believe what he was hearing. Then he gave her a lopsided smile and said, "Okay, do you have any other booby traps rigged to pop out in defense of your honor?"

He seemed completely comfortable now, relaxed and friendly. His eyes were crinkling at her in a kind and sympathetic way that was slowly easing her embarrassment. Now she felt only a little foolish. She gave him a wry smile of her own in return. "If I did, I wouldn't tell you about them, would I? It would defeat the purpose." And then, when his look narrowed dangerously, she lowered her lashes demurely and capitulated. "Oh, all right, I guess I'd better tell you about King Henry. It might be a shock if you were to come up the walk one dark night and step on him—not to mention the damage it would do Henry!" she added in horrified afterthought. It had just occurred to her that some people have violent reactions to snakes.

"I'll bite," Cam said dryly. "Who's Henry? Or should I say, *what*?"

"Henry is a king snake," Suzanna said earnestly, "and if you do find him, please, *please* don't hurt him. He's lived and hunted in this yard for as long as anyone can remember, which is another reason why there aren't any mice. It's also nice to be able to walk barefoot in the orchard and through the gardens without having to worry about rattlesnakes. This is his kingdom. We don't see much of him—just once or twice a year he shows himself to let us know he's—"

"In his kingdom and all's right with the world," Cam finished under his breath, still staring at her in what she imagined must be horrified fascination. "Are you a zoologist, or is it just some kind of hobby, collecting wild things?"

It was her turn to stare at him. "I don't collect things; they just go with the house. Some of them have been here longer than I have. Angel's Walk is big enough for all of us."

He stood up abruptly and went to turn on the overhead light. The sudden illumination made his hair gleam like polished metal; she found herself remembering how soft it had felt to her fingers, and how warm.

"This is quite a house," Cam said. He was roaming the room with an odd restlessness, touching the rich fruitwood moldings, looking up at the high ceiling, the peeling wallpaper. Maggie the bat, Suzanna noticed, had disappeared. "It really *was* built to last."

"Yes," Suzanna said with a warm glow of pride. "Papa—my grandfather—said that with care it would last forever. Only—" She shrugged sadly. "I'm afraid I haven't been able to give it the care it needs. But some-day—" She broke off, and he turned, lifting his eyebrows at her.

"Someday?"

She took a deep breath. "Someday I'll have the money to restore it." Her eyes went automatically to the pile of photographs and papers she had left on the floor.

Cam's gaze followed hers. He made a small gesture and said, "This looks like a project. Something for the mu-seum?"

She gripped the edge of the piano bench, rocking back and forth and biting back the automatic protest that clutched at her throat. "Not really," she said tightly. "It's . . . personal."

He looked from her to the pile and back again and then said softly, "May I?" At her reluctant nod, he dropped to his heels and selected a picture at random. He looked at it for a long time in silence and then held it up so she could see and said, "Your grandfather?"

Suzanna looked at the photo of the big square man in overalls and nodded. "Yes, that's Papa. He's quite young there."

"Looks strong."

Suzanna laughed. "Oh, yes, he was very strong, in every way. People used to tell stories about him. . . ." Her voice trailed off. Cam looked at her curiously and poked through the pictures some more.

"Most of these are of him, aren't they? What are you planning to do with them?"

Suzanna tensed and was silent. Cam continued to stare patiently at her until it seemed she had no choice but to lick her lips and say in a low, tense voice, "I'm, uh, writing a book."

"What?"

A little more firmly, she repeated it. "I'm writing a book."

His face lit with surprise and interest. "Really! Why do you say it like that, as if you were afraid I'd laugh?"

"Maybe I was. I've never told anyone before." She spread her hands and gave a nervous little laugh. Her heart was pounding again, a jittery, butterflies-in-the-stomach kind of rhythm. "I felt a bit strange about telling anyone. So, you're the first. I've wanted to do it for several years, but I only really got started last winter."

His eyes seemed very intense, holding hers with a deep, unreadable look from across the expanse of carpet. "Come tell me about it," he said softly.

There was something very compelling about the man from the Corps of Engineers, Suzanna decided. Something in his eyes, or in his voice, perhaps. How else could she explain what made her do as he asked, join him there on the floor, tell him of plans and dreams she'd never even revealed to her family? Why did she keep finding it necessary to remind herself that he was a stranger?

"He looks like a big man," Cam said, tapping one of the old photographs. "When did he die?"

"Let's see—three, no *four*, years ago in April. He was eighty-seven."

"And your grandmother?"

Suzanna smiled. "Oh, she's very much alive. Ninety-two, and as stubborn and independent as a mule."

"What are these?" Cam indicated the scattered notes.

"Papa's stories." She took a deep breath. "The reason for the book, really. They were—are—living history." She leaned forward, trying to make him understand, wondering how someone as rootless as Cam seemed to be ever could understand. "Papa was a storyteller. He and others like him, the old-timers I knew when I was a small child, they *lived* the history we can only read about. Papa loved to tell stories—the same ones over and over. We all heard them so many times that after a while we stopped listening. And it wasn't until it was almost too late that I realized that what he was telling was history. He was giving us all his greatest legacy—our family's story, yes, but also the story of this valley, and even of the settling of California and the West—firsthand. And we almost let that gift be lost forever."

She fell silent. There was a painful constriction in her throat, and she couldn't look at the man sitting so quietly across from her. This was all so personal, so moving to her; she felt almost unbearably exposed and vulnerable.

He waited in silence, too, not prodding her, and after a moment she took a little breath and went on. "His name was Harland Day, but everyone called him Weaver. He used to like to say he got his name because someone once said, 'That old man Day can sure weave a tale!'" Suzanna smiled. "It wasn't true, though. Weaver was just his real middle name."

"Tall tales?" Cam asked, lifting his eyebrows.

Suzanna threw him a quick, defensive look. "Oh, no, his stories were true. He loved a good yarn as much as anybody, but he always made it clear from the beginning whether a story was true or not. If he said something was true, it was. I know that because so many of the stories he told me have been verified. He had a fantastic memory. He could remember places he'd lived when he was a little tiny child, and he could actually go back and find them again, after all the years and the changes. Here's an example." Suzanna picked up a color snapshot and handed it to Cam.

"About ten or fifteen years ago, Papa decided he wanted to try to find the house where he was born. His parents homesteaded in the Sierra Nevada foothills of the San Joaquin Valley, near White River. *Their* parents had come across the prairie in covered wagons in 1850, and when they found the gold fever had died down, they became teamsters. They drove bull trains over the mountains, carrying loads of supplies from camp to camp. Papa could tell you stories about that—" She stopped and gave Cam an apologetic smile. "I'm sorry. I get sidetracked. Back to that picture. Anyway, the amazing thing is, Papa did find the old homestead. The house was a shack, and the yard was full of old junk, but the palm trees his mother had planted nearly a century ago were still there. You can see them in the picture. And that's the well his father dug by hand." She leaned back on her hands, shaking her head and smiling, remembering, hearing again her grandfather's rich, storyteller's voice.

"That well nearly cost his father his life. He'd got down to water at about twenty feet, and there was a boulder in the bottom of the well. He loaded it with dynamite, and when he was ready, he fixed a rope on the windlass so that his wife could windlass him out of the well with his help. Well, he had lighted the fuse and hollered for his wife to pull him up, and the windlass broke. His wife threw herself onto the windlass to keep it from turning, and Papa's father came out of that well hand over hand. When he reached the top, he had strength enough to grab the top of the curbing. Then his wife let go of the windlass and grabbed him by the seat of the pants and hauled him over the side, and the blast went off and threw rocks a hundred feet in the air!"

Suzanna came back to the present in the middle of warm, soft laughter, both hers and Cam's. She stopped to brush at her eyes and draw a long, steadying breath. "Oh, he liked to tell that story, and he'd laugh...."

"I think you have a lot of the storyteller in you, too," Cam said softly.

She hugged her knees, embarrassed suddenly and very self-conscious. "I'm sorry; I know I get carried away. I can talk on and on sometimes."

"It's all right. I like listening to you." His voice sounded gravelly, almost gruff. His hand stirred idly through the notes and pictures. "So you've decided to write it all down."

"Yes." She was staring at his hand, suddenly remembering that he had slipped it under her... fanny; remembering the feel of it cupping and lifting, an intimate and presumptuous warmth. Why hadn't she minded? If Ron had done such a thing—She coughed and looked quickly away. "I'm going to write it all down, because I have something of my grandmother's side of the family in me, too. She writes everything down—in diaries, letters, family Bible. Now Papa's story will be recorded, as well, even if it's never published." She was busy as she spoke, gathering up the scattered pieces of her dream.

Cam got unhurriedly to his feet and stood looking thoughtfully down at her. "It's very important to you, isn't it—the past?"

She didn't answer, and he walked slowly to the bay window and fingered the dusty brocade draperies, faded now to an indeterminate gray. "Suzanna?"

She looked up at him unwillingly and found that he was frowning, watching the reflection in the dark glass. "Sue, tell me something. Why did your grandfather give you this house? Tony's told me a little about your family. I know it's very large. He could have left it to any one of dozens of people, including your grandmother. He left it to you. Do you know why?''

"Maybe," Suzanna said softly, "he knew that I needed the house as much as it needed me."

"Did you know," he said harshly, turning from the window, "that it's sitting on government property? On lake bottom?"

"Yes." She hugged herself, suddenly frightened without admitting why. He seemed so grim. "But they bought more land than they needed when they put the lake in. The water is over the spillway. The lake can't rise any higher. Isn't that right?"

He was silent, regarding her steadily and soberly, his deep-set eyes shadowed and unreadable. "Isn't it?" she demanded, her voice rising a little.

He walked slowly over to her and extended a hand. After a moment's hesitation, she put her hand in his and let him pull her to her feet. Her hand wasn't quite steady in his, and he stood for a minute, frowning down at it.

"Suzanna," he said as if he'd just had a brilliant idea, "would you like to go out with me?"

He was still frowning at her hand, and consequently so was she. At his unexpected invitation she jerked her eyes to his face and muttered stupidly, "Out?" She caught his smile just as it slipped sideways.

"Out," he repeated. His thumb had begun to rub absently over her knuckles.

"You mean, like a date?" Except for Ron, she hadn't been asked out on a date since high school—and rarely then.

"Yeah. Like dinner."

"Tonight? We . . . we have so much food. . . ."

Cam laughed and released her hand finally. "Tomorrow, then."

Suzanna seriously doubted whether one day was going to make much of a dent in the amount of food they had stockpiled, thanks to their shopping sprees, but she was so bemused by the invitation and the oddly tense little eddies that were swirling just under the surface of their conversation that she found herself nodding. "Yes . . . all right. Tomorrow."

Cam stooped and picked up her box of notes and placed it in her arms. "Tomorrow," he said, and left her.

"THREE FEET," Tony O'Brian said with a snort of disgust. "Three damn lousy feet."

He was bent over a large aerial photographic survey map spread across his desk, and his pencil beat an angry tattoo on the irregular red-shaded area that surrounded the existing lake. "Look at this, Cam." He pointed a long, bony finger, tapping the map here and there for emphasis. "You've got the airport here, marinas here, here, here and *here*. And this one's got a restaurant besides. And there's a trailer park here that'll have to be evacuated, and you know some of these mobile homes aren't very mobile! Are you listening, Cam?"

"Of course I'm listening," Cam said irritably. "I drew the damned map. Don't tell *me* what it means!" He could feel the park manager's eyes on his back but refused to turn from the window. Out of the corner of his eye he saw Tony O'Brian walk around the desk and stop.

"Cam—" Tony's voice came again, more gently. "You do know about Angel's Walk? You're going to flood it."

Cam turned on him in unreasonable fury. "*I'll* flood it? Don't put this onto *my* back. *I* didn't put fifty feet of snowpack in those mountains and then send a heat wave! *I* didn't put a city in the middle of a dry lake basin. My job is to save a whole *city*! I can't weigh one broken-down old house that never should have been allowed to stay on that land in the first place against the welfare of a quarter of a million people, for God's sake! She—all these people *knew* they were on designated lake bottom!"

"Bakersfield sits in an old lake bottom, too," Tony said softly. "If it didn't, we wouldn't have a problem." He sighed. "Look, Cam—I'm sorry, man. It's just—"

"No, I'm sorry," Cam said quietly. Still without turning, he asked, "Tony, why in the hell did you send me to her? You must have known from the first minute I mentioned the possibility of raising the spillway what it would mean to that house."

Tony came to stand beside him. He gave a little snort of irony. "Well, you were just so arrogant. You just kept shrugging off 'a few marinas, some flooded fields' like they didn't matter. I guess I wanted you to know on a more personal level who'd be getting hurt. These are real people, Cam. I've known most of 'em all my life. Damn it, they matter."

Cam swore viciously under his breath, and Tony moved to the desk to begin rolling up the map. He glanced up at Cam every so often but didn't say anything more. After a few minutes, Cam abruptly turned, frowning.

"Will she have a place to go?"

Tony looked surprised. "Suzanna? Oh, sure—there's family all over the valley. Any of us'd be glad to have her."

"Maggie and Henry, too, I wonder?" Cam muttered under his breath, and then hastily brushed it aside when Tony looked puzzled. "Nothing. Forget it."

"Of course, living with relatives isn't like having a place of your own," Tony said, continuing to regard Cam with a worried frown. "And then—well, to Suzanna, Angel's Walk isn't just a house."

"Look, dammit," Cam rasped. "It doesn't make any difference; can't you get that through your head? I can't let it make any difference. It's got to be done. And it doesn't make one particle of a difference how I feel!"

"How *do* you feel?" Tony asked pointedly.

"How the hell do I know!" Cam shouted, and then, angry with himself, he muttered crossly, "That's none of your business."

"Suzanna is family," Tony said flatly. "I may be old-fashioned, but I think that makes it my business. And I'm fond of her. I'd, uh—I'm asking you to lay off of her, Cam."

"What?" Cam stared at him, his eyes narrowing.

Tony looked uncomfortable but determined. "I said lay off. Leave her alone. She's a nice girl. And you'll be moving on soon. I don't want her hurt any more than she has to be."

Cam felt his face twist in what he knew must be very close to a sneer. It fit the way he felt inside. He practically snarled. "You should have thought about that before you sent me to her, old buddy! It's a little bit late, isn't it, for the big-brother routine?" He felt the other man's wince like a kick in the stomach and almost wished Tony would haul off and let him have a good one, right in the jaw.

"I'll be going to Sacramento tomorrow," Cam said crisply. "I know who to push to get this expedited. Expect the crew here day after tomorrow. Those new spillway sections will be here by the end of the week, by army chopper. We'll crane 'em into place over the weekend." He was on the way out of the office when Tony's quiet voice stopped him.

"Shall I tell the paper? They've been calling me. So has the chamber of commerce. And the sheriff will have to get going on the evacuations."

Cam looked at him, counting slowly to ten to give the helpless rage in his belly a chance to settle. "Keep it till to-morrow," he said finally in a hard voice. "I want to tell her first."

Tony nodded, and Cam started out once more. And stopped again. "By the way, is there a hospital in the valley?"

Tony looked startled. "Well, sure, yeah. What—"

"Where is it? Show me on a map."

Tony, looking more bewildered by the minute, did so. Cam studied the map, measuring the distance from Angel's Walk to the hospital, and then shook his head. "Okay, now—where's the nearest pharmacy?"

"Pharmacy?" Tony looked half scandalized, half alarmed. "Why do you need a pharmacy?"

Cam gave a bark of joyless laughter. "Not for what you're thinking, so relax." He grinned unpleasantly at the color that was suffusing the park manager's bony face, hating himself, hating Tony for putting up with him. "Though maybe that's not a bad idea, after all!"

He slammed the door and dived into the late-afternoon heat, wondering whether he'd ever been more unhappy with himself and with his life.

SUZANNA WAS SINGING in the kitchen; rather, she was humming, putting in words only when she felt like it.

Just a song at twilight, when the lights are low....

She wondered whether there had ever been a time in her life when she'd been happier.

As idiotic, silly and schoolgirl romantic as it seemed, she was fairly certain she was falling in love with a perfect stranger—the man from the Corps of Engineers named John Campbell Harris.

Of course, never having been in love before, she couldn't be absolutely certain that was what it was. But if there was anything she could say about herself, it was that she was honest and straightforward. She never tried to deny her feelings or, except to spare someone else's, to hide them. And she knew that no one in her life had ever touched so many feelings deep inside her as he did. *John.* Or Mr. Harris. Somehow she liked calling him that. It had an odd, sort of old-fashioned intimacy, almost Victorian.

It occurred to her suddenly to wonder if he thought she was some sort of Victorian prude, reading old love letters, living in a Victorian house, singing old songs. But there wasn't anything prudish about the way he made her feel. He was so brash, so vital; from the first time he'd touched her, brushing tears from her lashes with his fingertips, she'd felt the energy flowing from him like power from a dynamo. And with his kiss he'd touched something deep inside her, awakening all sorts of hungers and yearnings that were blossoming inside her now the way a seed stirs to life when touched by a drop of rain.

No, Suzanna wasn't a prude. She was too honest and down-to-earth for that. She was a live-and-let-live kind of person. People and animals simply were what they were. She either accepted them as they were or left them alone. And she had grown up too close to the earth to have very many illusions about human or animal behavior. Basic and natural desires, like feelings, were never wrong; they just *were*. She accepted them. It was only actions that were right or wrong, and actions were only wrong when they hurt someone. It was a simple philosophy, and up till now it had worked just fine. It was interesting and something of a shock to her to discover that actually experiencing those desires and feelings was something else entirely.

At first she'd been frightened, but she thought the fear was mostly a holdover from her adolescence. It was fear of rejection. She'd been attracted to him from the beginning and painfully aware that she wasn't the sort of woman likely to appeal to him. She'd been bewildered by his flirting and even a little resentful of what she was sure must be just habit on his part. But last night he'd kissed her. And she'd felt the raw desire vibrate through his body and had seen it in his eyes. She'd felt exhilarated, even awed. For the first time in her life, she understood the power of those feelings.

But that wasn't all. Cam Harris had *listened* to her, really listened, as if he genuinely cared and was interested in what she had to say. No one had ever paid attention to her like that, and in some ways that had touched her more deeply than his kiss.

What an exciting, dynamic, fascinating man he was, and how incredible that she, ordinary, unremarkable Suzanna Day, should be "going out" with such a man! No wonder she felt like singing!

She'd been singing this morning in the museum when Ron had stopped by unexpectedly to ask her to dinner this evening. He'd commented on it somewhat testily. Poor Ron, he wasn't used to being turned down.

Poor Suzanna, she wasn't accustomed to dealing with two invitations for the same evening. She hoped she'd handled it tactfully. She really didn't want to hurt Ron. He was fond of her, in his way, and it really wasn't his fault that he had never ignited skyrockets in her.

Suzanna was making gingerbread, and the whole kitchen was warm and filled with spicy smells and golden afternoon sunlight. There was no trace of skunk today; they'd been quiet for two nights in a row, which was most unusual for this time of year. Suzanna was frowning a little as her glance returned to the glimmer of lake waters beyond the kitchen windows. Was it possible the water *was* coming? Had the animals sensed it?

The front door slammed as she was taking the pan of gingerbread out of the oven. She hastily wiped perspiration from her forehead and turned with a smile, hoping she didn't look too hot and disheveled.

Cam came into the kitchen, and she felt her smile vanish as if a light had been switched off inside her. How fragile a thing was happiness. Just like that, her euphoria was gone, and all her fears and uncertainties returned, as the darkness returns when the light goes out.

Chapter Five

Cam halted just inside the door. His face was impassive, almost wooden, and his eyes were like flint. He gave her one brief, hard glance and then kept walking, straight to the refrigerator, nodding and murmuring a polite hello as he passed.

He was carrying a small white paper bag. He took a red plastic box out of it and started to put it into the refrigerator, then appeared to change his mind and instead slapped it down on the table. He fixed her with a steady, considering gaze.

Suzanna licked her lips and waited tensely, wondering desperately what could have happened to change him from the laughing, charming man of the day before to this coldly brooding stranger. Was it something she'd done? Or not done? She looked distractedly down at Cat, who had been licking the mixing bowl clean and was now washing her front paws.

Cam followed her glance. And all at once something seemed to give in him, like a spring uncoiling. He rubbed a hand over the back of his neck and released a long breath, almost a sigh. His eyes softened to gray-green. Now he merely looked tired.

"Smells good," he said, gesturing toward the cooling pan of gingerbread. "What is it?" The words were friendly, but his manner still seemed forced, stilted, as though he were trying to atone for the brusqueness.

"Gingerbread," Suzanna said huskily, knowing he probably didn't really care.

"Ah—" He nodded and fell silent.

After a moment, Suzanna cleared her throat and gestured toward the red box on the tablecloth. "What is that?"

Cam looked at her for a moment longer and then straightened and picked it up. He broke a paper seal with his thumbnail and opened it, then held it out to her. She stared at the neatly packaged hypodermic syringe and other mysterious objects without comprehension.

"Ever seen one like it?" Cam asked, watching her.

She shook her head. "Are you diabetic?" she ventured, still puzzled. "I told you to give me a list—"

"No, and I'm not allergic to food of any kind. Just—" his lips twisted in a wry little smile and he jabbed a finger toward the windows "—to bee stings."

Suzanna sank into a chair, forming a prolonged, silent "Oh..." with her lips. Her legs felt shaky for some reason. Relief, she supposed; she hadn't realized how shaken she'd been by his coldness. But it was only the bees! He was worried about them, worried about how she would feel. The idiot, she thought lovingly, gazing at him. Why didn't he say anything before?

"I thought I'd better show you how to use it," he was saying as his big hands took small packets out of the box and arranged them on the tablecloth. "I carry a kit with me, and I'm capable of injecting myself if the need arises. However," he went on with chilling calm, "there's always a chance I won't be able to get to it before I stop breathing, in which case it's nice to know there's someone around who can do it for me. Here—'' He pointed to the packets, naming them. "Alcohol, to wipe before and after injection. Forget that tourniquet; you don't need it. The syringe contains two doses of epinephrine in case one doesn't do the trick. You give one, turn this, and the other is primed and ready. The tablets are antihistamines. Ever give an injection?''

Suzanna could only manage a headshake. "Do you mean," she said in a horrified voice, "that you could die? Just from a bee sting?''

"I don't know," Cam said, grinning at her, his natural buoyancy apparently restored. "I've never cared to put it to the test. But I've come close enough to be smart about precautions. Come over here a minute."

Suzanna went unwillingly, on shaky legs. He was taking another syringe, this one empty, out of the bag, and when she had come to stand at his shoulder, he removed the last item, a small bottle labeled "sterile saline solution." With growing apprehension, she watched him fill the empty syringe with the saline solution, working with tight-lipped concentration. When he held it out to her, she flinched away in horror.

"Go on—take it," he said firmly.

"Oh, no. Please.'' Suzanna swallowed, feeling herself go cold. "I can't."

"Of course you can," he said softly, his eyes, with a glint of laughter in their depths, holding hers. "You wouldn't let me die. Not a woman who feeds skunks and hummingbirds. A woman," he added in undisguised challenge, "descended from one who hauled her husband out of a well by the seat of his pants."

When she still could only stare at him, he said gently, "It's very easy, really, once you get over the trauma of the first time. That's why I want you to do it now, when I'm in shape to talk you through it.''

Suzanna gulped. "I'll get rid of the bees."

"There will always be bees. Come—let me show you." His voice was so patient, so warm. Suzanna felt his hands take hers and caress them, molding them as he showed her how to hold the syringe. "Like a pencil, see?" he murmured. "Now swab the area with alcohol. Let's see—this arm muscle is fine. Any large muscle will do."

Suzanna was assailed by a wave of dizziness, more the result of his nearness and the feel of that firm, heated flesh beneath her hands than by what she had to do. She tried to concentrate very hard on what she was doing, carefully sponging the smooth mahogany skin with an alcohol wipe. As she blew on his skin to dry it, she glanced up to find his eyes smoldering only inches away from her face. She jerked back as if they might burst into flame at any moment and said sharply, "All right—now what?"

"Take the muscle in your hand and squeeze it," he murmured. "Like this."

She put her hand on the bulging biceps. It felt like rock.

"Come on," he teased softly. "I said *squeeze* it."

"Then relax it," Suzanna exclaimed with annoyance. "I *can't* squeeze it like that!"

He laughed, his eyes shifting to caress her cheeks. "Sorry, how's that?"

"Better," Suzanna murmured, swallowing. She stared at the tanned bulge of muscle and was aware of a desire to feel the warmth and firmness of it with her mouth. She licked her lips and raised the syringe.

"Now just stab with it—like a dart. You won't hurt me. The needle is very small. See," he murmured, softly triumphant, "that wasn't so bad, was it?" His eyes were holding her, guiding her, like luminous silver beams in the dark. She clung to them and whispered, "What now?"

"Pull back on the plunger just a little bit to see if there's any sign of blood. If you see blood it means you're in a vein. You don't want to be in a vein; you want muscle. Okay, you're fine. Now just push the plunger. And then pull the needle out. Fine. That's great. Now, was that so terrible?"

"No," Suzanna said in a low voice. She made a helpless little sound of relief and closed her eyes and felt Cam's hands close on her waist. It was incredibly easy to let him draw her down into his lap and into the haven of his arms. So incredibly natural to hide her face in the warm hollow of his neck....

His arms tightened around her almost reflexively, holding her close to his body. She felt his cheek resting on the top of her head. He chuckled, making her body move with it, too, and murmured, "'Oh, Suzanna, don't you cry for me....'"

She said, "I'm not crying." The words moved her lips against the smooth, heated skin in the curve of his neck. It seemed so natural to press her lips to that skin and then to open her mouth and touch it with her tongue. It tasted salty and smelled of hardworking man, a musky and intoxicating blend of sun, sweat, soap and masculinity. It must have gone straight to her head like vintage wine, because she'd never felt so reckless. Her mouth moved across the taut muscle at the base of his neck until it met the neck of his T-shirt, followed it downward to the hollow at the base of his throat, then moved upward along the cord of his neck to a place where his pulse jumped against her lips like a wild thing.

Cam groaned. "Suzanna, what are you doing?"

She laughed softly as the sound vibrated through her lips, tickling. "Tasting," she said huskily. "You taste salty. Like potato chips." She leaned forward in his arms, reaching to the other side of his neck, chafing her face against the roughness of stubble before leaning even farther to find the smooth roundness of the biceps where the needle had punctured his flesh.

"Sue, you'd better stop." His hand stroked down her spine and back upward in a rough caress, then swept away the tumble of hair and closed on the nape of her neck.

"You know what they say about potato chips, don't you?" Suzanna murmured against his skin. "You can't eat just one."

He drew a quick breath and pulled her roughly back against his arm. In the instant before his mouth found hers, Suzanna saw that his eyes were closed and that there were strain lines etched into the coppery forehead. And then she let her own eyelids drift down and gave a little sigh that became a part of his kiss.

He took her mouth with a curious mixture of urgency and restraint; his lips, his tongue, his mouth, were vibrant with trapped energy, hard and yet unexpectedly gentle. His tongue plunged deep and then withdrew, then invaded again with renewed passion, almost, Suzanna thought later, when she could think again, as if he couldn't stop himself....

Except that he could. His fingers tangled in her hair, and he tore himself away, leaving her trembling and breathing in sobs. For an instant she stared into eyes that looked like summer storm clouds, dark and threatening. Just for an instant. And then he pulled her face down and cradled it against his neck while his hand smoothed her hair back from her cheek.

"Sorry," he said after a moment, his voice dry. "You tasted salty, too. And you know what they say about—"

Suzanna sat up abruptly, pushing against his chest with her hands and looking around her for a place to hide. She felt sick—dizzy and weak and filled with vague and consuming aches—and the tension in her neck and jaws was forming itself into an inexplicable urge to cry. Why did being in Cam's arms always seem to end with her feeling like this—empty, aching and embarrassed?

But he wouldn't let her go. He said, "Hey, come here," and folded her into his arms. She felt his hands on her back, stroking her as if she were the cat, murmuring soothing, gentling things that weren't really words. After a while, he said huskily, "Okay now?"

She nodded against his neck, not quite truthfully. She stayed where she was because she was still too confused and embarrassed to look at him and because there was something she had to ask him while she still felt the reassurance of his arms around her. "Why—" she began, and then went on tensely, "Why do you always stop? Don't you want— I mean—"

His arms tightened almost convulsively, and she felt the pressure of his lips on the top of her head. "Yes," he said almost immediately, "I do. Believe me. But I have to be able to stand myself." He gave a tight little laugh that bumped against her chest. "Hey, listen—I move around so much, about the only constant company I've got is Cat—and myself."

"But it was me," she said, slowly sitting up. "You didn't—"

"Yeah, Sue, I did." He rubbed his hand over his eyes and then looked at her, searching her face. "And I don't know why; I don't make a habit of seducing innocents."

She struggled briefly, searching for the floor with her feet, and this time he let her go. When her back was to him and he couldn't see her face anymore, she attempted a denial. "What makes you think—"

"Oh, Sue." That was all he said, very softly. She felt him come up behind her and place his hands on the rounds of her shoulders. When he turned her, she couldn't bring her eyes up past the base of his throat. "You are a surprising woman in many ways, but I'm not wrong about this. Am I?"

She shook her head, still not looking at him. "It doesn't matter."

He put a knuckle under her chin, lifted it and kissed her, just a stirring of warm breath and supersensitive nerve endings. "Yes, it does," he whispered. "You're soft and vulnerable and beautiful and sexy and unprotected."

She didn't pretend not to understand. She looked straight into his eyes and said, "That doesn't matter, either."

For just a moment his eyes were soft, and a smile jerked at the corners of his mouth. And then suddenly his mouth hardened and twisted sardonically, and she couldn't read the expression in his eyes at all. With deliberate brutality, he said, "It does to me. I do move around a lot, but I try not to leave a trail of progeny wherever I go." At her shocked gasp he winced, then made an angry, disgusted sound and started for the door. Without turning, he stopped and said harshly, "Don't make this so damned hard for me. I'm not a saint, and you are...very tempting."

He disappeared into the shadowed hallway. When he came back a moment later, Suzanna was still standing where he'd left her, in the middle of the kitchen. He came as far as the doorway and leaned against it, giving her a

long, brooding look filled with hungers and longings she
was just beginning to understand. And then he smiled
wryly and said, "I'm sorry. Do we still have a date?"

She nodded slowly, and he left again, and still she stood
there. When Cat began to brush sympathetically against
her ankles, she collected herself and went outside to change
the hose in the orchard. A quick run through the sprinkler might be just what she needed to cool her body and
restore her good sense.

If she'd surprised Cam Harris, it was nothing compared to the shock she'd given herself. She was no prude,
true; and she hadn't gotten to be a twenty-seven-year-old
virgin on purpose. But the things she'd just done and
said... It was true that she'd never been too concerned
about what people thought of her, but to even consider
having a child— A child deserved a complete set of parents. She, of all people, should know what it was like to
grow up without a father. She had had Papa; what would
her child have? No. She'd been wrong, dead wrong, and
Cam was right. It did matter. A child deserved stability,
security, a rock to lean on. Someone like Papa.

Someone like Ron?

But something in her cried, *What about me? Papa was
an exciting, dynamic man as well as a dependable one.
Why can't I have someone who will stir and excite me?
Someone like... Cam.*

In the end, it wasn't a dash of cold water that restored
her sensible perspective. It was an audience with a king.

In Suzanna's childhood a white rail fence covered with
climbing roses and bordered with flower beds had separated the orchards from the front lawn. The fence had
vanished long ago, and now only a thick bank of iris and
creeping myrtle remained. About halfway along this border there was a gap where the gate had been, and at the

corner of the gap was the faucet, marked and protected by a stubby post. It was always wet there when the sprinkler was going because the connection was old and leaked in a fine spray. It was a favorite watering hole for bees and hummingbirds and frogs.

As she approached the faucet, Suzanna saw what looked like a striped cane lying across the gap in the border. *Henry.* She froze, but it was too late. At the first vibrations of her footsteps, the snake began to move, slowly and with regal dignity. She stood very still, holding her breath until the beautiful black-and-white creature had disappeared into the orchard grass. As always, after a rare glimpse of his elusive majesty, Suzanna felt shaken, strangely humbled and blessed.

Forget Cam, she told herself fiercely. *He's about as stable and dependable as . . . as the Kern River! I'd rather not marry at all. I'll go on living here in Angel's Walk for the rest of my life. I'm happy here.*

But that same little voice inside her said sadly, *I was happy. Before he came. . . .*

THEY WENT TO DINNER in Suzanna's twelve-year-old Dodge, a more appropriate mode of transportation for an evening out than a Corps of Engineers' four-wheel-drive pickup. Suzanna handed Cam her keys and got into the passenger seat without waiting for his gentlemanly assistance. The tension between them was electric; it seemed safer not to risk having him too close.

As he adjusted the seat to accommodate his frame, she studied him covertly, as if an analytical evaluation of him might help to dilute the attraction. She decided that he looked different in the soft blue polo shirt and gray slacks. He looked younger, somehow, more carefree and less like a jock.

No, she amended, he really wasn't a jock. Not in that cliché sense, anyway. He had the build for it, certainly, but not the face or the soul. He was too intelligent, too sensitive, too caring.

She cleared her throat and looked away. Obviously, critical analysis wasn't the answer. She concentrated on adjusting her dress and fastening her own seat belt. Coincidentally, she was wearing gray, too, a cool striped shirtwaist in a thin crepelike fabric that floated around her legs with the soft breezes of evening. Funny, she'd never noticed before the way the dress caressed her skin; she'd bought it for its versatility and comfort. Now it was as if every nerve in her body was awake and working overtime. She felt her hair lying against her neck, her eyelashes brushing her cheeks when she blinked, her nylons hugging her legs, her nipples pushing against the fabric of her bra. And just that thought, that awareness, was enough to make them tingle and contract. She glanced over at Cam and then quickly out the window. Obviously, comfort wasn't going to be a realistic goal for either of them this evening. Cam drove in brooding silence, his elbow on the windowsill, his hand across his mouth. Suzanna didn't attempt small talk; she was no good at it, anyway.

He took her to a place she knew only by reputation; she and Ron had never eaten there. Known only as Road's End, it was above the town, and its dining room overlooked the churning white rapids. Suzanna knew that it was one of the valley's more popular night spots, with a rowdy bar and a small dance floor, a video arcade and a recent addition, a mechanical bull. On weekends they had live music—country, mostly—but on a Monday night the jukebox was providing the cover noise, with a fluctuating background accompaniment of raucous laughter and the space-age percussion of the arcade.

Cam guided her through the darkened barroom with a hand at the small of her back. That outwardly casual warmth at her waist was so distracting she was barely aware of anyone else in the place.

They took their seats at a window table. Cam ordered beer, a brand with a Spanish name. Suzanna, who wasn't accustomed to drinking, dithered over her order while the waitress fidgeted and glanced around at the other tables. Finally, Cam suggested a margarita, and Suzanna readily agreed.

As the waitress hurried away, Cam settled back, smiling at her across the table. Suzanna sat with her hands folded and looked around self-consciously, her nervous gaze finally settling on the rushing river that was still visible as a white froth in the growing darkness. The Kern River was the only river in Southern California to flow year-round and had one of the steepest drops of any river in the world. It was considered extremely dangerous because of the treacherous nature of its white water.

"The river is higher than I've ever seen it," she said with a shiver. "Even the old-timers are saying it's never stayed so high for so long. It's been known to wash out the bridge through town, but that's only during a flash flood, and the last time it happened was before I was born."

"Were you born here, in the valley?" Their drinks had arrived. Cam poured his beer and waited for the foam to settle while Suzanna sat contemplating her wide, frosted glass and wondered whether she was supposed to drink it with a straw or through the crystallized stuff that was clinging to the rim.

"No," she said, touching her tongue to the crystals and finding them salty. "I was born up north, in the San Joaquin Valley. My mother was teaching at the time, near Modesto." She sipped, considered the intriguing combination of tastes and said, "Hmm," in cautious approval. "But both my mother and her mother were born here in the valley. In fact, my grandmother's people were the first settlers here. Even before gold was discovered here, in Whiskey Flat, they were ranching out on the south fork. They still are."

"What happened to your parents?" Cam asked very casually.

Suzanna lifted one shoulder and took another sip of her drink. His eyes were clear and interested, focused on her and waiting for her answer, but she wasn't used to talking about herself. She always worried that she might be boring people. Cam was the first person she'd ever met who seemed to really want to hear the story of her life. It was easier with Ron; he always had so much to say.

She took a deep breath and began matter-of-factly. "Well, my mother died when I was in high school. She'd been fighting cancer off and on for years." She smiled wistfully, looking inward on the poignant sunshine glow of memory. "That was hard. We were good friends. And she was so courageous. But we'd been living with my grandparents since I was two years old, and I just went right on living there, so it wasn't as disruptive as it might have been."

"That's why you're so close to your grandfather, I guess. Is your father alive?" It was a cautious question. Suzanna answered it with detachment.

"As far as I know. He didn't keep in touch." Funny, how the little twinge of pain was still there, even now that she was grown. Perhaps, deep down inside, she would always be the little girl who had pestered her mother with endless questions about her daddy. *Why doesn't he ever come to see me? Why doesn't he write to me? Doesn't he want a little girl?* "I don't think he wanted either a wife or a daughter very much in the first place."

"So," Cam said softly, "your grandfather took his place. I can see why you call him Papa."

She nodded, smiling. "Since I lived with him and heard so many others call him Papa—including my grandmother—it was just natural that I call him that, too. In my earliest memory he was a giant in overalls, too big for my arms to reach around. I used to trudge along at his heels through the deep dust in the watermelon patch. We'd come to a melon that had burst in the heat, and Papa would take out his pocket knife and stoop over and cut the heart out of it and give me half. We'd eat it standing right there, with the juice running down our chins."

Suzanna stopped. She was looking at Cam through a dancing, shimmering tear glaze; one blink would betray her. "My, what a patient listener you are," she said with forced brightness. "I'm sorry."

"For what?" he said harshly, and then shifted restlessly, as if she'd irritated him. His deep-set eyes regarded her somberly, reflecting the glow of the table lamp with sympathetic softness, and something else. "Don't you have any idea what you sound like when you talk? Hasn't anyone ever told you that your voice is—that you have a way with words?" He smiled crookedly at her. "I like listening to you. You tell a pretty good story yourself, you know."

"Oh, no," Suzanna murmured, abstractedly touching her cold, moist glass to her hot cheek. "I'm extraordinarily dull."

He muttered something under his breath and shifted again, impatiently. Suzanna watched him while vague and uncertain fears and tensions grew inside her. He seemed so angry she actually flinched when he leaned across the table to touch her face.

"Balderdash," Cam said distinctly, and carefully brushed salt crystals from her cheek.

Suzanna burst out laughing, half in relief. "Now there's a Victorian expletive if I ever heard one! It must be contagious."

Cam grinned. They were both surprised to find the waitress at their elbow, ready to take their dinner order.

Suzanna didn't feel hungry, so she was content to leave the ordering to Cam while she let her gaze roam around the dining room. A burst of laughter from the bar suggested the evening was just beginning to warm up in there. The sound made her uneasy, bringing back old insecurities she thought she'd outgrown. She turned back to Cam the way a child reaches for an adult hand in a dark room and found him watching her expectantly.

"I'm sorry," she mumbled. "Did you say something?"

"I hope you like your prime rib rare. Where did you go? You were a million miles away."

She smiled and tucked a strand of hair behind her ear with her finger. She didn't answer his question directly, not immediately. She didn't mean to answer it at all, but there was something almost seductive about that focused attention of his. Even so, she only meant to make conversation when she said lightly, "Funny, I always wanted to travel."

Cam snorted. "Take it from me; it's not all it's cracked up to be."

"But I didn't just want to be a tourist. I wanted to see the whole world. I wanted to *live* in every country, speak the language, understand the people and customs. You know?"

"Why didn't you?"

She shrugged and looked away. "It was a ridiculous notion, completely impractical."

"But," Cam persisted quietly, "didn't you travel at all? Even as a tourist?"

She shook her head. Amazing how hard it still was to talk about it.

"Why not?"

He was Cam, and his eyes were as soft and reassuring as dawn skies. She looked at his face and thought how familiar it had become to her in so very short a time. So familiar, and so dear. She opened her mouth and heard herself say, "I couldn't."

He frowned. "Couldn't? What do you mean? Couldn't afford it?"

"No. I mean I just can't travel."

"That's ridiculous," Cam snorted, sitting back in his chair. "You can do anything if you want to badly enough."

"That's not true!" Suzanna cried, stinging with the pain of a newly reopened wound. "It *isn't*! You don't know how many times I told myself that and what an idiot I felt like. If you can be allergic to bees, why can't I be allergic to travel?"

"Allergic?" He was frowning intently.

She hunched her shoulders defensively and murmured, "Well, it has a name. It's a phobia, agoraphobia. I get upset in unfamiliar places. And I really *can't* help it."

"Maybe you can't, but somebody could."

"You mean a psychiatrist?" She made a gesture of rejection. "Oh, sure, but at what cost? That would be like spending a fortune to remove a blemish that only shows in a bathing suit. It doesn't really bother me or affect the way I live. I'm perfectly happy."

He regarded her so steadily it made her uncomfortable. After a while, he said softly, "This place—you've never been here before, have you?"

"No, I haven't," she admitted resentfully. "How did you know?"

"You've been as nervous as an animal sniffing a trap ever since we came in here. I just thought it was me you were uncomfortable with. But it's not, is it? It's just because this is a strange place to you. How can you tell me it doesn't affect your life if you can't even enjoy dinner in a new restaurant?"

Suzanna looked down at her hands, feeling as silly and neurotic as she used to when she'd had to turn down invitations from friends wanting her to spend the night. She'd lied then to keep them from knowing. She'd felt so childish, so weak. She should have been strong enough to overcome it. "I'm only a little nervous," she said, laughing exasperatedly. "For heaven's sake, don't let it bother you."

There was no immediate answer, and after a moment Suzanna looked up to find him frowning at his reflection in the dark window. "So," he said slowly, "you became a time traveler instead."

She stared at him, shaken. It seemed to her an incredibly sensitive and perceptive thing to say. In those few quiet words she heard both understanding and acceptance. Something inside her that had been closed up tightly relaxed and opened, like a flower bud unfolding to the sun. She smiled and touched his hand.

"Perhaps I did," she said softly.

The food arrived. They spent the dinner in relaxed conversation, like two old friends renewing an acquaintance after a long separation. Cam told Suzanna about places he'd been and jobs he'd worked on, and Suzanna told Cam more about her family's history. When they were ready to go, he asked, "Care to stay awhile? We could sit in the bar if you like—have another drink."

Suzanna agreed, just because she didn't want the evening to end. She didn't want another drink, and she didn't like the rowdy atmosphere of the bar, but she did want to stay with Cam, talking and listening to him talk. So she nodded and allowed him to guide her to a padded leather chair beside a small round table near the dance floor.

The jukebox was playing a plaintive country waltz, and a red-gold light revolved over the handful of couples shuffling around the square of hardwood. Over at the far end of the room the mechanical bull stood motionless. It was the weekend tourists who felt the urge to prove their manhood on a lurching dummy made of wood and leather; too many of the locals had ridden the real thing to be very impressed with the facsimile.

It just wasn't Suzanna's kind of place. She felt so uncomfortable she kept looking around like a guilty child with one hand in the cookie jar, hoping she wouldn't see anyone she knew. But as her eyes raked the patrons leaning against the bar, she drew in her breath in a tiny, involuntary gasp and quickly turned her face back to the dancers.

"Someone you know?" Cam said lazily, his eyes narrowing.

Suzanna shrugged. "Just an acquaintance. Nobody, really." But she could still feel those sooty little eyes staring with studied insolence at the back of her neck.

His name was Elwood Matson, and she'd known him, as she had known most of the people in the valley, since childhood. Elwood was built along the lines of a truck—he had always been an overweight child—and had a notorious mean streak. In high school he had given the football coach dreams of glory until it became apparent that Elwood would be a chronic eligibility problem. Suzanna was one of many who had been pressed into service as tutors in a continuing effort to keep Elwood eligible for important games. Her flesh still crawled at the memory of some of his suggestions of how they might better spend their time together. She didn't see him often these days, but she knew he worked for Ron as a security guard at one of the marinas.

"Suzanna," Cam whispered without disturbing his lips, which had curved in a chilly smile, "say hello to the nice man."

She jerked her head around to see Elwood rolling toward them, shifting his shoulders and grinning. "'Lo, Suzanna," he said with the kind of familiarity bolstered by alcohol. "Long time no see. What are you doin' here?" His eyes had narrowed, but he was still grinning. It wasn't a pleasant grin. "Seen Ron?"

"Hello, Elwood," Suzanna said with resignation. "No, I haven't seen Ron this evening."

"So who's your friend?" Elwood asked rudely. "Stranger, huh?"

Suzanna cleared her throat and glanced at Cam. His eyes were half closed, and he slowly and deliberately lifted his glass and took a sip of beer. With great reluctance, she said, "This is Cam Harris. He's with the Corps of Engineers. Cam, this is Elwood Matson."

Elwood's head was bobbing as he absorbed the information. "You workin' up at the dam?" he asked suddenly, thrusting his jaw forward and narrowing his eyes.

"That's right," Cam said lazily.

Elwood's head bobbed again, and Suzanna saw an unpleasant smile spread slowly across his face. "Be seein' you, Suzanna," he muttered, and ambled toward the bar.

A few minutes later, Suzanna saw him in the foyer, hunched over the pay phone.

She shivered and drew her fresh drink toward her. She didn't really want it; she wasn't used to drinking, and already her head felt tight and achy. It was so terribly crowded and noisy here. Conversation was impossible, and Cam suddenly seemed disinclined to talk, anyway. In fact, he seemed to have fallen into the same black, brooding mood that had shaken her so this afternoon. Her stomach was knotting with tension when she opened her mouth to suggest that they leave.

"Don't look now," Cam drawled in a low voice. He nodded toward the entrance, and Suzanna, following his gaze, groaned softly. "It's just possible we've got trouble."

Chapter Six

"Oh, Lord," Suzanna breathed. "It's Ron."

"How jealous is your boyfriend?" Cam asked with dry amusement.

"Ron wouldn't make trouble," she said quickly. "It just isn't his way. But—"

"But you don't know about the bodyguard," Cam murmured. His posture was relaxed, his face placid, but Suzanna could feel tension and energy radiating from him like heat.

But before the two men had reached their table, there was a little flurry at the bar's entrance. A tall blond vision in black designer jeans and white silk western shirt sailed toward them, hands outstretched in an old-chums-well-met kind of greeting.

"Suzanna!" the woman gushed, "what a surprise to find you here! Isn't this place a blast?"

Suzanna swallowed surprise and murmured noncommittally, "Lucy...Lucy Tate." *D'Arcy*. She must remember that her name was Lucy D'Arcy now that she was editor of the local weekly newspaper. In high school she'd been just plain old Lucy Tate, gossip columnist for the senior class newsletter and darling of the English teachers. But then Lucy had gone off to some college in the

Midwest, shed thirty pounds, married well and divorced even better, and had come back to take over the local paper, sporting a new name and an old flair for the sensational. Since her offices were right next to the museum, Suzanna ran into her quite often. On those occasions, Lucy had very little to say to Suzanna, which made her behavior now all the more puzzling.

"Actually, I had no idea *you* came here," she said, pulling up a chair without waiting to be asked. She turned a glittering smile on Cam, who was leaning back in his chair, legs extended, watching developments with that deceptively bland expression on his face. Suzanna noticed uneasily that his eyes had that dangerous, flinty look. She also noticed that Lucy's eyes, for all her cheery friendliness, were shrewdly calculating. She was obviously here with a purpose.

Ron and Elwood had arrived. Lucy looked up and cried, "Well, Ron! This *is* gettin' interesting, isn't it?"

"Hello, Suzanna," Ron said, glancing distractedly at Lucy. He pulled up a chair beside Suzanna and fastened a wary gaze on Cam. Elwood took his place behind Ron's chair and promptly took on the approximate shape and facial expression of a bunker.

"Why, I think I know you," Lucy said coyly to Cam. "Haven't I seen you up at dam headquarters?" She was leaning toward Cam now, flirting openly. Her sleek blond head obscured his face, so that Suzanna couldn't, in that noisy place, tell what he had replied.

Suzanna turned to Ron, who was frowning moodily at her. "Hello," she said, not knowing what else to say. She might have found the situation amusing, in an embarrassing sort of way, if it hadn't been for the undercurrents and tensions she didn't quite understand.

"Suzanna," he said, pursing his lips. His frown deepened, and he cleared his throat. "I have to say, I'm a little bit floored. I sure never would have expected you to be in a place like this."

Suzanna didn't answer. His attitude was beginning to irritate her. He hadn't any real claim on her; she'd been his regular Saturday night dinner date for ages but to the best of her memory had never made any commitments or promises.

Ron shifted uncomfortably in the face of her silence, and the set of his jaws became mulish. He jerked his head toward Cam. "That's the guy I saw at your place, isn't it? I kind of got the impression he was a relative. Mind tellin' me just who the hell he is?"

"Not at all," Suzanna said, fighting rising anger. "Ron, Lucy, I'd like you to meet Cam Harris, U.S. Army Corps of Engineers."

Ron Weed looked startled, but he half rose to reach for Cam's hand. It was automatic on Ron's part. Suzanna knew from the narrowed eyes and the pugnacious thrust of his chin that he wasn't at all pleased to make Cam's acquaintance.

Lucy, on the other hand, was clearly delighted. "Well," she crowed, "isn't that the most extraordinary coincidence! Here we made a special trip down to the dam this afternoon just to see you! We were so disappointed when Mr. O'Brian told us we'd just have to wait till tomorrow to get the story on what you people plan to do about this runoff problem. And then here I run right smack into you! Well, now, how about it, Mr. Harris? Care to give us a hint—on or off the record?" When Cam just returned her keen blue gaze and shook his head, she gave a musical little groan and placed her fingers on Ron's forearm. "Have a heart, please, Mr. Harris. I know Ron, here, would be especially interested in hearing what you plan to do. Ron is president of our local chamber of commerce, you know. He owns several businesses that are directly affected by the level of the lake. So how about it, Cam? A sneak preview?''

''No comment,'' Cam drawled, sipping beer.

Behind Ron, Elwood shifted slightly. Lucy gave him a quick glance, and Suzanna saw a gleam in her eyes. ''Is it true,'' she said with exaggerated sweetness, ''that the corps is thinking about increasing the capacity of the lake?''

Suzanna's heart thudded and then stood still, waiting.

''Another 'no comment,' I'm afraid,'' Cam said easily. ''I'm sorry; you'll just have to wait until the press conference tomorrow morning. Tony O'Brian will be able to answer all your questions at that time.''

Lucy leaned forward, suddenly dropping her party gloss. ''You know, Mr. Harris, I have an idea *you're* the man with all the answers. I'm sure you realize that if the corps does raise the water level of our lake, it would have some drastic consequences for a lot of people around here.'' She waved a hand toward the crowd at the bar. ''In fact, just as a guess, I'd say that most of the people in this room right now would be *very* interested to know if that's what you have in mind.''

Ron leaned forward, his hands clasped together on the tabletop. ''I've got three marinas myself. You raise the water level any more and you put me right out of business. In the first place, there's no more room between the water and the highway. In the second place, you flood the campgrounds around the lake and the tourists have got no place to stay. You put half the valley out of business—a lot of people out of work. Seems to me we've got a right to know what's going on.''

"Elwood," Lucy said as if the thought had only just struck her, "you work at Ron's marinas, don't you?"

"That's right," Elwood rumbled, crossing his arms on his massive chest and rocking back on his heels. "And there ain't no damn outa-town college boy gonna come in here and take my job away from me."

The atmosphere had suddenly grown ugly. Suzanna felt a menace that stirred the skin on the nape of her neck like a prickle of electricity. Cam stretched lazily and pushed aside his empty glass. "Well, now, I'm sorry to have to disappoint you folks, but the answers will just have to wait until tomorrow." He lifted his eyebrows at Suzanna. "Shall we go?"

Before Suzanna could reply, before anyone could move, Elwood had planted a huge, meaty hand on Cam's shoulder. "You ain't goin' nowhere, college boy," he snarled. "Not until you give us some answers." He lifted his head to grin at Ron. "And they better be the right ones, huh, Ron?"

Suzanna didn't have time to be afraid. What occurred next happened so fast she was never certain just what *did* happen. Just a little flurry of motion—and suddenly Elwood was bent double with his arms clutching his body, wheezing and retching. Cam was on his feet, his hand on Suzanna's wrist, pulling her up beside him as he carefully eased the huge, helpless man into the chair he had just vacated. He patted Elwood's shoulder and said to Ron, "Take care of him. He'll be all right in a minute or two— he's just a little short of breath. Suzanna?"

He took her by the elbow so that she had to almost run to keep pace with him. Outside, in the cool, pine-scented night, she angrily jerked her arm out of his grasp.

"What did you *do*?" she gasped, stopping in the middle of the gravel parking lot so that he was forced to stop, too.

"I neutralized a troublemaker," Cam said shortly. "Now let's get the hell out of here."

"That was…it was…well, it wasn't very sporting!" She was beginning to feel chilled and shaky with reaction.

He gave her a long, heavy-lidded look. "You're right; it wasn't *sporting*. In my experience, sporting is noisy and messy. Things get broken, like windows and noses and the small bones of the hand. Is that what you want?"

She opened her mouth, but he made an impatient noise and took her arm again, and his hand wasn't gentle as he hurried her to her car, unlocked it and half shoved her inside.

When they had left Road's End far behind and there were no lights in the rearview mirror, Cam settled back in the driver's seat and ran a hand across his face. "Look…I'm sorry," he said, expelling his breath in a gusty sigh. "You probably didn't realize it, but we were about ten seconds away from a full-scale brawl back there. Believe me, I've been involved in enough of 'em to know."

His voice sounded distant and tired and muffled slightly by the hand that still rested across the lower half of his face. Something inside Suzanna gave a queer little lurch.

"It's all right," she said softly, wanting to erase the fatigue and the sadness from his voice, and reached across the space between them to place her hand on his thigh.

He jerked as if she'd startled him and glanced down at her hand. And then, shifting his hands on the wheel, covered her hand with his and pressed it hard against the firm muscle of his thigh. He held it there for a long moment while pulses throbbed and raced at the points of contact and then lifted it, squeezed it gently and laid it back on the seat between them.

"I wish to God it was," he murmured.

IN THE SILVERY DARKNESS, the house looked lonely and brooding, its darkened windows like sightless eyes reflecting the moonlight.

"You didn't leave a light on," Cam said at last, breaking a long silence.

He felt Suzanna jerk slightly; he seemed to have startled her out of some unhappy reverie of her own. "Oh, no, I never do," she murmured vaguely. "I've never thought it was necessary."

"You're not afraid of the dark?" He could feel her turn to look at him and knew that her eyes would be shadowed with worry and uncertainty. He could hear it in her voice.

"No, of course not. I've never had any reason to be afraid."

Until now, he thought, getting out of the car. He had to accept responsibility for putting the fear in her eyes and the uncertainty in her voice, but he knew that the ugliness he'd just introduced into her serene little world was nothing compared to what he was about to do to her.

Suzanna got out of the car without waiting for him to come around and help her; instead, he stooped to open the gate, holding it for her to pass through. She paused while he latched it, and then they strolled up the long, pale ribbon of the front walk, side by side but not touching, together but miles apart.

"I'm sorry," Cam said wearily.

"For what?" He heard the silken whisper of her hair on her shoulders as she turned to glance at him, but she sounded curious rather than surprised.

"For tonight." He shrugged and made an impatient gesture with his hand. "For getting you into that mess." *For bulldozing my way into your home, your nice quiet life, and for the hurt I'm going to cause you.*

She reached for his hand, the same trusting, childlike gesture she'd made in the car, and again the gesture grabbed at his heart, making him wince with unexpected pain. "I told you, it's all right. It wasn't your fault, anyway. That Elwood—"

Cam shook his head. "He was only part of it. I shouldn't have..." He let his voice trail off. *Shouldn't have what? Shouldn't have heard your voice, shouldn't have found out how soft your hair is, how good you smell? Heaven knows, I shouldn't have kissed you....*

He could feel her eyes on him, hear the hurt feelings in her silence. The hand in his curled, seeking its release, and he clasped it tightly and then impulsively carried it to his lips. He thought sadly, *She thinks I'm sorry I asked her to go out with me.*

And he was, but not the way she thought. The more he was with her, the more he wanted her, and the more he knew she was one girl he had to leave alone. She wasn't for him in any way, and every minute he was with her eroded his resolve to keep his distance, especially at times like this, when she was walking so close to his side that he could feel the warmth and movement of her body. He could sense that the lightest touch from him would bring her into his arms. Why, he didn't know; for some reason she was his for the taking. Every sense, every nerve in his body, knew it.

And, he thought wryly, looking up at the gabled windows of Angel's Walk, *the damned house knows it, too.* He wondered if, after all, it might be haunted; it seemed to wait with a brooding and hushed expectancy.

They had reached the porch. Suzanna was saying in a stilted voice, "Thank you for dinner. I'm sorry it wasn't—I wasn't—"

Cam interrupted her with a snort of self-reproach. "It wasn't your kind of place. I knew it wasn't. Video games and mechanical bulls..."

"It's all right," she said steadily. "I know what you were trying to do."

"You do?"

"Yes. You think I'm sort of hung up in the past. What was it you said? 'The Golden Long Ago'..." Her soft laughter had a catch in it. "You were trying to bring me back to your time—*this* time. Weren't you?"

"Sue—" Relief made his voice sound hollow. He found himself holding her hand tightly in both of his. "I never meant to make you unhappy or uncomfortable. I didn't know—"

He felt the violent shake of her head. "Don't make me sound like some sort of emotional cripple! I'm *not*. I'm happy. I really do *like* my life."

"I know." He was surprised at the sadness in his own voice. Or was it envy?

"And you know, being in touch with the past isn't such a bad thing. Sometimes it's not as long ago and far away as you think."

"No?"

"No." Her voice sounded breathless and hopeful. "In fact, it's as close as next weekend."

"Sue—" He sighed, tired out by tension and frustration. "What are you talking about?" It didn't matter, because long ago and here and now, he was the snake in her Eden, and he knew it.

"My family always has a picnic on Memorial Day. A real, old-fashioned family get-together. I thought maybe—" she cleared her throat nervously "—you might like to come. With me. Just to see—"

"Sue—"

"We spruce up the old pioneer cemetery, make home-made ice cream, play baseball, do all that old-fashioned stuff. I thought, since I'm going to be there, and you do have to eat, anyway, that you might just as well..." She took a deep breath, and Cam could feel the vibrance of her entreaty in her hands. "Oh, please come." And then, with a smile he could only hear, "You owe me one, Cam."

Maybe so. But Memorial Day—a week from today. In a week she wouldn't be able to stomach the sight of him. And in a week more she probably wouldn't even have a home to go to.

Tell her. You have to tell her now.

But instead he heard himself sigh and whisper, "Okay, Sue."

There was a pause, as if she were replaying his words in her head, and then she said huskily, "Does that mean—?"

"Yes, I'll come. If I can."

He heard the soft expulsion of her breath, a whispered thank-you, and then she kissed him.

He wasn't a tall man, and she wasn't a small woman; she only had to raise herself a little on tiptoe to do it, leaning across the barrier of their clasped hands. She wasn't an experienced seductress, either, so the kiss was a feather's touch, both impulsive and tentative. Cam reacted to it instinctively, before he could remind himself that he wasn't going to get any more involved than he already was. His mouth softened, becoming warm and welcoming. Hers clung as if caught in some inescapable magnetic field, then parted sweetly.

Warnings of every kind were resounding through his head, but it was already too late. A shaft of pure desire skewered him from throat to groin. He snarled silently at the clamor of his conscience. *Just once, damn it—just this one kiss!* And with an audible groan, he took her in his arms.

He wanted to tell her everything in that kiss, that one, last kiss. Of the loneliness and isolation of all the rootless years, of the frustration and futility, the anger and the regret, and of other things, too—vague hungers and poignant longings even he didn't understand, yearnings that ached in his throat and tingled in the backs of his eyelids. He crushed her to him, trying to imprint the shape of her on every nerve ending in his body. He filled his mouth with the taste of her, his nostrils with the scent of her, as if somehow he could fill himself up, take enough of her with him to last the rest of his life, and then leave her alone. What he wasn't prepared for was that the more he had of her, the more he seemed to need.

So he plundered her mouth with a kind of desperation that appalled even him, holding her head in his hands, tangling his fingers in the weight of her hair. He was only dimly aware of her breasts pressing against his chest, her fingers clutching at the muscles of his back, the soft whimpering sounds she made deep in her throat. He was drowning her, sweeping them both away with the intensity of his passion.

A groan of frustration and bitter resolve vibrated through his throat, and he tore his mouth from hers and buried his face in the fragrant masses of her hair. He couldn't do it. Not to her, not to himself. His need of her was so acute it was agony, but he still had to live with himself. For a few more moments he held her while he listened to the twang of his taut nerves and overstimulated senses and then reluctantly and with a supreme effort separated himself from her.

She said his name, "John," in a sigh that was almost a moan, and then seemed to collect herself. "Cam, I—"

He interrupted her with an utterance that was meant to be her name. *All right, tell her. Tell her now, you coward!*

And that's just what he was—a coward. He couldn't bring himself to tell her, not with all that appeal and confusion radiating from her like body heat.

He started to speak just as she did the same and quickly touched her lips with his finger, asking for her silence. Beneath the hand that still rested on the curve of her shoulder, he felt her body quiver.

"Look, Sue," he said, wishing his voice didn't sound so harsh. "I've got kind of an early day tomorrow—"

He felt her stiffen and turn away; he let his hand drop from her shoulder as she moved. "What time will you be wanting breakfast?" Unlike his, her voice sounded cool and detached.

He hesitated, then reached around her to push open the door. He shook his head and then, realizing that she couldn't see him, said, "Don't bother. If it's all right with you, I'll just help myself. No need for you to get up that early."

She murmured, "I see. All right, then. That's fine." Neither of them made a move to turn on the light in the hallway.

Cam said, "I'll be going away for a few days."

"Oh?"

"Yeah. I've got to go to Sacramento. Don't know exactly how long I'll be gone."

"Oh. Well, thank you for letting me know."

He wished she'd quit being so polite. She was hiding her hurt behind her inherent class, and it made him feel more than ever like a dirty low-down lying wolf in sheep's clothing. "Listen, I hate to ask, but would it be okay if I left the cat? I know—"

"Oh, sure. No problem."

"I think she'll be happier here. She'd be alone in a hotel room."

"Of course you can leave her. She's no trouble at all."

"All right, then. Thanks." There was a moment of silence alive with unspoken tensions and yearnings, and then Cam murmured, "Night," and took the stairs in the dark, two at a time. In his room, he punched at the buttons of his portable tape deck with barely contained savagery and sat down on the bed in a rectangle of moonlight. After a moment, he sighed deeply and lay back, letting the earthy wail of a saxophone and the rusty-voiced passions of Bruce Springsteen's lyrics speak for him.

SUZANNA AWOKE late the next morning and immediately felt the emptiness of the house close in around her. Outside her window, the sun was warm and golden and redolent with the scent of lilacs. The birds were singing just as usual, and the bees would be humming busily between the apple trees in the orchard and the hole in the wall. And inside, the house felt chilly and abandoned.

Funny, Suzanna thought, feeling anything but. *I never felt lonely before Cam came.* Now it seemed almost as if the only time she didn't feel lonely was when he was here.

She hadn't slept well last night, and that was something else she'd never had trouble with before. Cam's music really shouldn't have kept her awake. It hadn't been especially loud, and Suzanna had been known to go to sleep listening to music herself now and then. Of course, she generally listened to a different kind of music. She wouldn't have chosen for herself lullaby music that stirred so many restless longings, music that left a fever in her skin and a vague, unexplained ache in her heart. Or maybe it hadn't been the music at all. Perhaps instead it had been undischarged energy left over from those few electric moments on the front porch, fallout from a kiss that frightened her and a man she didn't understand.

Downstairs the phone was ringing. Suzanna muttered a mild protest; short of sliding down the banister, there wasn't much chance of getting to it before the caller gave up, and she really didn't feel up to a wild and fruitless dash this morning. She got out of bed and padded to the open window, counting rings while she warmed her bare toes on the patch of sunlit linoleum. Five, six... Oh, well. If it was important, they would try again.

From behind her came a faint scratching noise. Mystified, she went to open the bedroom door. With a soft trill that sounded oddly like a question, Cat padded into the room, pausing to sniff delicately at Suzanna's feet, touching her briefly with a cold, moist nose.

"Morning, Cat," Suzanna offered, and received a quick, hopeful look and another little trill in reply. "Are you looking for your large, noisy friend?" Feeling less alone, Suzanna gave the cat a scandalized look and said with mock severity, "Might I ask why you think you'd find him in here? Please, I'm not that kind of girl." Cat didn't bother to dignify the remark with a reply, and Suzanna snorted in rueful agreement, "The heck I'm not." *She* wasn't the one who'd slammed on the brakes last night. As before, it was Cam who'd pulled back before their escalating passions could pass the point of no return. Strange, she could have sworn it wasn't what he'd wanted to do.

Shaking her head distractedly, she reached for her robe and went off to the bathroom, leaving Cat staring into the attic doorway, ears alert and tail twitching.

"Suzanna. Oh, good—you *are* home. I didn't think you'd have left for work yet. Where were you?"

"Hello, Meg. Upstairs. You never let it ring long enough, you know. This place is—"

"I know you never run to pick up the phone; that's why. If you think you can't reach it, you ignore it. You know, Suzanna, someday you're going to miss something important."

Suzanna shrugged and tucked the receiver between her ear and shoulder, leaving her hands free to pour orange juice. "If anyone wants to get hold of me badly enough, they'll call back."

Meg O'Brian sighed, but her heart obviously wasn't in it. "Well," she said briskly, shifting gears, "how are you?"

Suzanna smiled into the receiver and murmured, "Fine, Meg; how are you?"

"Suzanna, please don't be inscrutable. You must know how concerned Tony and I are about you."

"Since when? As of Sunday you were tickled to death with my new tenant."

There was a moment of silence, and then, cautiously, Meg said, "Oh, yes. How is that working out?"

"How is what working out?"

Meg sighed and enunciated with exaggerated patience, "How are you getting along with Cam Harris?"

"Mr. Harris is fine." Cat had come into the kitchen. She sat in the doorway like a china figurine, with her tail curled around her paws, watching Suzanna with round, accusing eyes. "He's gone out of town for a few days."

"Hmm. After the press conference, I suppose you mean."

"What press conference?"

"At dam headquarters. You know they're announcing plans to control the flow—"

"Oh, yes," Suzanna murmured. "The press conference." She sipped orange juice and stared through the Virginia creeper at the blue gleam of lake water.

"Didn't Cam say anything to you about what they plan to do?"

"No, nothing."

"Tony, either. Suzanna, he seems so worried. *I'm* worried. He won't talk about it at all. Are you going to the press conference?"

"No, of course not. Why should I?" Suzanna drained her juice glass and abruptly turned her back on the windows.

"Aren't you interested? I mean, your house is sitting on lake preserve."

"Yes, but above the high-water line. I don't see how the water can get any higher if it's already over the spillway, do you? And I'm sure Cam would have told me if I was going to be directly affected by their plans." *Wouldn't he?*

There was silence on the line. Suzanna prompted, "Wouldn't he?"

Meg said softly, "Yes, I'm sure he would. You're right." And then, sounding more like herself, she asked, "What's he like, Suzanna? Tony won't say a word except that he's reliable, trustworthy and so on. So is a Saint Bernard."

Suzanna stifled rueful laughter. "Well, the 'saint' part isn't too far off."

"What?"

"Never mind. Nothing."

"Well?"

"Well, what?"

"*Suzanna!* What does he look like? You know, tall, dark, handsome...what?"

"He's not tall."

"Short isn't all that bad."

"Not short, either. Taller than I am."

"So far so good."

"Not dark."

"Blond? Listen, Robert Redford would be—"

"Not blond, either."

"Oh, no—bald?"

Suzanna covered the receiver to hide her laughter. "Not bald. Meg, you'll have a chance to meet him. I've invited him to the picnic."

"To the picnic? Fantastic—wait, you mean I've got to be in suspense for a week?"

"Meg, I've got to go. I'm going to be late for work."

"Suzanna, wait. You didn't mention—"

"Bye, Meg."

"Wait—what about *handsome*—?"

What *about* handsome? No, she wouldn't call John Campbell Harris handsome, but it didn't seem pertinent, somehow. Handsome seemed too smooth, too polished, too lightweight for a man like Cam. It would be like calling a woman "pretty." Cam was so very much more.... What *would* you call a man with such strength of personality that his going left a great gap in the lives he touched?

Suzanna cradled the receiver, gently cutting off her cousin's exasperated wail. Cat, she noticed, had vanished from the kitchen doorway. It was odd the way that animal seemed to sense Cam's absence. Surely she was used to being left alone in strange places while he worked, but she seemed to know that this time she'd been left *behind*.

THE UNSEASONABLE HEAT WAVE was continuing. May in the valley was often cold and nearly always windy, but this morning's air had the brassy stillness of mid-July. A

beautiful day, the tourists would call it. Perfect weather for
being out on the lake. And out there they were, by the
hundreds, their sleek speedboats slashing across the mir-
rored surface in elongated Vs, the dumpier fishing boats
crouched in the shallows amid the foliage of newly inundated trees.

It was too lovely a day to be indoors. It would be a quiet
morning at the museum, which was all right with Suzanna. She was looking forward to getting back to Isabelle Potter's love letters, to losing herself in another time.

Escape, she thought in astonishment. *Is that really what
I'm doing?*

Suzanna was just fitting her key into the lock in the
museum's front door when she heard her name called in an
impulsive and breathless hail. Lucy Tate—no, what was
her last name now? Something improbably French.
D'Arcy—that was it. Lucy had just parked in front of the
newspaper office next door and was struggling to extri-
cate herself, several notebooks and shoulder bags, a camera and a tape recorder from her Japanese sports car. She
looked flushed and disorganized, a most uncharacteristic
state for Lucy.

"Suzanna, sweetie, wait up. You're just the person I
wanted to see." Lucy nudged the car door shut with one
hip and marched up the steps of the wooden boardwalk
that fronted the western-style buildings.

Suzanna unlocked the museum door and stood waiting
for the newspaperwoman to join her. She was thinking,
*How extraordinary. Lucy glad to see me twice in twenty-
four hours? I wonder what's got into her.* Suzanna had always felt uncomfortable around Lucy. She had exactly the
kind of cool sophistication that Suzanna found most in-
timidating, but even in high school there had been a cer-

tain world-weariness about Lucy that had made Suzanna feel slightly foolish, and very naive.

It was only slightly cooler in the museum. Suzanna switched on the portable fan and the overhead fluorescent light and then turned to confront Lucy, who was helping herself to a paper cup filled with water from the cooler.

"Ah, that's wonderful." Lucy sighed and crumpled the cup in her hand. "You wouldn't believe how hot it was up there on that damn dam. Excuse my French." She closed her eyes for dramatic effect and managed to look elegantly exhausted in spite of the flush of health and excitement across her cheekbones.

Suzanna hid a skeptical smile and murmured dryly, "Why did you want to see me, Lucy?"

Lucy, who was giving herself a critical inspection in a compact, arched her brows in surprise. Sparing Suzanna a brief glance over the lid of the compact, she responded, "Why, I want an interview, of course."

"An interview?" Suzanna gave a little laugh of genuine surprise. "Whatever for?"

Lucy snapped the compact shut and tucked it back into one of the shoulder bags she had unloaded onto Suzanna's desk. Carelessly pushing aside a pile of maps to points of historical interest, she made herself comfortable on a corner of the desk and regarded Suzanna with mild annoyance.

"Come on, Suzanna. How do you feel about the Corps of Engineers' plan? Of course I mean to interview as many as possible of the people directly affected by it, but you *have* to be at the top of the list. Tell me—"

Suzanna said faintly, "Why me?" *Directly affected?* Behind the cynical glitter of Lucy's blue eyes lurked a shadow of compassion that was more disturbing than hostility. Almost like a premonition, a trickle of perspiration rolled down Suzanna's neck and was instantly cooled by the fan's blast, chilling her. She shivered involuntarily. "I don't really have anything to say, Lucy."

And now hostility replaced the compassion in Lucy's eyes. Arching her brows, she said coldly, "Is that a 'no comment'? Look, I know you think you're too good to talk to someone as *vulgar* as a reporter, but I'd think for Ron's sake at least—"

"Ron! What does he—"

"Yes, dear, *Ron*. I should think you might at least have something to say about the fact that your fiancé will be put out of business if the corps proceeds with its plans to—"

"Lucy, he's *not*."

"Not what?" Lucy had stopped, hand poised over her notepad, a curiously intense look on her face.

Suzanna passed a hand distractedly over her forehead. "Lucy, what are you talking about? Nothing you're saying makes any sense. In the first place, Ron isn't my fiancé. We're just friends."

"Oh, yeah?" Lucy examined her pencil with studied indifference. "Does Ron know that?"

The quick pink flush in the other woman's cheeks gave Suzanna a sudden flash of insight. The cool and unflappable Lucy seemed to have lost her professional objectivity. Suzanna said softly, "I've never given him any reason to think otherwise, Lucy." And then more forcefully, she added, "Of course, even as a friend, I'd be concerned about his welfare, but for heaven's sake, Ron's not going to be bankrupted by this. Even if the high water does mean he'll have to close the marinas temporarily, he has so many other businesses. There are the motels, and with the campgrounds all flooded, the motel business should be terrific." She gave a dry laugh. "Really, Lucy, Ron will manage."

"You and Ron aren't—" Lucy had to pause to clear her throat.

It was Suzanna's turn to feel compassion as she watched the woman she'd always thought cold and hard-boiled adjust her professional detachment around herself like a cloak. The revelation had left her feeling distracted and amazed, and she had to shake herself in order to reply firmly, "No. Honestly."

Lucy cleared her throat again. "All right. Well—" She made a notation on a tablet that Suzanna rather imagined was more for the purpose of restoring her composure than providing her with any useful information. She looked up, frowning. "But there's still *your* house. I would think—"

"My house?" Suzanna said blankly. The icy premonition returned to settle in the backs of her knees, giving them an unnerving tendency to buckle. She groped behind her for the support of a glass display case.

"Yeah, that old run-down place that sits out on the east end of the lake. That's yours, isn't it? You must be—"

"What about my house?" Suzanna heard herself ask in cold, measured tones. Her lips felt funny, rather stiff and numb. Her gaze was so tightly focused on the other woman's face that it seemed oddly disembodied. All she really saw was the look of dawning realization immediately followed by consternation.

"Oh good Lord." Lucy's voice sounded flat, horrified. "Don't tell me you don't know. Listen, Suzanna, I'm sorry. I just assumed you knew—I mean, you were with him last night, and I figured he'd have told you. You know—I thought that was why—"

Why he was wining and dining a plain Jane like me? Because he had to tell me—what, Lucy? Please . . .

"Well I'm sorry to be the one to tell you. Suzanna, they're raising the spillway, increasing the storage capacity of the lake. Honey, that house of yours is going to be sitting in about six feet of water."

Chapter Seven

"Six feet of water." The words went echoing on and on while Lucy's face swam away into a pale blur. Suzanna was mentally tracing a line six feet up the white clapboard walls of Angel's Walk. She was watching with agonized helplessness as thick brown water stinking of rotting vegetation and floating debris poured through paneled doors and leaded casement windows, turning the flocked Victorian wallpaper in the sitting room to mush, rotting the beautifully handcrafted cherry-wood moldings, the fireplace, the newel posts and banisters, eating away at the foundations....

"Sound as the day it was built," Papa always said. But no house was built to survive indefinite submersion.

"Suzanna—why me?" Lucy's voice retreated muttering dire oaths and imprecations. A moment later, Suzanna felt a hand on her shoulder. "Here—take a sip."

"What ...?" Suzanna stared dazedly at the small white paper cup and then murmured, "Oh. All right. Thanks." She felt her own hand close around the cup's coolness, felt the paper give a little under the pressure of her fingers but didn't think to lift the water to her lips. Frowning with the effort to concentrate, she said, "Lucy."

"Yes."

"That's impossible."

Obviously relieved that Suzanna wasn't going to faint or become hysterical, Lucy returned to her perch on the corner of the desk and said with grim certainty, "Nope. Apparently not. You've got to admire that man's ingenuity. He does know how to get a job done, and fast. Sorry, Suzanna, but I've never seen red tape cut with such dispatch." She consulted a notebook. "He's flying out of here today with the specifications. Prefab sections of the new spillway—steel-reinforced concrete—will be ready by Friday. They'll fly them in by U.S. Army chopper—you know, the big ones with the two rotors that they use to move trucks and tanks and things." Lucy, who always had been one to talk with her hands, raised both arms and described small circles in the air with her index fingers. "Over the weekend the sections will be lowered into place over the existing spillway and anchored—"

"Excuse me," Suzanna interrupted, pausing to clear gravel from her voice. "*When* did they decide to do all this?"

"Just yesterday. And they say it'll all be finished by Memorial Day. Just a week, start to finish. Can you believe it? Who says a bureaucracy can't move fast when it wants to!"

"Oh, not a bureaucracy, just one man," Suzanna said ominously, adding in a furious undertone, "And yes, he certainly can move fast when he wants to." She downed the previously ignored water in one gulp. "Mr. John Campbell Harris," she said with precision, "is a cowardly rat fink." She crushed the soggy cup and hurled it at the wastebasket, missing it by at least a yard. Uncharacteristically, she felt no impulse to pick it up. "An *unmitigated* coward and rat fink," she amended, staring reproachfully at the litter and then adding, in a wretched whisper, "*Damn* him. . . ."

Suddenly, Suzanna was acutely aware that she wasn't alone; in a public place, in the presence of another person, her natural reserve wouldn't allow her to lose her control over the emotional violence boiling inside her. Shock, rage, despair, the pain of betrayal—she felt so many feelings, as though a major war, complete with heavy artillery, were being waged inside her head and chest. She knew all at once that she had to be alone, if only to work out some sort of cease-fire.

"Lucy," she said decisively, "would you mind? I'm going to close up here now."

"Close? You just opened." Lucy had never been known for her sensitivity.

"Something," Suzanna said grimly, "just came up."

"Oh. Right. Sure, I understand. Look, if there's anything I can do. . ." Lucy hopped off the desk and began assembling the paraphernalia of her profession. Suzanna switched off lights and fan and picked up her purse and keys.

At that moment, the bell on the doorknob gave a violent clang. Ron Weed exploded through the door, nearly bowling Lucy over in the process. He steadied her with both hands, muttered distraughtly, "Oh, sorry, Luce," and setting her aside, looked past her to Suzanna. His face was bright red; it occurred to Suzanna, with a kind of detached fascination, that she'd never before seen him in a rage.

"*There,*" he announced with an air of triumph. "I warned you about that guy!" Suzanna couldn't recall his having done any such thing, but she only lifted one eyebrow and gave a neutral reply.

Ron hooked one hand on his belt buckle and used the other to make angry gestures in the air. "Well, he's sure put it to all of us, hasn't he? The whole damn valley—we don't count for more'n a whole hill of beans! *Politics,* that's all it is—just plain old politics! Mathematics! There's more voters down there in the big city than there are up here in the sticks, so we're expendable; that's what we are!"

Suzanna didn't even try to point out that Cam Harris wasn't an elected official, nor did she stop to think why it should occur to her in his defense. She only knew she wasn't in any emotional state to deal with Ron, or any kind of tirade. Acting on inspiration born of desperation, she took his arm and steered him gently but firmly to where Lucy was standing, looking like anything but an unbiased reporter. Suzanna said with determination, "Ron—what a coincidence. Lucy was just saying how much she'd like to do an in-depth interview with you, weren't you, Lucy? Since you do seem to have a lot to say, I'll just leave you both to it." She pulled the door wide and held it, just in case her suggestion was too subtle an invitation.

Ron frowned and began to protest. "You're closing up? It's not even noon." He and Lucy, Suzanna decided, would make a perfect pair. "Where—"

"Home," Suzanna said flatly. "To Angel's Walk."

"Well now look—"

But Lucy had clearly regained enough composure to grasp opportunity when it was handed to her on a plate. Taking Ron's arm in a determined grip, she exclaimed, "Ron, I can't tell you how glad I am to have a chance to get your statement concerning this tragic situation. As one of the most influential members of the business community as well as one of the most respected men in the valley, your opinions will be of great interest to our readers." She maneuvered the perspiring businessman past Suzanna and out onto the boardwalk. Suzanna could hear Lucy's voice, in top professional form, slowly retreating. "I'm so thrilled you've agreed to allow me a little of your precious time. Let's just step into my office, shall we? It's a whole lot cooler in here—Say, how 'bout something from the Coke machine? My treat."

Suzanna smiled wryly as she locked up the museum and headed through the late-morning heat to her car. Ron didn't stand a chance.

Shut into her stifling car, alone at last, Suzanna sat very still and let reaction catch up with her. Her mind went blank. All she could think was *My house, my house, my house.* All she could feel was overwhelming pain and grief. Gradually, though, the mists dissipated, burned away by the heat of her anger; and with the anger came denial.

No. It's a mistake. No way are they going to destroy my home. Cam wouldn't do that to me. He knows how much Angel's Walk means to me. He wouldn't do that to me.

Finally, and inevitably, came the bitter chill of reality. Why not? Why wouldn't he do it? What was she to him, anyway, but a harmless flirtation? She wasn't even that, but a recent acquaintance, practically a stranger. If he had a job to do, why would she be a stumbling block?

I'm a consultant. I go where there are problems and try to find solutions.

So he'd found his solution, and there was no mistake. Lucy might be annoying, but she was a conscientious newswoman, and her weekly paper was very reliable. She would have her facts right. Her editorial comment was right on the money, too. "That man" did indeed know how to do his job. Well, she just hoped he was pleased with himself.

"More often . . . it's just painful."

Oh, how much she didn't want to remember that! She didn't want to remember the bleakness in his eyes. And there was something else: that strange, violent, almost-desperate kiss of the previous evening. It had turned her bones to water. It had stirred vague fears in her even as it awakened unbelievable passions; the fear clutched at her heart even as the passion tied knots inside her. No, it was too unbearable to remember.

Suzanna realized that she was still sitting motionless in her car and that the car was like an oven. She drew a shaky breath and started the engine, and after carefully wiping the moisture from her cheeks, drove slowly home.

Home, but for how much longer?

Steeped in midday sunshine, the house didn't look haunted or mysterious or even run-down. It was masses of vibrant color, vivid green lawns—in need of mowing, Suzanna noted—climbing red roses, clouds of white apple blossoms. And fragrances—lilac and grass, honeysuckle and rose, with not even the faintest lingering hint of skunk. And permeating it all, like the low pulsing of a heartbeat, were the sounds of life—insect hum and bird song. To Suzanna, Angel's Walk was alive, and she felt as if she had just been told that a dearly beloved friend was terminally ill.

Suzanna heard the telephone ringing as she was coming up the walk. She counted rings automatically but didn't quicken her steps. She had counted eleven rings by the time she reached the kitchen, put her purse down on the table and picked it up.

"I let it ring—" Meg sounded breathless, as if *she* had just run to answer it "—twenty-one times."

"I only counted eleven," Suzanna said with a note of apology. "I just got home."

"I *knew* you'd be home, that's why I let it ring. I called the museum, and nobody answered, so I figured you'd be home sooner or later. Suzanna, I just heard—Tony called right after the press conference. I can't believe it. Is there anything I can do?"

"No," Suzanna said gently, "I don't think so."

"But where will you—what are you going to do? You'll need help moving. Have you thought—"

"I don't know. I haven't really had a chance to think yet. I just found out myself."

"Who—?"

"Lucy Tate—uh, D'Arcy. You know, from the newspaper."

"Oh, Suzanna. What a way to find out. I'm so sorry."

So am I. "Oh, well, I guess there really isn't any good way to hear bad news."

"No, I guess not. Listen, Suzanna. You know you can come and stay with us. You can move in with Laurie, and then, when she goes to college in the fall, you'd have her room all to yourself. You know we'd love to have you."

"Yes, thanks, Meg." Suzanna looked desperately around her familiar kitchen, wishing she could cry, wondering how in the world she was going to stand the pain another minute.

"Listen—are you going to be all right? Should I come down?"

"*No.* No, I'm okay. I have a lot to do, Meg. I'll be fine. Really. Don't worry about me."

"Oh, Suzanna—" Meg's voice broke.

Suzanna whispered, "Bye, Meg," and hung up. She stood motionless, listening to the silence, recognizing in it the empty echo of her world crashing around her ears.

"Her room all to yourself." Was this the way she was destined to spend her life, dependent on the generosity of

others, never again to have a place of her own? Angel's Walk was more than just her home. It was all she had, the only thing in the world that she owned, the only place she really belonged.

She'd told Meg she had a lot to do, and she probably did. But it was impossible to concentrate, to make herself do anything. All she seemed capable of doing was wandering from room to room, sometimes just standing in one place, staring into emptiness while the emotional war raged on inside her.

She was in so many pieces! Part of her was still shell-shocked, wandering gaunt eyed around the battleground, chanting "Myhousemyhouse," in pointless litany; and another part of her had already broken and was running from the field in panic, crying, "Where will I go—what will I do?" Of course, there was also a big part of her that was so full of rage it wanted to go charging blindly into cannon and volley armed only with futile bravado: *I won't let him do it. He'll destroy my house over my dead body!*

Then, and most intolerable, there was the unbiased observer, the part of her that would always watch with an impartial eye and record the suffering of both sides. That part insisted on reminding her that the enemy wasn't the poor man in the trenches. John Campbell Harris, the observer pointed out sadly, was as much a victim as she was.

She found herself in Cam's room without any memory of how she'd come to be there. The bed wasn't made; only the bedspread was tossed over the jumble beneath. Suzanna half expected Cat to be curled up in the middle of it, but she wasn't. Her litter box was in the far corner, and nearby a water dish and an opened can of cat food remained untouched. Suzanna sighed, suddenly wishing for the undemanding companionship of the little gray animal. She could have used something warm to hold on to just then.

Cam's clothes were scattered around the room, on the floor, on the dresser, draped over a chair. Suzanna gathered them up automatically and stood holding them in her arms. Well, he'd said he wasn't neat.

Oh, Cam... John. Why couldn't you have told me? It might have been true, what she'd said to Meg about there being no *good* way to hear bad news, but some ways were less bad than others. Why hadn't he told her? After the things she'd revealed to him about herself and Angel's Walk, he probably knew better than anyone how much her home meant to her.

Her eye was caught by the glint of silver, a large portable stereo tape player on the floor, half under the bed. Suzanna dropped the bundle of clothes and lifted the tape player into her lap. She pushed the Play button and heard the same passion-hoarse voice that had haunted her in the night. She listened, then turned it off and set it back on the floor.

Of course he understood how much Angel's Walk meant to her. That was why he hadn't been able to bring himself to tell her.

Oh, John, Suzanna thought, laughing a little, sniffling a little. *You couldn't bear to hurt me, I suppose. You're still a coward, but I do understand.*

It occurred to her to wonder how she would have felt, seeing the suffering in his face when he broke the news. Would it have added to her own anguish or distracted her from it? Would her first impulse have been to comfort *him* instead of wallowing in her own misery? And if that was the case, what did it mean? Why should the feelings of a relative stranger matter so much to her?

She did know one thing, remembering that one long famished kiss: if they had comforted each other last night, they would probably have comforted each other right into bed.

And what, she demanded, is so wrong with that? It wasn't such a bad reason to go to bed with someone—solace, mutual need. In any case, since she couldn't allow herself to fall in love with the footloose civil servant, it would probably be the best reason she'd ever have.

With a prolonged sniff, Suzanna curled up in the middle of Cam's unmade bed and finally allowed herself to cry.

She was so wrapped up in her troubles that it was Wednesday evening before she could bring herself to face one more unthinkable but undeniable fact: Cat was gone.

CAM FLEW IN from Sacramento Thursday in the early afternoon, the hottest part of the day. After supervising his plane's moorings and checking in with the airstrip office, he tossed his suit bag and overnight case into the jeep he'd left parked in the meager shade of a bull pine and opened both doors wide. While he waited for the cross-breeze to blow the furnace blast of heat from the jeep's interior, he stood tapping his fingers on the rooftop, considering.

He felt obliged to go straight to dam headquarters. It was early yet, and there were still things he needed to do. But that wasn't where he wanted to go.

He needed to talk to Tony, to go over some figures with him, to work out a few things before the choppers got here. But Tony's wasn't the voice he wanted to hear.

He was hot and tired and wanted a shower and a change of clothes. He could get that at dam headquarters, but he longed for something more. At Angel's Walk he knew he would find a kind of peacefulness, a tranquillity that was like a cool, refreshing shower to the soul.

He wanted to go home.

Suzanna's car wasn't parked in front of the house, and Cam's sense of disappointment was acute, something he felt as physical pain. Where was she? Could she possibly be at work, business as usual? The house looked exactly the same, completely unchanged. He didn't know what he'd expected, but it was almost a shock to find everything looking so normal, so untouched.

As he pushed open the gate, he checked abruptly and then went on, shaking his head and silently laughing. In the section of lawn nearest the orchard, a bright orange power mower had cut in an inward spiral, coming to rest at the edge of a neat rectangle of lush emerald grass. Cam was still chuckling as he walked through drying grass clippings to stand looking down at the silent machine, but now there was an unfamiliar ache in his heart. Who but Suzanna would mow a lawn that was soon going to be part of a muddy lake bottom?

At first he thought that irony might have occurred to her belatedly and that was why she had left the job unfinished. But no, closer inspection revealed an empty gas tank. She must have just gone for gasoline.

Obeying some obscure impulse, Cam turned and went back to the jeep. Tossing his suit bag and case across the front seat, he lifted the heavy gasoline can from the back and returned to the stalled mower. It took him only a moment to refill the empty tank. When he pulled the starter cord, the motor fired instantly. He adjusted the throttle, and with a strange feeling of satisfaction, moved into the patch of unmowed grass.

It was hot, and in a matter of minutes he was drenched with sweat. He removed his shirt and let the slight breeze cool his body. Sweat trickled into his eyes, stinging. It tickled as it ran down the side of his face, and he lifted his arm to wipe it off.

Pain jolted him like a high-voltage electrical charge. It was excruciating pain and with it came shock, horror, revulsion and dread. For one numbed moment he could only stare at the small golden brown insect writhing its own death throes on the inner bend of his elbow, and then he quickly dashed it to the ground and scraped the stinger from his skin. His movements were calm, his hands steady, but inside a cold, unnerving fear was already clutching at him: Was this it? Would this be the time he couldn't get to his kit before it was too late? And he thought frantically, *If Sue doesn't come back in time, she'll find me . . .*

He wouldn't let that happen. On top of everything else, he couldn't do that to her. Besides, he had too much to do; there were jobs unfinished; he had to try to make things right, somehow, for her.

His kit. Where was it? There was the one in the kitchen, of course; it seemed a long way to go. His shirt pocket. He always carried one in his shirt pocket. But the sweat-soaked shirt he'd abandoned in the grass was empty. In his suit bag, then—in the jeep. And that was a long way to go, too, when already he could feel his head, his chest, his throat swelling, blowing up like a balloon, cutting off his air, blinding him. He no longer felt hot. Instead, he was cold and clammy. He knew he was going into shock, but if he could just get to the jeep . . . find his kit.

The door handle was hot. It was awkward, opening it with his right hand, but his rapidly swelling left arm was hanging like so much deadweight. It was going to be awkward trying to inject himself with his right hand, too. Everything was clumsy; the zipper on his suit bag seemed unbelievably stubborn, almost hostile. But the kit was there, in the pocket of his other uniform shirt, if he could only grasp it. His hand had begun to shake, and his breath was already coming in long, labored gasps.

He had the plastic case in his hand but was just a little too hasty. He fumbled the case and dropped it on the ground. He sank down in the shade beside the jeep and picked it up again, and this time he began silently to pray.

Chapter Eight

For Suzanna, the first shock was in finding a Corps of Engineers jeep parked at her front gate. She'd known Cam was expected back today, but nothing could have prepared her for the painful constriction in her chest at the solid reality of his being here. She'd heard the quaint expression "Her heart turned over." Now she knew what it meant. Willing herself to calm, unhurried movements, she got out of her car, opened the trunk and lifted out the gallon-size gas can. There was absolutely no reason why her heart should be hammering and her stomach filled with butterflies. *None.*

She had her hand on the latch of the gate when she got her second shock. It was a sound, a faint croak, that was barely more than a whisper: "Sue...I need...you."

For a few heartbeats she didn't see him sitting there in the deep shade with his back against the front wheel of his jeep. And when she did see him, it didn't register at first that anything was seriously wrong. Just hearing his voice was enough to deliver a numbing jolt to her system. She said, "Cam...? What—" And setting the can of gasoline carefully on the ground, she started toward him.

One good look at him gave her the biggest shock of all. She whispered, "Cam—oh, Lord," and in the next instant found herself on her knees in the dirt beside him.

His face was barely recognizable, but he made a valiant effort to smile. "I guess...I wasn't..." He couldn't finish. His breath was making a funny whistling sound. Suzanna found herself staring with dreadful fascination at the movement his chest made as he struggled to drag air through constricted air passages.

She knew what had happened. He'd tried to prepare her for this. He'd taught her exactly what to do during that emotionally charged, strangely erotic afternoon in her kitchen. It seemed like a dream now—his skin warm, brown and so smooth. But the reality—who could have prepared her for *this*?

The hypodermic—where was it? There, in his hand. But he seemed to be slipping into semiconsciousness. What if he stopped breathing? What if his heart stopped? She didn't know CPR! She looked wildly around for help, knowing there was none, knowing that there was no one but her. Cam's life depended on *her*.

She took the syringe from his fingers, trying to remember to turn it the way he'd shown her. *Hold it like a pencil.* The muscle of his arm that had been so warm and resilient, inviting the exploration of her mouth, now was cold and clammy and mottled with hives. It didn't even feel like human flesh, and that made it easier.

Suzanna sat weakly back on her heels, still holding the half-empty syringe. She didn't know she was crying until her nose began to run, and then she sniffed and whispered tensely, "Cam—don't you die. Don't you dare die." She drew a shaky hand across her eyes and wiped her cheeks on the sleeve of her T-shirt. But except for the labored contractions of his chest, Cam didn't move.

The other half of the adrenaline—he'd said to turn the syringe another notch if the first dose wasn't enough! Suzanna was taking no chances. She emptied the syringe into Cam's unresponsive muscle and then, tossing it away, took his swollen face between her hands and said furiously, "John Campbell Harris, you are *not* going to do this to me! I'm not through with you yet; do you hear me? Come on back here and face me like a man, damn it!"

Was his color better? Did the whistling sound seem fainter, his chest muscles less strained, or did she only want to think so? Did her hands, smoothing damp hair back from his temples, feel currents of warmth and vitality returning to his skin?

"Cam," she muttered, punching the words between her teeth. "Come on, say something. *Talk* to me, damn you. *Cam...*" She put her hands on his shoulders and tried to shake him, but fear had turned her to jelly; it was like trying to move a boulder. "Come back here, you rat. You're not going to get away that easily! You're not going to go and die and leave me with no explanation! Cam, *please.*"

A voice near her ear, husky but steady, said, "Explanation for what?"

Suzanna's eyes flew open, and she sank abruptly onto her heels, pressing the back of one hand hard against her mouth. His breathing was quiet, almost normal, and the eyes that stared back at her through heavy, still-swollen eyelids were bright and alive. A smile twisted his mouth sideways. Suzanna's heart turned over yet again.

"Oh... you," she murmured, relief and chagrin washing through her like cold water. "Are you—? I can't believe—" And then, in ridiculous accusation, she asked, "Were you faking?"

Cam's laughter was soft and a bit worn, but it wrapped her in warmth and comfort. "No, the stuff just works that fast. A real miracle cure, huh? Hey, do you think you could hand me a couple of those antihistamine tablets?"

"Oh, sure." Suzanna removed the tablets from the cellophane packet and held them out to him. When he made no move to take them, she placed them between his parted lips, shivering as warm puffs of breath touched her fingertips. She whispered, "Um...do you need water?" Her own mouth was bone-dry.

"No." He shook his head. "Not right now. In a minute, maybe."

She couldn't look at him enough. "Are you really all right?"

"Yeah, I'm fine. Will be." His voice was quiet and gentle. He lifted one hand and touched her cheek with the backs of his fingers. "Were you crying?"

Suzanna uttered a rather liquid-sounding "No!" and looked away.

His head tilted, and a quizzical half smile pulled at his mouth. "Hey, I think you just missed your best shot at me. I'm the guy who's ruining your life, remember?"

Suzanna ducked her head and wiped her eyes on the tail of her T-shirt. "That's a rotten thing to say," she said tightly.

"Yeah, it was. I'm sorry." Cam's voice was soft again. He sounded tired, and when Suzanna looked at him again, she saw that he had leaned his head back against the fender and closed his eyes. His color and features were almost normal, but there were purplish smudges under his eyes.

She longed to touch him again, to run her hands over the bones of his face, the roughness of his jaw, the warm brown column of his neck, the bumps and hollows of his collarbone, the hair-crested mounds of his chest. She loved his chest. She wanted to lay her cheek on it, to touch a nut-brown nipple with her mouth, to tickle her nose with his hair. She just couldn't think of an excuse to touch him again.

Cam didn't seem to suffer the same restraint. His hand stroked her cheek, then dropped to her throat just in time to catch the movement of her nervous swallow. "What do I need to explain?" he asked again, gently probing.

"Why you left me."

"Left you?"

"Why you left," Suzanna gulped, frantically back-tracking, "without telling me." She reached out a clenched fist, unable to help herself, and then drew it back before it could touch him. She shook her head in quiet anguish and met his eyes. "Why didn't you tell me, Cam?"

Now it was his turn to look away. Neither of them seemed to be breathing. "I couldn't," Cam said harshly. "I'm sorry. I should have told you. I wanted to. I meant to. But I couldn't."

"Why?"

"Ah, Sue..." There was a long moment of tense silence, and then he sighed, and hooking his hand around her neck, gently drew her head down onto his chest. "I just couldn't. Do you know what I mean?"

Suzanna shut her eyes tightly, trying desperately to hold back the trembling that would betray her feelings. "Yes," she murmured against the strong, reassuring thud of his heart. "I guess I do."

But she was thinking, *Why? How? When?* Why should she understand? He was destroying her life's founda-tions! Because she loved him? How could she—he wasn't anything like what she wanted in a man! And when could it have happened? She hadn't had time to fall in love. She hadn't known him long enough to get acquainted! And in a few days or weeks he would be gone....

For Suzanna, time had always been a nebulous thing. She'd been close to people whose lives had spanned stage-coaches and communications satellites, the horse and buggy and the space shuttle. The people she knew best were born, grew up and grew old in the same place, and most relationships were for a lifetime. But a few minutes ago she had been reckoning the lifetime of the man she loved in single heartbeats. Time had telescoped, and suddenly a few weeks, even a few days, seemed a very long time.

"God only knows why you should understand," Cam rasped, echoing her thoughts. The hoarse, ragged sound of his voice was a jarring reminder of the strain she must be putting on him, when only minutes ago he'd been struggling for every breath. She sat up but couldn't resist touching his chest with a lingering hand under the pretext of brushing away a few clinging blades of grass.

With a sudden, almost-violent movement he caught her hand, holding it hard against the heat of his body. The air between them boiled with turmoil and confusion, like water where two opposing currents met. Without knowing precisely when it had happened, Suzanna was aware that they had crossed some sort of threshold; their relationship had acquired a new dimension, and no matter how much they might have wanted to, there was no going back.

She coughed and said, "You must be uncomfortable."

Cam gave her a look of fierce intensity. His voice sounded incongruously mild. "Yeah, I think I'm about ready to go inside. Give me a hand up."

Suzanna turned her hand and gripped his tightly, bracing herself against the drag of his weight. The pull on her hand wasn't just a token; he really did seem to need her help. She asked doubtfully, "Are you sure you're all right? Maybe I should call—"

"I'll be fine. Joints are a little stiff and sore, that's all. Couple of aspirin and a hot shower and I'll be fine."

But he looked so tired and moved like an old man, sort of bent forward at the waist. He kept rotating his neck and shoulders as if the joints didn't fit together properly. Suzanna suddenly remembered the first time she'd seen him here, right in this spot, the day he'd come to introduce himself into her life. How alive he'd been! He'd seemed almost to crackle with power and energy, like a dynamo. And how afraid of him she'd been. He had been pure electricity, dangerous to get close to; if she had touched him, she would have gotten badly burned. That was why she'd fought to keep him out of her house—the skunks were only an excuse. Cam Harris had been a high-voltage live wire; she'd been afraid that if she grabbed it, she wouldn't be able to let go, and he would burn out all her circuits and then leave her lifeless and empty.

But now the power had been turned off. He was only a man—skin, bone, muscle and sinew, mortal and vulnerable. A man with frailties and shortcomings, a man she could understand, a man she could love.

She stepped close to him and slipped her arm around his waist, and again there was that feeling of having stepped across a threshold. She felt a strange possessiveness, a protective instinct that wasn't at all maternal. Her mind wasn't able yet to put the concept in logical form, but her heart was telling her, *This man is mine*. To hell with time, to hell with the future; today he was hers, and today was forever.

Cam hesitated a moment and then dropped his arm across her shoulders. Suzanna looked up at him, but he was looking determinedly straight ahead, eyes slightly

narrowed and jaw tensed. His whole body felt stiff, as if he
had tightened himself against her.

*But that's all right, John Harris, because I understand
you now.* Suzanna directed the thought at his rigid profile
and smiled a private, inner smile. He might be a rootless
wanderer, a man who took care to leave no part of himself behind, but she had touched him, she knew. She had
made him care. He might try to mask his feelings, but he'd
given himself away by not being able to tell her about
Angel's Walk. And he'd given himself away with that last
desperate kiss, when she'd felt deep inside him the unmistakable tremors of passion and pain.

THEY HAD REACHED the foot of the stairs.

"Okay, I'll take it from here," Cam said with a crooked
smile. "Thanks for the lift, and, uh, for saving my life."

She murmured, "Oh, sure, anytime," gazing at him
with a look that had a stranger effect on his heart than the
bee venom.

Cam gave her shoulders a brotherly squeeze. "Just one
more thing—"

"Yes?"

"Think you could find me an aspirin or two?"

She whispered, "Sure."

Realizing that his fingers were describing sensuous circles on the skin of her upper arm in a manner that in no
way could be called brotherly, Cam reluctantly lifted his
arm from her shoulders. He muttered something vague
and unnecessary about trying the shower and then took the
stairs two at a time, just to show her he could.

In the sanctuary of the shower, Cam soaped his body,
shampooed his hair, measured and then dismissed the
stubble on his jaws, all on automatic pilot. He was thinking, *You can't hurt her anymore, Cam. You just can't use*

*this one. This one's a hell of a lot more than a warm body
and a good time. This one's not just a temporary antidote
for loneliness. You can't love this one and then leave her
behind without a backward glance.*

It was while he was standing with his eyes closed, letting water as hot as he could stand it cascade over his
abused body, that he bitterly acknowledged the real source
of his inner struggle: the very last thing in the world he
wanted to do was leave her behind.

But you can't take her with you, either, he reminded
himself, turning off the faucets and reaching for a towel.
*She has anxiety attacks in strange restaurants. How is she
going to follow you?*

She only thinks *she can't travel,* he argued back with
stubborn arrogance, drying himself energetically and only
belatedly remembering to be careful of his swollen and
tender left arm. *If she was with me... If she loved me...*

*If Suzanna loved him, she'd go with him in a minute if
he asked her to. He'd bet on it—she was just that kind of
person.*

And she could be happy. I'd make her happy..

*That's nothing but ego talking, you jerk. You'd make
her miserable.*

He knotted the towel around his waist and combed
through his damp hair with frustrated fingers. She was like
a precious stone, and this was her setting. Removing her
from it would diminish her, and it would probably destroy her. It was a chance he just wasn't willing to take.

So, he thought, turning on the water in the sink before
he remembered that his toothbrush was still in his overnight bag outside in the jeep, *you can't love her and leave
her, and you can't take her with you.* He turned the water
back off and stared hard at the steam-shrouded figure in
the mirror. *That brings you right back to square one: leave*

*her alone. It may just be the most worthwhile thing you
ever do.* It would certainly be the hardest.

He left the bathroom and padded across the landing,
wearing only the towel and an expression of bleak resolve. In the doorway of his room he stopped, stifling a
groan, feeling as if he'd just received a karate kick to the
solar plexus.

The room was heavy and languid with afternoon sun
and shimmered with golden motes. And in the middle of
it stood Suzanna, holding a bottle of aspirin in one hand
and a tube of something in the other. And if ever the term
"ripe" could be applied to a time, a place and a woman,
this was it. Everything about her—her skin, rosy tan and
dewed with moisture, her hair, burnished by the sun to the
color of ripe wheat, her body looking more voluptuous in
T-shirt and jeans than she could possibly know—seemed
to evoke sensual images and tactile memories of tropical
beaches and endless summers and sweet, rapturous loving.

"I brought the aspirin, and this cream." Her voice hit
his chest and spread into his belly like hot mulled wine.
"Papa used to use it for his arthritis. I thought it might
help your aches and pains. You massage it in."

"Thanks—" He cleared his throat and repeated it.
"Thanks a lot. I appreciate it."

She didn't move. Cam reached out a hand to take the
tube of ointment.

Suzanna shook her head and smiled. "You can't very
well massage your own back, especially with that arm.
Come—sit down. I'll do it for you."

"Sue . . ." Cam could feel his resolve eroding like adobe
in the rain. He waved a helpless hand in the general direction of his towel. "Look here, I—"

Her laughter was a silken ripple down his spine. "Mr. Harris, don't tell you're embarrassed. It looks to me like you're every bit as 'decent' as you were the other night when you invited me in here. Come on, sit." She patted the bedspread in a no-nonsense manner.

Cam glared balefully at her and wondered what had become of her blush. There was a tinge of pink across her cheeks, but it wasn't the full flush of embarrassment he'd come to adore. It was just enough, along with the sheen of perspiration, to give her face a kind of glow. Wisps of hair clung to her damp forehead, and her mouth looked firm and sweet, full of moisture and promise, like some exotic fruit. And if he didn't take positive action of some sort, he was going to eat her alive....

Cam sat gingerly down on the edge of the bed and then, after a moment's consideration, carefully turned and stretched out on his stomach, raising his upper body on his elbows.

"Uh-uh," Suzanna said severely, prodding at the hard ridges of muscle on either side of his spine. "You'll have to lie down. I told you before—I can't do anything with you when your muscles are tense. Come on, now, lie down all the way.... Right. Now just relax."

He tried. He employed every relaxation technique he'd ever heard of. He counted backward from one hundred, imagined himself going numb, beginning with his fingers and toes. He thought of himself floating in an inner tube on a sun-dappled pool; lying in a field of clover while white clouds drifted lazily across a cerulean sky. He tried matching his breathing to hers, which didn't work, because hers seemed to be strangely erratic. Her breath kept catching in her throat; then she would seem to forget to breathe altogether for a while, and finally she would release a long, uneven sigh. In Cam's mind, those soft expirations became whispers of love, sighs of fulfillment; puffy clouds and sunlit waters had a way of melting into visions of her face, lips parted, swollen and moist from his kisses, eyes heavy and glazed with passion.

I'm losing my mind, he thought gloomily. *What in the world is keeping me from making love to her here and now? When did I develop such restraint?*

She hitched herself farther up on the bed in order to reach his neck, and her denim jeans scraped along his ribs. As her hands manipulated the small muscles in his neck and lingered in the hair on his nape, he worried that she would feel the telltale pulse in his neck or hear the grinding of his teeth. Her fingers moved relentlessly over his body, and every touch was like a small electric shock. Wherever her hands smoothed the cooling medication, his skin burned and tingled with cold fires, but he burned and tingled, too, in parts of his body she hadn't touched. And when he felt the heels of her hands press into the muscle ridges in the small of his back and her fingers fan out to stroke the ticklish sides of his waist just above the edge of the towel, he thought in desperation, *If she goes any farther . . .*

It occurred to him to wonder if she had any idea what she was doing to him. And then he thought, *Of course she knows. Nobody's that innocent.* He felt a surge of anger that she should be making this so difficult for him. Why should he have to be strong for both of them, damn it?

He willed himself to breathe slowly, deeply, evenly. He was thinking, *Damn this job. Damn this weather, this place and this infernal house. And damn you, Suzanna Day, for making it all so hard.*

After a while, blessedly, she got tired of looking at the back of his head, and thinking he was asleep, she quietly left him. But her going left a cold emptiness in the sun-baked room. Cam dropped his good arm over the side of the bed and groped for his tape player, then rolled over, pulling it onto his chest. He punched a button and settled back, shaking with silent, rueful laughter. *Oh,* the voice on the tape groaned softly, *I'm on fire....*

IT WAS AFTER DARK when Suzanna heard Cam's footsteps on the stairwell. The footsteps retreated in the direction of the kitchen and then returned, coming to a halt at the edge of the puddle of light that spilled from the living room into the dark hallway. She drew a long, careful breath, and placing her pen on top of her notebook, lifted her eyes to where she knew he would be—leaning against the cherry-wood door frame, watching her. And as a bolt of electricity shot through her, she gulped and thought, *Oh, help.*

His hair was tumbled, his jaws shadowed, and there was a bedspread mark across one cheekbone. He'd dressed, more or less—worn Levi's and a short-sleeved khaki shirt left untucked and unbuttoned—but he still had the damp, mussed-up look of someone just awakened. And he looked as surly and restless as a bear in early spring. His particular brand of vitality had never seemed more raw and untamed.

"Hello," she ventured, more bravely than she felt. "How do you feel?"

His reply was a grunt. "I'm okay."

"Would you like an aspirin or—"

"Just some more antihistamine. Got any cold medicine?"

Suzanna shook her head. "Sorry. I never get colds. Shall I—?"

He mumbled, "It's okay. I'll get the stuff from the kit in the fridge." He began to scratch his arm mechanically, then realized what he was doing and stopped. "You didn't wake me," he said, frowning.

"You didn't ask me to," Suzanna said logically, a little puzzled by the aura of anger around him.

He gave a dry snort, and pushing himself off the door frame, entered the room. "I didn't know I was going to fall asleep."

"Well, you must have needed the rest," Suzanna ventured, being cautious and reasonable, "or you wouldn't have dropped off so quickly."

"Quickly?"

"Yes, while I was massaging your back. You were sound asleep before I'd barely begun."

Cam stared at her, a hard, stormy look. She thought, *Why on earth do they always symbolize love with hearts and flowers and sunshine and pretty pastels? What it really is, is lightning bolts and thunderclouds.* And as for color...all she could see at the moment were black doubts and gray uncertainties and the rich, vibrant purple of pain....

She faltered. "I'm sorry. I thought under the circumstances—was it important?"

He stared for a moment longer and then made an impatient gesture, as if shaking off a persistent fly. "I just had a lot to do, that's all. It was time wasted." He began to prowl the room like a restless tiger, touching things, picking up knickknacks, pausing to peer through the leaded glass doors of the built-in bookcase beside the fireplace. And then he whirled on her suddenly and demanded with testy irrelevance, "Do you *always* work like that—on the floor?"

Thinking, *What on earth is the matter with him?* Suzanna gave a nervous laugh and began to chatter. "Yes, I guess I do. I've never liked chairs. I can't seem to stay in them. No matter how hard I try, I just sort of slip off before I know what I'm doing, and there I am—''

He interrupted her. "Yeah, I remember.'' He strolled slowly toward her, thumbs hooked in his pants pockets. His voice was softer but still carried those bewildering undercurrents of tension and anger. Suzanna's heart began a slow, painful rhythm that she could almost hear, and she thought, *Be patient. Be calm. He'll get around to what's bothering him*.

"You were on the floor the first time I ever saw you. You were under a desk, with your nose in the past.'' With the last word he gave a pile of photographs a rude nudge with his toe, and she gasped and put out a protective hand.

"Damn it, Sue.'' He dropped abruptly onto his heels beside her, picked up her notebook and then laid it back down with a restraint that only underscored his anger. His good arm shot out, pointing beyond her shoulder toward the west, toward the lake. "Don't you know what's going on out there? Don't you know what's happening? I mean *here* and *now*. Last winter enough snow fell in the Sierra Nevadas to bury this house twice over. Now it's melting faster than anybody's ever seen it melt before. That's water, Suzanna, and it's got to go somewhere. Right now a whole lot of it is going over that dam down there—enough in the time it would take you to sneeze to wash this house off its foundations and clear into next week! And do you know where it's going after that?''

Suzanna swallowed a lump in her throat and nodded automatically, but he ignored her assent and took her arms in a painful grip.

"It's going right on down the canyon and into a tule slough, where somebody had the wonderful intelligence and foresight to put a *city*. A quarter of a million people! And my job—*my job*,'' he grated when she would have interrupted, giving her a little shake, "is to keep it from doing that. Okay? After all the acts of God and the stupidity of men have done their worst, somebody comes and says, 'All right, Harris, your mission, should you choose to accept it, is to *fix* this mess!' And Suzanna...that's what I'm gonna do. All that water is going to stay right here in this lake, and that means that the lake is going to have to get *bigger*, and that means this house, which had no damn business being here in the first place, is going to be in the middle of it. Do you understand that?"

Inevitably, if belatedly, anger came to her rescue. Damn it, her world had been sunshine and pastels; *he* had brought the purple and the gray. And quite suddenly she hated him, not so much for what he was doing as for what he *was*. Not for destroying her home and her peace but for making her love him in spite of it.

"I'm not a child," she said stiffly.

Cam threw his hands into the air and brought them down with a slap on the taut muscles of his flexed thighs. "Then quit acting like one!"

"I beg your—"

"Look at this place!" Cam was on his feet again, pacing, flinging an arm out to take in the cozy, lamplit room. "You haven't done a damn thing to get ready to evacuate. Nothing." He made a furious gesture toward the bookcase. "It looks exactly like it did when I left. What do you intend to do? Leave it until the water's lapping at your front doorstep?"

Stung to defensiveness by guilt, Suzanna shot back, "I've been busy! You don't know what I've been doing. You weren't here!"

"Oh," Cam said, his voice quiet now that he had her shouting, "I can see what you've been doing. Mowing lawns that don't even matter anymore and burying yourself in this stuff. You know, Sue—'' He paused to look down at her, a long hooded gaze. "You're like an ostrich, except you stick your head in the past instead of the sand.'' He rubbed a hand over his face, and Suzanna was struck by the strain and tension in its lines and hollows. The gloomy colors he'd brought to her world had touched him, too.

"It's coming," he said after a moment, the anger draining out of him as she watched. Now his eyes were shadowed and unhappy, his voice gentle. "I'm sorry. There's not a thing you can do about it. It *is* going to happen, and ignoring it won't make it go away." He waited a while longer, and when she only continued to sit in stubborn, hurt silence, he touched the top of her head with the tips of his fingers and went off to the kitchen, absently scratching his bee-stung arm.

Oh, no you don't, Cam Harris. Don't you go gentle on me! I want to stay mad—it doesn't hurt as much.

She swallowed hard several times, shoring up her defenses. *Who do you think you are, Cam Harris! You don't even know me. Where do you get off, telling me what I'm like!* Scrambling to her feet, she followed him.

Cam was leaning against the kitchen sink, eating ice cream from a half-gallon carton with an iced-tea spoon. When Suzanna came through the door, he pointed the spoon at her and scowled. He had to dispose of a large bite of chocolate-chocolate chip before he could speak, but when he did, Suzanna felt her fortifications crumble into sawdust.

"Where the devil is Cat? I haven't seen her around."

Suzanna halted and clapped both hands over her mouth. She thought, *Now I really do know how he felt. I'm a coward, too.*

But for her there was no escape from the job. Cam was watching her, waiting for her reply. She had to tell him. She lifted her hands and let them drop, then said helplessly, "Cam, I wish I knew."

His frown deepened. "What do you mean?"

"I mean she's missing. I can't find her anywhere. I keep thinking—"

"What'd you do, let her out?" He didn't sound angry or even alarmed. Just curious. After the one pause to ask his question, he had renewed his attack on the carton of ice cream and was giving it the benefit of his focused concentration.

"No," Suzanna said, clearing her throat. "I didn't—"

"Well, then, she's got to be in the house somewhere. She's probably just hiding."

"Not necessarily." Suzanna lifted a hand to touch her hair, then her lips, and then, to still its nervous wandering, tucked her hand into the hip pocket of her jeans. "There's the attic," she said wretchedly. "I forgot about the attic."

"The attic?"

"Yes, the door—remember?"

"Okay, so you think she's in the attic. No problem— she'll come out when she's ready. I wouldn't worry about it."

"No—you don't understand." *Damn it,* Suzanna thought, *quit making this so hard. I'm trying.* All in a rush she blurted, "It's been almost three days. I've been in the attic looking for her, and—Cam, see, there's a pane missing in one of the dormer windows. There used to be an owl living up there—"

"Oh, for—"

"Well, it isn't there anymore!"

"So you think the cat went out the window?" Cam said carefully.

"It's the only thing I can imagine. She could have gotten from there onto the roof, I think, and from there—" She shrugged helplessly. "Cam, I'm sorry. I feel terrible."

Cam muttered, "Stupid cat," and took a spoonful of ice cream.

Suzanna looked miserably at the floor. "I've been putting food outside for her just in case. *Something* always eats it, but of course—"

Cam took two more bites, giving them his undivided attention, then turned abruptly and dropped his spoon into the sink. One shoulder lifted and then dropped. "Look, don't sweat it. It's not your fault." His voice was light and carefully controlled.

Suzanna stared through a haze of misery at the back of his neck. "I know how much she meant to you, Cam. I wish—"

He put the ice cream back into the freezer, slammed the door and turned abruptly. His face was expressionless, his eyes carefully veiled. "Look, I told you, don't worry about it. The dumb cat didn't even belong to me, anyway. I told you she was just a stray." He shrugged and looked away, mumbling something that sounded like "Nothing but a nuisance...."

Suzanna was silent, remembering the tone of indulgent affection he always used when referring to the cat, the way he spoke to her as if to another person, a friend. She remembered, too, how touchy he'd been when she had probed too deeply. He'd said then, too, "She's just a mangy old cat." Everything in his voice and in his face contradicted the denial.

"Cam," she said softly, "why are you afraid to admit that you care?"

He spun back to her, his eyes bright with anger. "What do you want me to say? She was a cat. An old stray cat, that's all. What am I supposed to do, cry?"

"She was your *friend*," Suzanna said tensely, "and you did care. You once told me she was the only company you have besides yourself."

He made a sibilant sound of disgust. "What do you do, jot everything down?"

"Well, it isn't hard to remember the way you felt about that cat. It was obvious. Why is it so hard for you to admit? Are you ashamed of caring?" *And is that why you keep pulling away from me every time your feelings get too close to the surface?* "Maybe you think it isn't manly to love a little kitty cat."

Cam made another rude noise and turned his back to her. Suzanna's anger boiled up and over. "Or maybe you can't admit that you need someone—even a cat. Cam the problem solver, the miracle worker, Cam the rootless wonder! You don't ever get involved, do you? You just stay loose—no commitments, no entanglements, no roots. No wonder you can't understand mine! No wonder you resent—"

"You don't have roots; you have anchors! *Anchors!* This place doesn't nourish you; it strangles you. It's dragging you down, holding you prisoner!"

"That's not true!"

"Yeah? Well, if what you have is roots, I'd rather be rootless. No strings, baby!"

"Well, if freedom is what you have, I'd rather have roots. You're like one of those balloons that goes higher and higher and finally self-destructs somewhere in the stratosphere. I may have attachments, but at least I'm not alone. I don't have to depend on a cat for company!''

Cam's fury became a slow, cold burn. He came toward her with that rolling masculine stroll, thumbs tucked in his pockets, a dangerous glitter in his eyes. "Now, Suzanna..." he drawled, deliberately lowering his gaze to the front of her T-shirt, "what makes you think I depend on a cat for company? Company is the easiest thing on earth to find; don't you know that? I've been in places you never even heard of, seen things you couldn't even imagine, done things you don't want to know about." He smiled, a slow, sensuous smile that didn't come close to his eyes. His hand came out to touch her shoulder and then moved first to the curve of her neck and then slowly upward until his fingers were moving in gentle massaging strokes at the base of her skull. Suzanna swallowed involuntarily and closed her eyes. She could still feel his eyes on her, calmly and coldly appraising her reaction to his insidious form of intimidation.

"Darlin', I've never lacked for company. I've tasted some of the most exotic fruits this world has to offer." His thumb began to move up and down her throat, and under his touch it seemed to swell and ache. His hand was so unbearably gentle, in tormenting contrast to the cruelty of his words. "And I eat sweet little things like you for breakfast."

Suzanna thought wildly, *I was right the first time I ever saw him. I can't handle men like him. I never could. Whatever made me think I understood him?*

His thumb exerted pressure just under her chin, lifting it. Suzanna opened her eyes and saw his face just above hers, fierce and dark and frightening. Then she looked into his eyes, those ambiguous eyes, shadowed now and filled with pain, and she knew that she did understand. And she licked her lips and drew a shaky breath and bravely whispered, *"Big... bad... John."*

For a few moments he and she and time all stood still. And then he swore softly and brought his mouth down to cover her parted lips. His hand, no longer gentle, held her head captive. His mouth was hard and bruising; teeth grated on teeth, and his tongue plunged deep, an unexpected intimacy that was meant to shock. Suzanna understood that the kiss wasn't intended to arouse or seduce. He was saying to her, "Look how bad I am—a terrible, dangerous man. If you have any sense at all, you'll stay away from me. And if you don't, you deserve what you get."

And what would he do if he knew about the bolt of pure desire that had just slashed through her chest and buried itself deep inside her? What was this surge of exhilaration she felt, a kind of strength and vitality unlike anything she'd ever felt before? She felt she could match his passion and exceed it, and his violence, too, if that was the way he wanted it.

But Cam suddenly tore his mouth away, leaving hers throbbing and swollen and tingling with cooling moisture. For a moment he just stared down at her, his face filled with horror and something like despair, and then he rasped, "Damn it, Suzanna—" and hurled himself out of the kitchen.

Suzanna heard the front door open. She and the house braced for the slam, but it didn't come. Instead, incredibly, incongruously there came the staccato explosion of a power motor! She clamped a hand over her mouth, stifling a sound that was half laughter, half sob, and raced down the hall and out onto the front porch.

Chapter Nine

In a rural nighttime accustomed to the soft harmonies of nature, the racket was an intrusion of sheer, shattering chaos.

Suzanna shrieked, "What are you doing?" but her voice was snatched away and buried in the avalanche of noise. She began to whimper with frustration. Somewhere out there in the darkness a madman was pushing a lethal machine through grass he couldn't even see, driven by devils to a fury beyond reason.

She hesitated, struggling with fear, and then threw herself off of the porch and into the night. "Cam!" she screamed. "Are you crazy? Stop it! *Stop it!*"

One minute she was in the center of a maelstrom of noise and confusion, pounding on the solid muscle of Cam's back with her fists, and in the next her blows were glancing futilely off his forearms, and her frantic cries were hanging alone in the stillness.

"You're crazy! Crazy—"

"*I'm* crazy? Take a look at yourself! Even the skunks have more sense than you do! They've already left; don't you know that? Even the damn *cat* knew better!"

"The cat left because *you...left...her!*" Suzanna sobbed. Cam had captured her wrists, and she struggled against him, trying to hit him again. For someone who had never in her life laid a hand on a living creature in anger, it was amazing how good it felt to vent her emotions in violence. "You left me...all alone...to face this. I didn't—I don't—I didn't know where to begin! I don't know what to do! I just don't know what to do...."

Blinded by tears and frustrated by the ease with which he warded off her blows, Suzanna gave him one last desperate shove. As he stepped backward to brace himself, his foot encountered the unexpected bulk of the lawn mower. The next thing Suzanna knew, she was falling with him, and his arms were around her, protecting her, while his body took the brunt of the impact with the ground.

There was one moment of shocked stillness. Suzanna was lying full length on top of Cam's motionless body, her heart beating a tattoo on his sternum. Her hands were on his shoulders; his were on her waist. And then her hands moved to touch his neck, his face; at the same instant, his hands moved upward to grasp her shoulders, and then her head. Their hands roamed urgently, exploring, seeking reassurance, and all the while they were both, in breathless, jumbled murmurs, saying exactly the same thing.

"Oh, Lord, I'm sorry. I never meant to hurt you. I'm sorry...."

Cam's hands tightened on her head. The muscles in his abdomen bunched and contracted against her belly as he lifted his head and shoulders to silence them both with his mouth. He took her lips with an urgency born of too much need and too much denial, and Suzanna's response was immediate and unrestrained. She made a small whimpering sound and opened her mouth in instinctive welcome. His tongue trapped the breath in her throat, but it didn't seem to matter—all she was aware of was his mouth, his breath, the pounding rush of his blood and the furnace heat of his body. When he groaned deep in his throat, she felt the vibrations in her own chest, and in her heart.

His arms held her tightly as he rolled them both sideways, cradling her partly with his body and partly with the cushion of cool, soft grass. Suzanna felt the urgency in him become less frantic and more focused; the dizzying blitzkrieg assault on her mouth eased and was renewed with control and purpose. His questing hands roamed down her back and found bare skin at the curve of her waist; and then, traveling upward over her ribs, pushing her T-shirt out of the way, discovered and dealt with the fastenings of her bra.

A tiny, involuntary spasm of shock caught at Suzanna's throat. Cam's hands stroked gently back and forth over her rib cage, just brushing the sides of her breasts while his lips and tongue bathed her feverish lips, soothing and reassuring.

He drew back, his face a greater darkness looming above her in the night. She laughed a little, trying to quell a tendency to tremble.

"Well," she said jerkily, "I guess you're all right...."

"Yeah," Cam said thickly. "The ground broke my fall."

Suzanna whispered, "Lucky you."

Cam whispered, "Lucky me."

Suzanna raised her hand and rasped the backs of her fingers across his jaw. "Is this what we were fighting about?"

He brushed her temple with his lips. "Yes, I think so."

Almost fearfully, she asked, "You aren't going to stop again, are you? Because—"

"Sue—"

"Because I don't think I can stand it if you do that again."

Cam said dryly, "Don't worry; neither can I."

"It makes me feel awful. Sort of ... sick."

His body rocked with his soft chuckle. He said fervently, "I know the feeling." He ducked his head, searching for her mouth. When he found it, she sighed and opened to him, more deeply and completely than ever before. Her body was melting, draining away into his.

"Cam," she whispered when he withdrew a little, "I'm not sure which is worse, when you stop or when you don't. That makes me feel—"

"What?" He dropped a kiss onto the corner of her mouth, tucked one under her jaw, then buried his face in the curve of her neck and throat.

Suzanna gasped, "Like I'm going to explode."

"It's all right," he murmured against her racing pulse. "We'll explode together."

"Cam, I think—"

"What, love?"

"I think—I'm frightened. I didn't think I would be, but—"

"Believe me, so am I," he muttered, and after a moment's hesitation, got to his feet and drew her up beside him. Suzanna clung to his forearms, feeling as though half of her had been rudely taken away.

"Cam, you said you wouldn't—"

"I know, love," he said with infinite tenderness. "It's just for a little while."

He was thinking, *Please, please don't let me ruin this for her, too.* Something itched and burned behind his eyes and made his voice come out sounding as if it had been strained through burlap. "Sue, are you really sure you want it to be me?"

"Yes."

Just like that, simply, without hesitation or equivocation. With one swift motion he lifted her into his arms and murmured into her hair, "I always said you were crazy."

"I'm not. I just know what I want. I want you."

I want you. He'd heard those words a good many times before in his life, but never were they spoken with such quiet and unadorned grace. The hot stinging in his eyes expanded to his throat, and a small earthquake shook his chest. Its epicenter seemed to be somewhere near his heart. "A determined woman," he said huskily.

"Yes. Descended of pioneers. One of whom pulled her man out of a well by the seat of his pants, don't forget." She made a sound—either a laugh or a sob—and added in a low, shaky voice that was a contradiction of her words, "I'm tough."

He cradled her head in the palm of his hand and pressed her slowly into his kiss. Her mouth was heated and open, her body boneless and pliant in his arms.

This time it was she who pulled away first. With her moist lips against his throat, she said in a slurred, inebriated murmur, "Oh, Cam. I've just thought of something. I'm not—"

He kissed the tip of her nose and then her mouth. "It's all right. Will you trust me to protect you?"

Protect you. As he listened to the ironic echo of his own words, she gave a little sigh and relaxed against him. He felt her eyelashes flutter against his neck like butterfly wings and drew a long breath.

"Sue," he whispered, "I don't want to hurt you any more than I already have. You're a forever kind of woman. You believe in roots, commitments."

"Anchors." The word was a soft exhalation.

"Yeah. And I'm the balloon without a string, remember? This can't be a forever kind of thing."

"I know that." She was silent for a moment. And then, very steadily, very gravely, she said, "I'm not an anchor, Cam. I wouldn't even want to try to hold you. I promise." He thought he could hear a smile in her voice. "Look, Ma—no strings."

No strings? He thought, *Sweetheart, if you only knew.*

He said huskily, "I don't want you to do something in the heat of the moment that you'll regret in the morning, do you understand? I want you to be absolutely sure."

"I am sure. Absolutely."

He looked at her while she gazed unflinchingly back at him, then carried her up the steps to the porch. He opened the screen door with his foot and swept neatly through it, but when he paused at the base of the stairs, she stiffened in his arms and protested. "Cam—"

"Hush," he whispered, tightening his grip. She gave a little gasp of breathless laughter and buried her face in his neck while he took the stairs, two at a time.

When he lowered her feet slowly to the floor in his room, she shivered and clung to him. "Are you cold?" he asked in a ragged tone, even though he knew better.

The breeze blowing through his open window was soft and balmy and alive with night sounds. His own skin felt feverish, his muscles tense and knotted, for although her innocence didn't seem very important to her, he was finding that it was very important to him—too important. Outside on the lawn, in the heat of violent emotions, he'd forgotten, but now he was so aware of it all he could think was, *Please, please don't let me hurt her.*

"No, I'm not cold," she said, seriously considering his question. "Shivery, though."

"Butterflies?" *He* certainly had them. He leaned forward slightly and brushed her throat with his lips. Her breath seemed to catch, and her voice became a whisper.

"No, I've had butterflies. This is different."

"Good." He touched the word into the hollow at the base of her neck. "I'd hate to think you were afraid of me."

"Not afraid. Nervous, though." He felt the cool hands on his neck, stroking, burrowing through the hair on the nape of his neck, but there was a kind of resistance in her, too, and he knew that she was fighting a battle with her own natural reserve.

He drew back and looked into her eyes and said gently, "Would you feel better if we turned off the lights?"

She licked her lips and then laughed and closed her eyes. "Yes, but it would probably do just as well if you kissed me. Either way, I'd stop worrying about—"

"What are you worrying about, love?"

"Oh, you know. Things. Like what I'll look like...."

His stomach muscles quivered and tightened with his efforts to control his laughter. He wasn't amused—it would have been a laugh of pure joy, sheer delight in her—but he was afraid she might not understand.

His hands rested on the sides of her rib cage, just under her breasts. Very, very slowly, he leaned forward, closing the gap between them an inch at a time until his lips were barely touching hers. As her lips parted in breathless anticipation, he moved his head, brushing his open mouth back and forth across hers. He felt her shiver under his hands and murmured, "Don't worry. You are very special."

But she heaved an exasperated little sigh. "I'm really not. And you are very attractive, you know." She took a deep breath. "I'm not very pretty or exotic compared to others you've—"

Damn. He'd earned that, with his stupid macho remarks.... "Sue," he growled, moving one hand upward, sliding it under her hair to cradle the back of her head, "'pretty' doesn't even come close."

She made one small relieved sound as he lifted her head into his kiss. And she made another, a deep-throated, hungry sound as she opened to him, meeting the deepening penetration of his tongue with her own. Cam felt passion envelop him, rolling over him like a summer storm, filling his ears with thunder and sending lightning bursts of desire zigzagging through his nerves. He felt her grow heavy and languid, felt the moist heat of her body penetrate thin cotton and melt into his pores. Her nearness frustrated him in strange and unfamiliar ways; even with the taste of her in his mouth, the feel of her imprinted on every nerve ending in his body, it wasn't enough. He felt as though he truly needed to become a part of her, to make her a part of himself, even if in so doing he ensured that he would never, ever again be whole without her.

At last, Suzanna tore her mouth from his with a little gasp, then cleared her throat and said almost primly, "Thank you. I think that's done the trick."

Silent laughter made a starburst inside Cam's chest. He bent to claim her mouth again, but before he could, she placed her hands flat on his chest and said solemnly, "Hadn't you better close the door?"

"Sue," he whispered, feeling very tender, very patient, "I think we're alone in the house."

With an absolutely straight face, she murmured, "Well, not entirely. We wouldn't want Maggie zooming across your back."

Cam choked and buried his face in her hair. He was thinking that making love to this woman was going to be a lot of fun if they could just get past this first time. But this—this was too important to him. It meant so much to him that he make it right and good for her, to atone at least a little for the pain and loss he was bringing her. He knew that he was going to have to keep a tight rein on his self-control, dampen his own responses and tune himself in to hers. He had to make her, from this moment, the only focus of his existence.

He'd left one light burning, the small one on his drafting table. Its low-angle illumination painted her body in dusky shadows and golden highlights and turned the small drops of moisture on her skin into diamonds. He swept her up in his arms, leaving her clothing in a puddle on the floor, and sat down on the edge of the bed with her in his lap. He kissed her deeply, pressing her head back against his arm, stroking the long silken curve of her hip and thigh with his free hand until she began to twist and turn as if searching for something. Finally, she tore her mouth away and gasped, "Cam, I can't—"

"Hush," he commanded, claiming her mouth again and again, his tongue and lips sliding over every part of her mouth inside and out, so that when at last he transferred his attention and his mouth to the tip of one lovely, swollen breast, she had no breath left to confound his heart with words.

He caressed the petal-soft underside of her breast, then covered the perfect hemisphere with his hand, leaving only the nipple exposed to the warm and gentle ministrations of his tongue. When he drew it deep and deeper into his mouth, she made a soft, moaning sound and arched her back, pushing toward him and yet fighting him still.

His hand swept down across her ribs to the taut valley of her stomach and rested there for a moment, feeling the jump and flutter of tightly strung nerves and muscles. And then he began to relax her, stroking and soothing, reassuring her, conditioning her to his touch. His fingers brushed downy curls, whispered along the satin inside of her thigh. And by the time he whispered against the racing pulse in her throat, "Sue, sweetheart, open for me now," it wasn't necessary. There was no resistance left in her at all.

Her breath came in quick, uneven gasps as his fingers gently parted her, seeking that first tender penetration. And she tensed again, writhing in his arms, pushing into his caress. "Shh," he murmured, moistening her parted lips with his tongue. "Relax... lie still."

"I can't," she whimpered after a moment. "I can't...." And then, on a new note of near panic, *"John..."*

"It's all right," he said huskily, cradling her close, absorbing the throbbing of her body with his own. "All right, sweetheart, let it come...."

A DROP OF MOISTURE quivered at the edge of her eyelash; he ducked his head and touched it with his lips, a tiny, wet kiss.

"Sue, are you crying?"

She sniffed and pulled her face up into the hollow of his neck. "I'm sorry. I just—"

"What is it? Come on, tell me."

"I don't know. I think I feel sad."

"Sad?"

"Yes. I felt I **had** something wonderful, something scary and wonderful and exciting, and now it's gone."

A tremor of seismic proportions shook Cam clear down to his core. He laughed softly and kissed the damp tendrils of hair on her temple, holding her so tightly he wondered that she didn't crack. "It comes back," he said with fierce resolve. "I'll bring it back for you, I promise."

Suzanna was silent for a moment longer, then gave an embarrassed little laugh and relaxed, nestling more comfortably against his chest. "I didn't expect to feel like that. I guess there's more to this sex business than I realized."

"Yeah, there is." And more, it seemed, than he'd realized, too.

He left her for a moment, and thinking it would be easier on her if he finished undressing in the dark, reached for the lamp. But he'd understimated her. She said quickly, "No—please, leave it on," and then watched him with the frank curiosity of a child.

Only when he sat down beside her did he see the movement of her throat that gave away her nervousness. "Sue," he said gently, "are you feeling threatened?"

"Oh, no," she assured him, gallantly deadpan. "After all, it's still *you*." She tilted her head and added thoughtfully, "Only more so."

Cam just couldn't help it. His chest and stomach began to shake. He leaned over, touched his forehead to hers and then drew her face into his neck and smothered his laughter in her hair.

He found ways then to tell her without words how beautiful she was, how rare and wonderful. When he had made her molten in his arms, pliant and heavy with liquid heat, glazed and incoherent with wanting, he introduced himself into her body with a tenderness and tact he hadn't known he possessed. And she took him in not as an intrusive stranger but as a long-awaited friend, sighing his name in joyful welcome:

"John . . ."

SHE WISHED she could have said more. She wanted to say, "John, I love you," but remembering her promise, kept the words prisoner in her heart.

Cam's hand was on her forehead, gently stroking. He said softly, "Yes, love, it's only me."

The tight, stinging feeling in her body was easing, relaxing into incandescence. The shivers inside her rippled through her belly and emerged in a small gust of laughter. "Hello, John."

His answering chuckle touched deep inside her. "Hello, Sue."

She caught her breath and said in an awed whisper, "I felt that. I felt you moving . . . inside."

His lips brushed her forehead. She opened her eyes and encountered a gaze of liquid smoke. "I'd like to let you feel me moving some more," he said through a smile of heart-swelling tenderness.

Her reply was a breathless whisper. "Yes, please."

"Sweetheart, relax and come with me . . . now." His breath and his words merged with hers as he eased slowly deeper into her mouth and her body. A shimmering mass inside her swelled and throbbed and became a rhythm that caught her up and carried her along as easily and naturally as her own breathing.

And then, without warning, the excitement, the tenderness, the warmth and the joy exploded inside her and became something else, something almost frightening in intensity. Emotions she'd only glimpsed before—fierce, elemental torrents of feeling—surged through her and ached and burned through every pore in her body. No more giddy effervescence—this was fire and turbulence, rocket ignition and lift-off. And somewhere in the stratosphere an errant balloon was swallowed up in the holocaust, leaving her to tumble slowly back to earth.

"Told you we'd get it back again," Cam said thickly, propping himself on one elbow and smoothing damp wisps of hair off her forehead.

Suzanna just nodded, for once unable to articulate a reply. She couldn't tell him about the emotional explosion that had left her dazed, disoriented and more than a little scared. She'd promised him there'd be no strings. But how could she ever stand it when he went away?

He was looking down at her with a sweet, tender smile. She nudged his chin with hers, delicately demanding, and he obliged her with a long, languid kiss that ended with a regretful sigh. She felt the muscles beneath her hands tense and tighten and pressed her palms flat, holding him close for a moment longer. "Do you have to?"

"Sue," he groaned, "do you know how good you feel, how good *I* feel, inside you? I feel...drunk." He kissed her deeply and drew back to admire the result. "On vintage Suzanna...."

She licked her lips and laughed. "Mmm. Me, too. I feel wonderful."

"*Now* you do." He kissed her again, gently, and eased away. "But if we don't take very good care of you..."

"I think there's an ulterior motive here," Suzanna said, snuggling into the curve of his arm and slowly sliding her hand down across his belly. "I think you're saving me."

"Yes, from yourself."

"No—I mean, for later."

His laughter erupted as he hugged her close and growled, "You can count on it."

"Cam," she mumbled sometime later, on the brink of sleep. "Have you ever...made love to...someone like me before?"

He thought, *She's calling me Cam again. I wonder why.* "Never," he said fervently.

"No, I mean, you know, a *virgin*."

He thought of all the ways he could answer that and knew that none of them would do. At last, he said truthfully, "Not in a very long time. I guess not since I was one myself."

"Oh! You were both virgins? That's nice." She sighed and kissed his chin. "Did you love her?"

Cam laughed, while memory warmed him like spring sunshine. "Yes, I suppose I did."

She was silent for so long he thought she had gone to sleep. Then she stirred and whispered against his chest, "Cam?"

"Hmm?"

"I'm very glad I waited—for you."

It was a while before he could trust his voice enough to reply. "So am I, love. So am I."

SUZANNA HAD A DREAM that night, such a stark, uncomplicated little nightmare that she remembered it clearly when she woke up. She had a balloon, a beautiful red-gold balloon, but no matter how hard she tried, she couldn't hold on to the string. The balloon pulled and tugged until it slipped from her grasp and went floating away into the sky. She cried and cried, the helpless sobs of a heartbroken child. The balloon looked down at her with Cam's face, and as it drifted out of sight, she heard it singing, "'Oh, Suzanna, don't you cry for me....'"

SHE AWOKE with a startled jerk, her throat dry and aching from the stress of dream weeping. She didn't know what had awakened her, but whatever it was, it had roused Cam, too.

"What—" she began.

"The front door," Cam said hoarsely, and cleared his throat. "I think."

"It can't be. Who—what time is it?"

Cam raised himself on his elbows and scowled down at her. "Not that late. Serves you right for not locking your door."

"But—"

"Hush. Listen."

From the front hallway came several well-defined thumps, as if someone were placing heavy objects on the floor. Footsteps creaked. A door clicked open. And then a strong voice with the timbre of great age drifted up the stairwell. "Yoo hoo, Suzanna—I've come home."

"Oh, good Lord," Suzanna gulped, and slid under the covers.

Cam lifted the edge of the sheet and hissed at the top of her head. "Who *is* that? Not—"

"Yes," Suzanna hissed back, and put a mortified hand over her eyes. "Mrs. Hopewell."

Chapter Ten

Suzanna clutched the sheet and stared round eyed at Cam over the edge of it. "What is she doing here? She's not due back from San Francisco for another week."

"Why don't you ask her?"

"I can't. She'll hear me!"

"Sweetheart, I think that's the idea." Cam was grinning shamelessly at her, but his eyes were warm with sympathy, so she knew she would probably forgive him—eventually.

"She'll hear where my voice is coming from, you...you..." Suzanna whispered, punching him smartly in the shoulder. "She knows I don't sleep in here."

"Hmm...she's right, you know."

"Stop that! This is serious!"

"It certainly is. If you don't answer her, she's liable to come looking for you."

"No, Mrs. Hopewell never comes up here. She doesn't like to climb stairs. She wouldn't—"

"Suzanna?" The voice that had quelled generations of rowdy schoolchildren definitely sounded nearer now.

Suzanna's voice rose to a horrified squeak. "Cam? What am I going to do? What will she think if she finds me here? In your bed?"

Cam lifted his shoulders helplessly. "Maybe you'd better go head her off at the pass," he suggested in a strangled voice, turning a very suspicious shade of purple.

"I *can't*—I don't have any clothes! What did you do with my clothes?"

Cam lifted his shoulders again and made a muffled croaking noise.

"I don't even have a bathrobe," Suzanna wailed in a distraught whisper. "I can't face Mrs. Hopewell without a bathrobe!"

Cam pointed meaningfully toward the door to the landing.

"I can't go across to my room. She'll hear my footsteps!"

The man at her side suddenly flopped over and pulled a pillow over his head. The bed began to shake. Suzanna regarded the large quivering form for a moment and then hissed, "Oh, you!" and pushed him out of bed. He hit the floor with a thud and a muffled exclamation.

"Suzanna? Is that you?"

"Uh, yes, Mrs. Hopewell—" Suzanna scrambled out of bed, pulling the chenille bedspread around her like a toga. "I'm, uh, doing some packing. I'll be right down."

"Are you all right, dear? I heard something fall."

"Yes, I knocked over a stool—nothing important." The last word issued from between clenched teeth as Cam's hand stole under the edge of the bedspread and caught her bare ankle. She grabbed a pillow and began assaulting him with it. "Really, Mrs. Hopewell. I'll be down in just a minute. I'm...so glad...you're back!" Suzanna called, trying to make her voice sound brightly normal while Cam's hand was creeping up her leg and stroking the back of her knee. "Cam, stop that—"

"What was that, Suzanna?"

"Nothing, Mrs. Hopewell. I'm just finishing something."

"All right—I'll be in the kitchen making tea," Mrs. Hopewell announced. "Do try to hurry, dear; we have things to discuss." Her footsteps clumped decisively down the hall toward the kitchen.

Suzanna collapsed onto Cam in a jumble of arms, legs, pillows and bedspread. With a deft twist of his body, Cam rolled himself inside her toga and tucked her beneath him. His attempt to kiss her senseless was thwarted at first by a tendency on both their parts to burst into helpless laughter. But inevitably, as warm breaths merged, lips nibbled and teased and bodies slid silkily together, guffaws became chuckles, then settling-down gulps and coughs and finally, soft sighs of sensual rediscovery.

Cam lifted his head, and framing hers with his hands, subjected her face to minute examination. "Yep," he said, shaking his head sorrowfully, "it's there, all right."

"What is?"

He drew three straight lines on her forehead with his fingers and said in a dramatic whisper, "A great big scarlet letter *A*—right there. Sue, I'm sorry."

He wasn't smiling. His eyes were gray shadows, and his voice was rusty with regret. Suzanna's throat tightened. She freed a hand from the tangled bedspread and touched the hair back from his forehead.

"Cam, I'm not sorry. I don't feel like that. Like I've done anything wrong."

"Then why," he said softly, "are you acting like you have?"

"I'm *not*. I just—" She stopped and said faintly, "Oh."

"Yes." He kissed her nose and then, very tenderly, her forehead. "You don't deserve that," he growled, rubbing the spot he'd marked with his finger. "So get rid of it."

Suzanna's heart liquefied. "Oh, good," she said, heaving an exaggerated sigh of relief. "I forgot to ask if you'd still respect me in the morning. You know," she whispered after a moment's consideration, "I think—it's just Mrs. Hopewell. I mean—"

"Mrs. Hopewell? Mrs. Hopewell, who taught biology when nice girls *didn't*? Mrs. Hopewell, who isn't afraid of bats and who gives the skunk's spring orgy her blessing?"

Suzanna chewed her lower lip and considered Mrs. Hopewell with new eyes. "You think maybe I'm underestimating her?"

"Well, misjudging her, anyway." His mouth brushed hers, and then he shifted his weight and smiled at her. "Come on, love—I'll cover for you. You get some clothes on and go downstairs; they're in a pile over there on the floor, by the way, right where we left them. I'll take a shower, and you can say I've been in the bathroom the whole time."

"I think," Suzanna said dryly, pulling the bedspread around her as Cam helped her to her feet, "that this is a clear case of the less said the better. Are you sure," she asked anxiously, pausing on her way out the door, "that it doesn't show? I don't look different?"

"No, love." Cam chuckled softly. "It doesn't show."

"Oh," Suzanna said, and went out feeling vaguely disappointed.

But it ought to show, she thought, wincing a little as she slipped into jeans and encountered unexpected tenderness. After all, it wasn't every day a girl lost her virginity at the ripe age of twenty-seven. And she did feel different. Though that, she reflected, was more a state of mind than of body. After all, it wasn't every day a girl discovered, at any age, that she had fallen hopelessly, madly and irrevocably in love.

"SIT DOWN, SUZANNA. Have some tea. It's a blend I found in the city. A touch of black currant—quite good."

Suzanna had never cared for tea, but it was pointless to argue with Mrs. Hopewell when she employed that tone of voice. Suzanna murmured a meek "Thank you" and sat gingerly opposite her tenant and former teacher, a guest at her own kitchen table.

Mrs. Hopewell had the same effect on everyone, from small boys to PTA presidents. She was a commanding presence at any time, but sitting in state behind a desk or a table, her back ramrod straight, her face austere, she could be downright daunting. Her dark auburn hair was in its usual bun, just untidy enough to give her looks a certain fierceness and energy not usually associated with elderly ladies. Her hands, though corded and age spotted, were firm and steady on the antique blue porcelain teapot. Her gloves lay on the table beside her handbag and traveling hat, the wide-brimmed, flat-crowned black straw that always made Suzanna think of Mary Poppins.

"Milk or sugar?"

"No, thank you." Suzanna took the cup of tea and sniffed its fragrance, wondering what she could say that would sound absolutely natural. She finally settled on "How is your sister?"

"My sister is quite well," Mrs. Hopewell said firmly, and then, with a stare that would probably cause ice to form on her teacup, added, "Suzanna, I'm very disappointed in you."

"In me?" It was as bad as she'd feared.

"Yes. After all that has transpired since I left here less than one week ago, it was left to your cousin Margaret to see that I was informed of the fate of my home and my closest friend. Dear Suzanna," the old lady went on, her bearing no less unbending, her expression no less severe, "it distresses me terribly that you didn't think to allow me to share this time of trial with you."

"Oh, Mrs. Hopewell," Suzanna said, wondering if she might start to cry.

"I have come home," Mrs. Hopewell announced, "to be of assistance."

"That's very kind of you," Suzanna faltered, jumping slightly as the sound of the shower began overhead.

Mrs. Hopewell glanced toward the ceiling, and when she turned her gaze back upon Suzanna, it carried the unmistakable twinkle of amusement—and understanding. Suzanna groaned inwardly.

"You are no doubt thinking that my presence may cause more problems than it will cure," Mrs. Hopewell said dryly. She raised a preemptive hand, silencing Suzanna's strangled protest. "In a sense, you are quite correct, and I shall, of course, leave the physical needs of your situation to someone younger and more able-bodied than I." Her lips twitched, and Suzanna closed her eyes, resigned to mortification. "However—" Mrs. Hopewell was firm and stern once more. "I have come, Suzanna, to offer you a different kind of help." She reached for her handbag, opened it and took out a long white envelope, which she placed without ceremony on the table in front of Suzanna. "I think this will be of some use to you. Certainly a great deal more than it is to me."

Suzanna stared at the envelope, feeling oddly shaky—almost frightened. Mrs. Hopewell nodded encouragingly and murmured, "Go on, dear. Open it."

Suzanna did and found herself staring at her own name on a small rectangular piece of paper—and at a figure with an incomprehensible number of zeros. Her fingers seemed to go numb. She dropped the bank draft onto the tabletop and rubbed her hands on her thighs. She whispered, "Mrs. Hopewell, I can't—what—where did you—"

"Suzanna." As always, Mrs. Hopewell could restore order with a word. Suzanna gulped, swallowed and listened.

"My dear, my late husband made some very good investments. With no effort whatsoever on my part, those investments have made me a great deal of money for which I have absolutely no need. My needs are simple, as you know. I have no children of my own, and my two grand-nieces are being very well provided for by their respective families. I have always intended that you should be a beneficiary of my will." Mrs. Hopewell smiled benignly. "However, I shall be only ninety my next birthday, and I fully expect to see my centenary in good health. Therefore, after Margaret telephoned with the news of your situation, I went to see my attorney. That, Suzanna—" she gestured toward the envelope "—you may consider to be your share of my estate. I wish you to have it now, while I am alive. I trust you will put it to good use, moving Mr. Neal's house out of harm's way."

"Move Angel's Walk?" Suzanna's numbed brain clutched at the idea, like a drowning animal clings to a scrap of wood.

"Oh, yes, indeed. I'm quite sure it can be done. This house was well constructed, and I daresay is still as sound as the day it was completed."

"Oh, it is, it is," Suzanna muttered distractedly, smoothing the envelope with her fingers, reassuring herself that it was real. "Papa always said it was. He even looked into having it moved when the dam was being built and the towns and ranches were being relocated. They said it could be done, but it—" But it had cost too much money. For the farmers in the valley, large lump sums of money represented bank loans to subsidize new crops or day-to-day living or investment in land and machinery. For her grandfather to accumulate enough in profits to justify an expenditure as frivolous as moving a Victorian mansion some people still considered an eyesore, he would have had to enjoy a string of consecutive ''good years''—a string that never seemed to come.

''Oh, Mrs. Hopewell,'' Suzanna whispered thickly. ''I don't know what to say.''

''A simple thank-you will suffice,'' Mrs. Hopewell said briskly, rising to her feet with stately grace. She gathered up her tea things and moved to the sink, gliding like a tall ship with furled sails. When she turned, there was a gleam in her clear gray eyes that could only be attributed to laughter. ''And now, Suzanna, do you suppose you might persuade your Mr. Harris to assist me? I have come for my things. I am moving out.''

Suzanna, who had chosen that moment to venture a sip of her tea, exploded in a fit of coughing. A solicitous hand, too hard and heavy to be Mrs. Hopewell's, settled on her shoulder and then began to massage between her shoulder blades. She managed to wheeze his name and then gave it up.

''How do you do, Mrs. Hopewell.'' Cam's voice, warmly amused, poured over her head like molasses. She felt his body heat as he leaned across her to take Mrs. Hopewell's hand while keeping a possessive and protective grip on the back of her neck.

''Mr. Harris.'' The old lady's voice was dry and cool; Suzanna knew that she was enjoying herself enormously. ''So nice to meet you. Margaret has, of course, told me about you.''

So that was it.

Cam said blandly, ''Oh, yes. That would be—''

"Suzanna's cousin. Anthony O'Brian's wife. Anthony and Margaret are both former pupils of mine, you know," Mrs. Hopewell explained with a smug, proprietary air. "Anthony was rather a serious child, but Margaret always did enjoy a mischievous bent."

She sounded almost chatty. Suzanna, regaining enough control to open her eyes, was stunned to discover that the old lady's face was openly beaming. She opened her mouth and emitted a strangled wheeze of astonishment. Cam patted her back sympathetically.

"Did I hear you say you needed help moving something?" he inquired genially over Suzanna's convulsing body.

"Yes," Mrs. Hopewell said, reverting to her customary verbal economy. "I have taken rooms with Roberta Rafferty."

"At the motel?" Suzanna managed to croak, wiping her streaming eyes and nose with her hands. Bertie Rafferty, another of Mrs. Hopewell's former students, ran a small grocery store, motel and single-pump gas station about a mile on up the highway, safely beyond the ultimate limits of the lake.

"Yes. The rooms are small, but I have a lovely view. I shall be quite comfortable." She patted Suzanna's hand and then tucked a clean white handkerchief into it and instructed sternly, "Blow your nose, Suzanna. You must learn to *sip* your tea, dear, not gulp it. Mr. Harris, I shall be waiting."

Suzanna felt Cam's body vibrate with suppressed mirth and checked an urge of her own to kick him smartly in the shins. "You—you were supposed to *cover* for me!" she sputtered when Mrs. Hopewell had gone.

Cam's laughter exploded against her ear, tickling. She gasped and tried to tuck it protectively against her shoul-

der, but he chuckled villainously and pursued it with las-
civious intent. His attack gave her chills and fever and left
her feeling like warm maple syrup. "Listen," he said when
he had her completely subdued, "I knew the minute I laid
eyes on her that we were dead ducks. That is one sharp old
lady."

Suzanna moaned.

"It's all right," Cam said, planting a noisy kiss on her
ear that elicited a desperate squeak and then consolingly
patting the top of her head. "You know," he said as he
went out, flashing Suzanna a sunburst grin, "I have the
damnedest feeling she *approves* of me."

After he had gone, Suzanna sat at the table staring at
nothing and asking herself, *Why? I have the same feeling,
but why?* It was the first time she'd seen Cam's charisma
unleashed on anyone beside herself, and she really
shouldn't have been so surprised at the results, but Mrs.
Hopewell? There wasn't a more practical, down-to-earth
person in the world or a more astute judge of character—
hardly the person to be taken in by a charming rogue.

And suddenly, listening to her thoughts' echo, Suzanna
knew that the word "charming," like "handsome," had
too little substance to apply to John Campbell Harris.
With a warm, fluttery ache in her middle, she remembered all the ways he had shown his gentleness and sensitivity. She remembered the quivering in his muscles that
betrayed his restraint and the tenderness that in anyone else
would be easy to mistake for love.

No, Cam Harris isn't a rogue, she thought sadly. *Just a
man running away from commitment.*

The irony of it hit her a little later as she stood watching
from the upstairs windows while Cam patiently tramped
up and down the front walk, carrying boxes and suitcases
to Mrs. Hopewell's car. He was wearing jeans and a T-shirt

this morning—How could a man look so wonderful in jeans and a T-shirt? His hair caught the morning sunlight and reflected it, like a beacon. He seemed to have recovered all his vitality and energy, and more, and she was back to being more than a little in awe of him. From this distance it was hard to believe that he was a human man, not a dynamo, and harder still to remember that just a few hours ago, for a little while, he had been *her* man, and so very human—tender and passionate, funny and exciting, sensitive and strong.

He has everything—is everything—I ever wanted in a man, except the one thing I know I can't live without: stability.

He was the runaway balloon, and it was all very well in the heat of giddy passion to talk of sailing away with him. But she was as earthbound as Angel's Walk itself, and when he moved on, as inevitably he must, she would be left behind.

Tony came while Suzanna was in the shower, and by the time she had dressed, both he and Cam had left for the dam to meet the arriving helicopters. And she remembered too late that she hadn't had a chance to tell him about Mrs. Hopewell's gift and the reprieve of Angel's Walk.

IT WAS A TWENTY-MINUTE DRIVE from the house to the dam, and for the first ten the silence in the jeep was deafening. After the third or fourth time his peripheral vision caught Tony covertly studying him, Cam blew a gusty sigh and said, "Okay, man—out with it."

Tony glanced at him, straightened up, rubbed his jaw, folded his arms, slid back down. Cam muttered dryly, "Look, I can hear questions perking around in there like popcorn. So let's have 'em."

Tony shrugged and cleared his throat. "It's not really any of my business—"

"And you don't believe that for a minute."

"Well, all right, maybe it is. She's my wife's cousin. I think a lot of her."

"So?"

"So I'm curious, that's all. This situation—you, her, the house." He was hopefully silent, but Cam didn't help him. After a moment, Tony said, squinting through the windshield, "My wife tells me you didn't even tell her about it. She found out from a reporter."

Cam said, "Yeah," on an exhalation and endured Tony's silent scrutiny.

"She'll forgive you, you know," the older man said honestly. "She's not one to hold a grudge."

Cam smiled wryly. "Yeah, I know."

"How's she taking it? I haven't seen much of her the past few days."

"Ignoring it, mostly," Cam said, frowning. "Like she's expecting a miracle—a stay of execution." He laughed sharply. "You'll never believe this—she was mowing the lawn!"

Tony laughed and rubbed a hand over his face. "Oh, I believe it." He turned again to study Cam for a long moment and then asked pointedly, "How are *you* taking it?"

Cam snorted. "Me? What the hell are you talking about? I'm just doing a job."

"Yeah, well, I've seen you look better."

"Yeah?" Cam lifted his shoulder in a shrug and rubbed at his still-swollen elbow. "Had a little run-in with a bee yesterday, that's all."

"Cam, how long have I known you? Since Peace Corps days, right? I've seen you take physical abuse and come up thumbing your nose. You want to know what I think?"

"Hell, no, but you're going to tell me, anyway." The happiness, the good feelings of last night and this morning, had evaporated like dew, leaving him feeling cross and tired, and not for the first time in the past few days, dreading the day ahead.

"It's not a bee that's got you chewing nails," Tony said, quietly triumphant. "It's Suzanna, isn't it?"

Cam jerked the jeep to a halt in front of dam headquarters, gave the emergency brake a savage yank and reached for the door handle. The park manager's bony hand gripped his shoulder.

"Look—maybe I'm way outta line, and if I am, I'm sure you're going to let me know about it. But let me tell you, it's one thing to go into a job, keep your nose buried in the facts and figures and never take a good close look at the people whose lives you're playing with."

"Damn it, Tony!" Cam hit the steering wheel with the heel of his hand. "Do you think I could do this lousy job— make decisions that cost people their homes, jobs—if I let myself get emotionally involved?"

"No," Tony admitted quietly, "I don't. But have you ever considered that maybe you've been doing this for too long? That maybe this job is costing you something too valuable to make it worth the price?"

Cam growled, "Like what?"

"Like the ability to get emotionally involved. With anybody. When's the last time you cared about anybody? When's the last time you let anybody care about you? How about your folks, Cam? When's the last time you phoned your parents? Saw your sister? If you ask me, if Suzanna's managed to get to you—"

Tony broke off, silenced by whatever it was he was seeing in Cam's face. Cam sustained the look for what seemed like an eternity before pulling away, and when he did, Tony released pent-up tension in a dry whistle. "Well, as a guess, I'd say she got to you...."

Cam got out of the jeep. Tony did the same, coming around to stand beside him in sympathetic silence. Together they looked out across the ultramarine expanse of lake.

"What are you going to do?" Tony asked at last in a voice rusty with compassion.

"What I have to do," Cam said bitterly, and turned away with a resigned lifting of his shoulders. "Let's go build a dam."

"SOMEHOW I THOUGHT I'd find you here," Cam said, laughing, "cross-legged on the floor."

Suzanna hastily tucked the book she was reading under another one and regarded him owlishly over the flaps of a cardboard box. "I'll have you know," she informed him righteously, "that I am packing."

"Oh, I can see that," Cam murmured, squatting on his heels beside her and nodding his head dubiously.

"I *am*. Mrs. Hopewell got me started. She told me to start with books and knickknacks, so—"

"So here we are, ten o'clock at night and up to our armpits in dusty books and empty boxes."

His voice was so solemn that Suzanna looked at him closely to see if he was angry with her again, but his eyes were soft and filled with smiles. She felt her chest grow warm. "Ten o'clock?" she inquired huskily. "Is it really that late?"

"Mmm-hmm. And I'm hungry." His voice had a purring texture that tickled her nerves and made her suddenly want to rub against something warm.

"Are you?" she whispered vaguely, caught in the tractor beam of his eyes.

"Uh-huh."

"I'll go fix you something."

"Uh-uh." His lips brushed hers. "What I'm hungry for is right here."

She felt his hunger in the pit of her own stomach and responded instinctively, offering her mouth like a cup to a starving man. Slowly, carefully, he leaned across the space between them to take her offering.

He touched only her mouth, and yet he touched all of her, inside and out and in the secret recesses of her heart. His lips were vibrant with self-control, the slow joining of their mouths the more poignant for the tension and restraint in his body. His tongue slipped inside her with exquisite delicacy, molding her mouth to his so perfectly and completely that it proclaimed his need more eloquently than raw passion ever could. Suzanna held herself still, giving, giving, until her throat began to tighten and her eyelids burn with the pressure of emotion. Her chest hurt, not with the white-hot stab of desire but with a gradually expanding, all-enveloping ache.

This is love, she thought, dazed. *I never knew it would hurt so much.*

She touched his cheek with her fingers, and it was as if she had released him from some kind of spell. He pulled slowly away but lowered his eyes so she couldn't read them, letting them sweep over the jumble of books on the floor and across her lap. As she watched his hand follow his gaze, idly turning a volume here and there, she fought for composure, swallowing repeatedly and thinking, *No strings, no strings. I mustn't let him see how much I care!*

Oh, how she wanted to say, "I'm hungry, too, John. I've missed you. You left this morning without saying goodbye." But those were hardly "no-strings" things to say, so she only cleared her throat and silently waited.

"*Girl of the Limberlost*?" Cam said finally, softly laughing. "*Anne of Green Gables*?" He picked up a book and flipped it open to the copyright page. "Sue, this stuff belongs in a museum. Is this what you were so engrossed in?"

Suzanna shook her head and casually shifted positions, trying surreptitiously to tuck one incriminating volume out of sight under her knee.

But Cam was too quick and much too observant. "Ah-hah, there it is. Come on, let's see what you've got."

"It's nothing, really," she murmured, making it worse, groaning inwardly as the heat of a telltale blush crept into her cheeks.

"Come on, sweetheart." Cam chuckled, gently teasing. "You've really got me curious now, so you'll have to let me see it. It can't be any worse than these, can it?"

"Umm, well, yes, as a matter of fact it can." Suzanna gulped, accepting inevitable defeat with grace. With her whole face a conflagration, she drew the small maroon volume out from under her thigh and placed it in Cam's outstretched hand. And she waited, hoping he wouldn't misunderstand.

"*Purity and Truth*," Cam read aloud, shaking with incredulous laughter. "*What a Young Husband Ought to Know*. Sue, this is a Victorian sex manual!"

"Well," Suzanna said judiciously, clearing her throat, "it's a marriage manual, I suppose, but I don't want you to think—"

"Incredible," Cam muttered, thumbing through the yellowed pages. "I didn't think there *was* such a thing. Where in the world did you get this?"

"There's an inscription—apparently my grandmother's mother gave it to her soon-to-be son-in-law. Papa."

"Probably hoping he'd fill his bride in on the facts of life she was too uptight to tell her," Cam said dryly. "They didn't usually do very well in the sex-ed department."

"I don't know how much help it could have been," Suzanna said doubtfully. "It doesn't tell you what to *do*. It mostly tells you what *not* to do."

"Oh, yeah?" Cam's eyes were bright with laughter. His obvious delight in the situation was beginning to dissipate the fog of Suzanna's embarrassment, and both of them were finding it increasingly hard to keep a straight face. "For instance?"

Still valiantly deadpan, Suzanna murmured, "You're not supposed to stimulate impure thinking."

"My thoughts are nothing if not pure," Cam said slowly, fingering aside the hair on her neck and planting a chaste—and utterly devastating—kiss on the nape of it. "Tell me—how do I avoid contamination?"

"Avoid novel reading, theater going, and round dancing," Suzanna whispered, closing her eyes. A series of kisses, each less chaste than the last, brought his mouth to her throat, and then to the V of her shirt. She lifted her hand and buried her fingers in the raw silk of his hair.

"No problem there." Cam's words made moist puffs in the warm hollow between her breasts. "I can handle that. What else?"

Suzanna's reply was barely audible, a breathy sigh. "Nude statues and suggestive pictures..."

His hand brushed her shirtfront, and under it her breasts began to tingle and tighten. His fingers traced the sharp outline of her nipples through the thin fabric. "Not a naked statue or back issue of *Playboy* in the house." He chuckled softly. "Looks like we're doing just fine...."

"I don't think so." Suzanna gasped as Cam easily dealt with her shirt buttons and the front hook clasp of her bra and finally cradled the warm weight of her breast in his hand.

"Why not?" he muttered against her skin, and then circled one hard and tender nipple with his tongue.

Haltingly, struggling for coherence, Suzanna quoted, "Avoid bodily exposure and immodest postures...."

"So much for pure thoughts," Cam whispered, and lowered his mouth over one tingling nipple. He made a cradle of his body and drew her gently back into it, opening her to his touch and his gaze.

"Talk about immodest postures," Suzanna murmured, laughing, a little embarrassed by the Indian-style position of her legs.

Cam began to stroke the taut denim covering the insides of her thighs, up one side and down the other, pausing momentarily to house the center of her body in the warmth of his hand. "Personally," he whispered against her ear when she groaned and turned her face into his chest, "I think your posture's perfect." His mouth lowered to hers; his tongue pressed into her, hard and deep. Her lips, and every place he touched her, felt hot and swollen. The rubbing was becoming narrower in focus, and her body was finding it impossible not to respond to its vibrant, unspoken demand.

His hand shifted to the zipper of her jeans, then flattened against her stomach in a warm, open-palmed caress that stirred her insides. When his fingertips burrowed through feminine down, gently probing, she couldn't stand it anymore and moaned softly, drawing one knee up and closing herself against him. It was a protective reflex, an involuntary protest against sensual overload, but it was enough to still his hand. Lifting his mouth from hers and then just touching her moisture-dewed lips with his, he whispered, "What is it? Am I hurting you?"

She shook her head and with an inarticulate moan of denial traced his lower lip with the tip of her tongue.

"Sue, don't ever be afraid to tell me. Are you sore?"

With effort she brought her eyes to focus on his face and smiled. "No, you took very good care of me. But—"

"But what, love?"

With careful solemnity she cleared her throat and murmured, "I think I ought to tell you—the book warns at length about the dangers of sexual excess."

There was a moment's shocked silence, and then laughter tumbled through him. From deep down in his throat he growled, "Guilty as charged. I need you excessively. I have an excessive desire to make love to you. I want—"

"If you don't mind," Suzanna interrupted fiercely, turning her face back into his chest while her hand searched for his shirt buttons, "I'll let you know if you're being excessive."

"Promise?"

"Promise." Her breath caught as his hand pushed downward, uncovering the velvety hollow of her stomach, the delicately draped bones of her pelvis.

"Your skin..." He spoke huskily, lifting his head to gaze with undisguised hunger at what he was revealing. "It has golden overtones...like peaches. But you know, I never saw a peach that really looked like this or tasted so good."

Suzanna's only reply was a whimper of frustration as her nerveless fingers, not as skilled as his, tried to undo buttons and belt buckles.

"Slowly, love," Cam said, his voice warm and smooth with tender passion. "I'm not going anywhere."

She sighed against him, pressing words into the soft hair on his chest. "Not even to bed?" She wondered if he would have to carry her; she felt formless and floaty— shimmering incandescence born on heat waves....

"No." His voice was thick, slurred. "I want you...need you...*here*, now."

"In the middle of all these dusty Victorians? It seems—"

"Yes, it's excessive, I know, and immodest."

"And sexy." She felt drunk, light-headed, a butterfly dancing in sunbeams. Under his sure and gentle hands every part of her shivered, shimmered and ignited.

"That, too—Oh, yes, love, kiss me *there*." With a deep-throated groan he pulled her over astride his lap; she didn't know just when he'd divested her of her jeans, but the shock of rough, unyielding textures against her unprotected softness made her gasp. "John..."

"Yes." His voice held a note of elation, almost of triumph, as though she'd said or done something he'd been waiting and longing for. "Yes, love. It's me...."

"DID YOU KNOW," Cam said lazily, "that Maggie the bat has been hanging up there in the corner, watching us?" He was lying on his back with his head propped on a two-volume set of the works of Kipling, covered only by a limp and languid Suzanna.

"Mmm-hmm," she murmured, tracing his collarbone with a finger. "She came in while I was packing."

"You mean while you were reading, don't you?" After a moment's thoughtful silence, he said, "If she's been in here all this time, why isn't she flitting around raising the short hairs on my neck, like she did the other day?"

Suzanna considered. "Probably because the lights are on. That other time, when you were playing the piano, it was twilight, remember?"

"Mmm. Right." Cam sang softly, "'Just a song at twilight, when the lights are low....'" And then, when there was no answer, he asked, "Hey, are you asleep?"

"No," Suzanna murmured, obviously not far from it. "I just love to hear you sing."

Cam felt an odd, stirring warmth in his chest and vocalized it with a chuckle. "Come on, love. Time to go to bed. I know it's almost summer, but we'll get cold if we stay here." He slid his hands down her back from her shoulders to her buttocks, savoring the satin feel of her skin. Her body moved sinuously upon his, in unconscious response to his touch, like a cat being petted. The air in his lungs seemed to clog up in his throat, and his voice moved through it as if through molasses. "Hey, sweetheart, if you do that, we might never get to bed tonight."

She moved again, snuggling, and his arms tightened around her almost convulsively. With a sleepy sigh she said, "I don't care. I don't ever want to leave you."

A cold, hard lump in his chest glowed and flared. "You don't have to leave me," he said huskily. "There's plenty of room for us both in my bed, or yours."

"No. Oh, no." She shook her head emphatically, bumping his chin. "The book says sharing a bed is absolutely the worst thing—"

"That book—" Cam sat up suddenly, rolling her off of his chest and into the crook of his arm. "That book," he growled, catching her behind the knees and lifting her so he could bury his face in the hollow of her neck. "Do you know what you should do with that damn book?" She was laughing and squirming in his arms and couldn't have answered if her life depended on it. "Dump it in the lake. Or better yet, just leave it here and let—"

And even before her body stilled, he was flaying himself and thinking bitterly, *Good job, Campbell. Way to ruin an evening, you insensitive jerk!*

But she was sitting up, her breasts just grazing his chest, her hands clutching his shoulders, and she was gazing into his eyes and looking *radiant*. She was shaking her head and laughing, and saying, "*No*, no, Cam. It isn't going to happen. It's not!"

"Sue," he groaned, but she kissed him joyfully, impulsively.

"I forgot to tell you. It's saved! Angel's Walk is saved! Oh, Cam, it's going to be all right."

Cam set Suzanna aside, not gently, and turned from her, reacting to the wrenching pain in his belly the only way he knew how—with anger. He said harshly, "For heaven's sake, Sue—" and reached for his clothes, feeling as Adam must have felt when he bit into the apple. It was so damned awkward—and cold and lonely, too—dressing like that in the middle of the floor, amidst piles of books and boxes, under the harsh overhead lights and the interested gaze of a flying rodent. He was furious with himself for reminding her of her impossible situation and even more furious with her for that pigheaded, stubborn optimism. How could an apparently intelligent woman be so neurotic about a damned house?

Once he had his pants on and was feeling a little less vulnerable, he turned to her, expecting, after her prolonged silence, to have to cope with hurt feelings, or even tears. He was bewildered to find her still sitting there on the rug, leaning on one hand and looking like the model for a study of Aphrodite reclining. Her eyes were soft and shining with compassion, as if *she* were sorry for *him*. It absolutely infuriated him.

Tossing her his shirt, he ordered, "Put something on. We have to talk." While he waited for her, he glared up at that ridiculous flying voyeur, angry because it seemed to represent everything about Suzanna that was making his life so painful. How could any sane person deal with a woman who let a live bat fly around in her house? She was impossible—obsessed with the past, obsessed with a crumbling monstrosity of a house! And maybe, just maybe, if he could wrap himself in enough layers of insulating anger, he wouldn't have to feel her pain.

"Cam," she said softly, touching him on the shoulder, "you don't understand. I'm not being an ostrich. I really do have a solution. Thanks to, of all people, Mrs. Hopewell."

He turned, and faced with her open gaze and shining eyes, felt his anger slough off like old skin. "Mrs. Hopewell—" He sighed, feeling beleaguered, and tried to pull Suzanna into his arms.

She resisted him, laughing with sheer delight. "Yes, Mrs. Hopewell! Cam, you're not going to believe this, but she gave me some money, an unbelievable amount—a legacy, she says. It's enough—more than enough—to move this house. I don't have to leave Angel's Walk, Cam; I'm going to move it! Isn't that wonderful?"

He stared at her while his brain spun its wheels and the first rays of hope crept over the bleak landscape of his heart.

"It can be done, can't it?" she asked, faltering a little in the face of his silence. "I mean, Papa checked into it years ago, but you're an engineer, and you probably would know."

"Yes," he rasped, and then cleared his throat and said gently, "Yes, it can be done. But Sue—" he rested his hands delicately on her shoulders "—it will take *time*."

"I know that—"

"Even after you find a reputable mover, you've got to have a place to move it *to*, grade the site, pour the foundation, wait for it to cure. And this place has to be secured—utilities and plumbing disconnected, windows boarded up, everything fastened down. And on the road power lines have to be taken down and obstacles moved all along the planned route. Sweetheart, this isn't something that can be done overnight.''

''I know that.'' She sounded breathless, and there was a spot of color in each cheek, a bright, almost-feverish stain. ''But *you* could—'' She stopped, licking her lips, beseeching with her eyes, and he understood what she wanted, what she was hoping for.

''You want me to buy you the time you need,'' he said woodenly, feeling bleak darkness creep back around his heart. ''You want me to postpone the job on the dam.''

''Yes,'' she whispered, and he saw that she had gone very pale. ''Just for a few days. Please.''

''Damn it, Sue, I can't,'' he rasped harshly, feeling as if he were being torn apart. ''I wish I could, but I can't. If I'd known this morning—but it's done. We worked all day and late tonight, and it's done. The new spillway is already in place.''

Chapter Eleven

"So," Cam said to Tony over coffee the next morning, "there you have it. Ironic, isn't it? I've made a career out of solving unsolvable engineering problems, and yet I can't give a woman—a friend—the one thing in the world she wants."

They were sitting in Suzanna's kitchen listening to the world wake up. Upstairs, Suzanna still slept; Cam had left her finally in the predawn twilight, accepting the fact that, this night at least, he wasn't going to be allowed the oblivion of sleep.

Tony gave him the dull, morose stare of a man whose first cup of coffee hadn't yet taken effect. He'd stayed on at the dam long after Cam had left and was on his way back there now after a few short hours' rest.

"What makes you think this house is the only thing she wants?" Tony asked, yawning.

"Well, it's sure as hell the thing she wants most!" Cam said with such violence that Tony stopped in mid-yawn to stare at him. After a brooding silence, Cam gave an impatient wave of his hand and got to his feet. "Let's go. Bring that coffee with you. I'll drive."

He needed something to do right then, something to demand his attention, if not his concentration. He'd spent a long, hot night coming to grips with the fact that he was in love with Suzanna. Now, if he could just figure out how to deal with the fact that his biggest competition was a ninety-year-old relic of a house with the ridiculous name of Angel's Walk...

SUZANNA DIDN'T MEAN to sleep so late. She'd slept deeply and well—very well considering it was only the second night in her life she'd shared her bed with another human being.

Memory stirred, making her feel wicked and delicious, like Scarlett on the morning after Rhett carried her up the stairs. Suzanna stretched and snuggled down in tumbled sheets, which now held Cam's subtle essence mingled with hers and with the clean, fresh scent of sunshine and soap.

She didn't feel guilty; it felt too good, and too right. How many more nights would she sleep with Cam's arms around her and the sound of his breathing in her ears? The spillway was in place. How many days before his work here was done and he moved on to the next job, the next disaster?

On that thought Suzanna got up, quickly showered and dressed for dirty work in old jeans and T-shirt. There was so much to do, and time was so short. It was Saturday, so she couldn't start contacting movers until after the Memorial weekend holiday, but she could get started with the packing. Cam would be leaving soon, and that was that; she'd promised no strings. She wouldn't think about that right now. She'd think about her home instead and focus on saving Angel's Walk.

She was clearing away her breakfast things when the front door creaked cautiously open and a voice floated down the hallway like a disembodied spirit.

"Hello, Suzanna? Are you—is anybody in there?"

It surprised Suzanna. Not the voice, which she'd recognized, but the uncharacteristic quaver of uncertainty. Angel's Walk had an odd effect on some people. "Yes, down here, Lucy," she called reassuringly. "Come on in."

"My goodness," the newspaperwoman exclaimed, dumping camera bags and notebooks onto the table before collapsing into a chair. "This *is* quite a house, isn't it?" She was craning unabashedly, peering upward to where carved moldings bordered the twelve-foot ceiling. "I had no idea—I just thought it was an old—Why, Suzanna, it's absolutely beautiful!"

"Thank you," Suzanna murmured meaninglessly, looking at her unexpected visitor keenly, wondering why she was there but too polite to ask.

Lucy dragged her attention from the house to Suzanna and encountered a direct and questioning gaze. She abruptly dropped her eyes and looked uncomfortable.

Suzanna cleared her throat and said, "Uh, would you like some coffee?"

Lucy made a gesture with her hand and shook her head. "No, that's all right. Actually, I'm here on business." She got up and took a couple of aimless paces.

"Business?" Suzanna murmured, thoroughly bemused.

"Yeah—I thought maybe—"

She looked so acutely uncomfortable that Suzanna felt sorry for her. She would have helped her if she'd had any idea what it was she was trying to build up to, but as it was, all she could do was wait with a kind of tense patience, the way one waits for a stammerer.

Suddenly, Lucy seemed to collect herself. She peered at Suzanna, a direct and searching look. "Hey—listen, are you okay?" Suzanna opened her mouth, but Lucy rushed doggedly on. "I wanted to do a story on you, on this house. You know, local landmark swallowed up by the lake—that kind of thing. But I just realized, you were so upset the other day when you found out, and now that I see this place, I know what it must mean—what you must be going through." She stopped and pressed her hand to her forehead, flattening a few errant wisps of blond hair. "Damn it, Suzanna, I can't stand those reporters who stick microphones into the faces of bereaved people and say, 'And how does it feel to lose everything you own?' That's one of the reasons I came back here. I'm sorry—I know I should have called first, but I figured I could take some pictures at least, even if you weren't here, or didn't want— I mean, I can still do the story. I really shouldn't have bothered you. Forgive me."

"Lucy," Suzanna said gently, holding out a steaming cup of coffee, "please sit down. I'm fine. Just fine." When Lucy hesitated, she smiled and added an emphatic "Really."

"Really?" The other woman lowered herself warily into a chair and accepted the coffee without looking at it. "The other day—"

"The other day I thought the world had come to an end." Suzanna sat down, too, while Lucy watched her as if she might detonate without warning. "Lucy," Suzanna said, laughing, "this is wonderful. Perfect. Unless you have your heart set on a disaster story. Listen—Angel's Walk isn't going to be swallowed up by the lake. I'm going to *move* it."

"*Move* it?" Lucy sat forward. "Move a house this size? Are you serious?"

Suzanna nodded. "Actually, it's quite a compact house; it doesn't sprawl. And it's very sound under all the peeling paint. I know it can be done, and I'm going to do it!"

Lucy whistled soundlessly. "It would cost a fortune!"

"Almost." Suzanna smiled and told her about Mrs. Hopewell's gift. "The only problem," she finished with a sigh, "is time. The new spillway is in place, and it just depends on the weather how fast the lake will fill up. I don't know if we can get the house moved before the water gets here."

"You're right," Lucy said briskly, searching through her bags for a notebook and pencil. "This is one hell of a story. The history of this place would be human interest enough; the move is *news*. And this 'race against time' angle—God, what a cliff-hanger."

For the next hour Lucy asked questions, scribbled notes and drank coffee. Suzanna had never talked so much in her life; she had to admit that Lucy Tate—D'Arcy—knew her job. She seemed to know exactly what questions to ask to stir the memories and free the tongue. She took pictures in all the main rooms of the house and in each of those rooms thought of more questions. Lucy was delighted when Suzanna produced old photographs of Angel's Walk in happier times, with sparkling white paint and bright green shutters and Edwardian ladies in Sunday best striking poses on its manicured lawns.

Suzanna's box of old photos and notes interested Lucy so much, and she was so skilled at drawing things out of people, that Suzanna found herself telling Lucy about her plans to write a book.

Lucy listened intently. "When you get down to writing it," she said as she moved into the hallway, "give me a call. I might be able to help you. Now let's see. Who else lives here? There's the retired teacher—"

"Mrs. Hopewell," Suzanna offered absently. "Help me?"

"Sure, I'm a writer, after all." Lucy's smile was curiously lopsided. "I actually make a living at it."

"Oh, I didn't mean—But why, Lucy? Why should you—"

Lucy shrugged. "Why not?"

"It's very nice of you," Suzanna said slowly. "But you hardly know me." She gazed in complete puzzlement at the sleek-looking creature whose cool sophistication had always made her feel so inadequate and thought that she had never really known Lucy Tate, either.

"Yeah, I know," Lucy said dryly. "Ain't it a shame?" And she turned her attention back to the stairs. "Now, who lives upstairs?"

"I do," Suzanna mumbled, and trying valiantly not to stumble over his name, added, "And, um, Cam."

"Cam. That's Harris, right? Corps of Engineers?" Her tone and expression were deliberately casual.

Suzanna nodded and hoped devoutly that she wasn't blushing. "Right...Corps of Engineers. Mr. Harris. He, um, rents a room. Two. Tony sent him—that's Tony O'Brian, my cousin. From the dam."

Lucy grinned suddenly, said, "Right," and pulled open the front door.

Ron Weed was standing there, hand upraised to knock on the frosted glass panes.

"Lucy!" he said, sounding surprised, though Suzanna knew he must have seen Lucy's car parked out front.

"Morning," Lucy said coolly, and marched past him and out onto the porch. "Suzanna, if it's all right with you, I'll just get a few exterior shots of the house."

Ron's eyes followed Lucy's tight black jeans down the steps until she disappeared around the corner of the house. "What's she doing here?"

"A story," Suzanna said, trying not to smile. "On Angel's Walk."

"On Angel's Walk? You mean this place?" Ron frowned in the direction of Lucy's disappearance, then at Suzanna's blush and back again to Lucy, as if he couldn't decide which problem to tackle first.

"Yes," Suzanna told him with satisfaction. "We're going to move it."

"Move it!" And then, in suspicious afterthought, he said, *"We?"*

"Yes. Cam Harris and I."

"Cam. That's the troubleshooter from the corps, isn't it? I heard you tell Lucy he's still staying here with you. Suzanna, I can't—"

A screech of sincere terror interrupted him. He and Suzanna looked at each other, and then both of them bolted for the backyard. At the corner of the house, Ron, who was in the lead, ran full tilt into Lucy. The impact knocked Ron back toward Suzanna, who put her hands on his back to steady him and then peered around him in dread. Suzanna wasn't sure what she'd expected, but nothing seemed to be amiss in the backyard.

Lucy, however, was sobbing hysterically into Ron's immaculate shirtfront. "Oh, Ron, it was *horrible*. It went right over my hand. I just moved the f-flower pot out of the way so I could take a p-picture, and there it was! It was *huge*, awful. I hate s-snakes!"

Suzanna muttered, "Henry!" and moved cautiously around Ron, who was patting Lucy's quivering back and murmuring soothingly. She could see Lucy's camera lying on the flagstones near the old hand pump, and beyond it, moving in his usual unhurried fashion along the base of the board fence, the full five-foot length of a black-and-white banded California king snake.

Suzanna didn't stop to think. It had already occurred to her to worry about what would happen to Henry when the lake waters began to invade his territory. She'd been afraid he might be forced closer to the highway, and be run over in the road or killed by someone who didn't understand or appreciate his value. She'd hoped she might find and capture him, then release him in a new, safe hunting ground. And so when she saw her chance she took it without hesitation. In the next moment, she had her hands filled with a large, disgruntled king snake.

She knew king snakes were constrictors and nonvenomous, but she also knew that even a king snake could inflict a painful bite in its own defense. Henry was hissing and coiling furiously, five feet of pure muscle and offended reptilian dignity, and it was all Suzanna could do to maintain her grip just below the slender head.

"Ron," she gasped. "Could you help me a minute, please?"

Ron's response was a horrified *"Suzanna!"* Lucy's was shocked silence.

"I just need something to put him in. A box—anything. Hurry!" she added in alarm as Henry gave a violent twist and coiled himself around her forearm. "Look on the porch," she gasped when Ron disentangled himself from Lucy and moved purposefully toward her. Behind him, Lucy wiped her eyes and watched with a mixture of awe and revulsion."Just find me something to put him in. Something with a lid!"

Ron nodded. A moment later he called from the screened back porch, "Here's a picnic basket. Will that be okay?"

"Fine. Perfect." She was breathing hard and perspiring freely as she gingerly lowered the seething reptile into the wicker hamper, shucked it off of her forearm and slammed the lid. "There!" She plunked a flower pot on top of the lid for added security and rose, dusting her hands, flushed and smiling in triumph.

Ron and Lucy were staring at her with undisguised horror. Ron had his arm around Lucy's waist. Lucy's hand was resting on Ron's shirtfront, as if for reassurance.

Suzanna cleared her throat, hoping she wasn't going to burst out laughing. "Gee, Lucy, I'm sorry. I hope your camera's all right. I'm sure Henry didn't mean you any harm."

Lucy managed a dry croak. "H-Henry?"

"Suzanna," Ron said severely, "what in the hell are you going to do with that snake?"

"Turn him loose," Suzanna said casually, "in a safe place."

Ron picked up Lucy's camera and handed it to her. Lucy, who was struggling to recover her lost composure, made the most of checking the camera for damage.

"Seems fine," she reported, taking a deep breath and smoothing wisps of hair back from her damp forehead. With a quick glance at Ron, she said, "Well, I think I have all I need. I'll just get the rest of my stuff and be on my way." In the kitchen she draped herself with her cameras and bags and turned to hold our her hand rather gingerly to Suzanna. There was a moment of silence, and then she said with quiet sincerity, "Suzanna, thanks for the story— and good luck. I mean that. I hope you do save this place."

"Thank you," Suzanna answered.

Lucy hesitated, turned to go and then turned back to Suzanna. There was a crease between her eyes that made her look oddly wistful. "You know, we never got to know each other very well in school."

"No," Suzanna agreed, and added truthfully, "I'm sorry."

Lucy took another deep breath and said softly, "Yeah—me, too." She waited a moment longer, then turned to go. "Listen, it was nice talking to you. We'll get together again, okay? I'd like to do a follow-up on the move, so don't forget to let me know when you get it all set up. And hey, I meant that about your book. Stop in when you're at the museum, okay? We'll have coffee."

"I'd like that," Suzanna said.

Lucy glanced at Ron and cleared her throat. Suzanna noticed that a spot of pink had appeared in each cheek. "Ron," she began gruffly, then gave a brief nod and left.

Ron stood watching Lucy walk down the hall and out the front door. When he turned back to Suzanna, his forehead was creased. He looked almost puzzled. He said abruptly, "Well, guess I'll be going too, Suzanna. Just stopped by to see how you were doing, but I can see you've got everything under control, so uh—"

"'Bye, Ron. Thanks for coming," Suzanna said gently. She followed him down the hallway and from the doorway watched him increase his pace to a jog in order to catch up with Lucy. She saw Lucy halt, half turn and then continue with him down the long walk. Suzanna noticed that Ron had placed a protective hand on Lucy's back and that he swept the front gate open for her in a touching gesture of gallantry.

"'Bye, Ron," she whispered. She drew in a long breath of air that was heavy with the scent of growing things and hugged herself. As she smiled up at the sky of flawless blue, she was thinking that life was good again; the grays and blacks and purples were gone. She was happy, Ron and Lucy were going to be happy, Henry would be safe, Angel's Walk would be safe, she was in love, and the world was a Valentine in soft pastels.

As HE GAZED DOWN at the swirling pinwheel cloud on the satellite photo, Cam was thinking dismally that his life had never looked blacker.

"It's the worst thing that could possibly happen," Tony was saying agitatedly. "The worst. Right now that storm is just sitting there off Cabo San Lucas, but if it starts moving north..."

Cam nodded bleakly. "It'll mean rain. Warm rain, and lots of it."

Tony paced, slapping his desk with his hand each time he passed it. It irritated Cam, but he knew exactly how the man felt. "A hell of a lot of rain. Cam, we're talking about a flood of major proportions here. Even without that snowpack, we'd have flash flooding out of every canyon in this valley. Add that damn snow, and we're talking about—"

"A hundred-year flood," Cam said. "I know, I know. Well—" he breathed tiredly, standing up "—looks like we got that spillway finished in the nick of time, doesn't it?" His mouth twisted in irony. "We've saved Bakersfield. Hell, we'll probably get medals!"

Tony just looked at him, the sadness in his eyes magnified by his glasses. "You know what this'll mean? That lake's going to fill up like somebody left the water on in the bathtub. Cam, I'm afraid there's just no way Suzanna's going to get that house out of there in time."

"Yeah, I know." Cam drew a hand across his eyes and muttered tiredly, "She was so close. So damn close."

"Well," Tony said doubtfully as they were leaving dam headquarters, "we can always pray. Maybe that storm will decide to stay put. Or move in the opposite direction...."

It was so late by the time Cam got back to Angel's Walk that Suzanna had given up on him and gone to bed. Stacks of boxes neatly labeled with a black marker lined the hallway and made a pyramid in the middle of the living room floor. She'd had a busy day—probably worn out.

He found her in bed, sound asleep with the lights on and a cloth-bound copy of *Rebecca of Sunnybrook Farm* lying open across her chest. She stirred when he slipped in beside her and murmured his name sleepily. When he took her in his arms, she lifted a hand to touch his neck and turned toward him, snuggling, responsive even in semiconsciousness.

"It's all right, love," he whispered gruffly, stroking her hair. "I just want to hold you. Go back to sleep."

She did, like a happy child untroubled by dreams. But Cam lay awake, staring into the darkness and letting Suzanna's hair slide through his fingers like warm rain.

THE FIRST THING Suzanna saw when she walked into the kitchen Sunday after church was the picnic hamper. It was sitting on the table. Its lid, minus the flower pot, lay on the table beside it.

Cam was standing at the counter, dicing celery with a knife the size of a machete. He was wearing an apron and no shirt, whistling "Camptown Races" and inserting "doo-dahs" in a mellow baritone.

Suzanna's heart dropped into her stomach and stayed there, cowering. She had to restrain herself from running to the back porch and burrowing wildly through trash bags and laundry hampers.

She must have made an involuntary sound of distress, because Cam turned around to bestow upon her a smile of heart-stopping beauty and innocence. "Hel-*lo* darlin'. Didn't hear you come in."

"H-hullo," Suzanna croaked, trying hard to keep her eyes from darting around the room. Where was he? "What are you doing? Is that a p-picnic lunch?" Her voice cracked on the upward inflection, and to cover it, she cleared her throat and coughed.

"No, m'dear," Cam intoned, doing W. C. Fields again, "this is not a picnic lunch; it is a culinary adventure." Using the knife as a pointer, he indicated the assortment spread across table, stove and counter. "We have shrimp salad served in individual cocktail glasses of genuine plastic; we have croissants, fresh baked, formerly frozen; we have smoked breast of turkey, cream cheese and olives; and we have fresh, succulent strawberries with whipped cream. Great little invention—comes in its very own spray can. And of course—" he swept open the refrigerator door and with a wine steward's flourish produced a moisture-beaded bottle of Chardonnay "—a modest measure of benefic spirits!"

"Oh, good," Suzanna said vaguely, edging toward the door to the back porch.

"Sweetheart," Cam inquired kindly, "is something the matter? You look a little pale."

"Hmm?" Suzanna murmured. She had opened the door and was trying to peer through it and look completely natural doing so. Finally abandoning pretense, she muttered, "Excuse me," and poked her head and shoulders cautiously around the door.

On the sagging wood floor of the porch, just where the picnic hamper had been, was a burlap bag tied with a length of twine. As Suzanna stared at it, the bag gave a single convulsive jerk and then slowly expanded upward, like an alien creature drawing breath.

She slammed the door shut and leaned on it, weak-kneed with relief. "Oh, good. I thought—" she breathed, shutting her eyes for a moment. When she opened them again, Cam was grinning at her and shaking his head.

"I owe you one for that," he said mildly. "I really do."
He shook the knife at her. "You took ten years off my
life."

"Well, you just took ten years off mine!" Suzanna retorted. "Can you imagine the shock when I saw that
hamper sitting there?"

"Yeah, well what about the shock I got when I lifted the
lid and found myself dancing with a six-foot snake? You're
lucky I didn't have a heart attack!"

"*Five*-foot. I'm sorry. I didn't have a chance to tell you,
and I didn't know you'd be planning a picnic! It seemed
like a good safe place. It seemed like a *perfect*—"

"Hey, it's okay." Cam dropped the knife into the sink
and folded her into his arms. "It was a perfectly sensible
place to put a snake. . . . I take it that's Henry?"

Suzanna nodded, bumping his chin. "I caught him yesterday when he frightened Lucy half to death. It's a very
long story. Can I tell you later? Right now I'd just like to
kiss you."

"Permission granted," Cam growled, and obligingly
lowered his head so she could reach him.

"You've been snitching olives," she murmured a few
breathless moments later.

"Guilty—sorry."

"It's all right. I love olives."

The next time he had an opportunity to speak, Cam
muttered thickly, "Hey, unless you want to waste a really
terrific picnic lunch . . ."

"I'll stop," Suzanna whispered, "for now. Where are we
going?"

"I don't know. I'm the new kid in town, remember? I
was hoping you'd know about some private, romantic
spot . . . by hearsay, of course."

"Of course." Suzanna sighed. It was hard to think of anything but how good it felt to be there, enfolded in the warm, intimate cocoon of his arms and body. She savored every intimate detail: the furry sound his voice made rumbling up through his chest; the crisp tickle of hair against her cheek and the springy resilience of muscle beneath her hands; the sweet-salt taste and the clean-earth scent of his skin . . .

"I know of a perfect place." Her lips made soft kitten tracks across his collarbone. "It's a beautiful place."

"Mmm, terrific." He pressed her hard against his body. "I can hardly wait."

"Um-hmm," Suzanna muttered happily, "it'll be just perfect. For Henry. We can take him with us."

"Sue," Cam said, tilting her chin and gazing wonderingly at her, "do you know that you're crazy?"

Yes, she was. Crazy in love. Crazy to be in love with a man she barely knew, a man who would drift out of her life as he'd drifted in, like flotsam carried along by a swollen river. *Crazy.*

"I know," she said, sighing, "but will you kiss me, anyway?"

Chapter Twelve

This time it was Suzanna who drove Cam's four-wheel-drive corps vehicle. When he asked whether she thought she could manage a stick shift, she loftily informed him that she'd begun driving tractors at the age of eight and that her first car had been an ancient Ford pickup with a four-on-the-floor gearshift, a hand choke and a hand throttle.

"Why did I even ask?" Cam inquired dryly of Henry as he carefully stowed the gunnysack and the picnic hamper behind the front seat.

They drove away from the lake on the two-lane blacktop highway that sliced through the valley of the river's south fork. This was cattle country, farming country. On either side of the highway, cattle grazed in natural meadows—not the purebred stock of gentleman farmers but sturdy range livestock, multicolored mixes of white-faced Herefords and black Angus, with a bit of Brahma thrown in for toughness.

Interspersed with the undeveloped grazing land were fields of alfalfa and oats. Modern hay-making machines moved ponderously through the fields like huge voracious insects, cutting, raking, baling and stacking the hay in neat rectangular blocks.

Beyond the fields on the left-hand side of the road, Cam could see the bank of cottonwoods and willows that marked the river bottom. On the right, on the arid hillsides, there were scattered developments of mobile homes and small houses surrounded by vegetable gardens and fruit trees. In spite of these, and the state-of-the-art equipment in the fields, Cam could see how general lifestyles here might not have changed much in decades. The school and post office faced each other across a sleepy intersection, not far from a little white clapboard church with a stubby steeple that reminded Cam of the child's game "Here's the church, here's the steeple..." Yellow sunflowers nodded over fences, and little yellow butterflies danced in the shimmering heat. Here and there an old barn huddled, gray and sagging, in a field of yellow mustard flowers. The midday heat and insect hum made the earth seem relaxed and sleepy, as if it were spinning just a bit more slowly.

They left the highway and the green fields and ticking sprinklers behind and followed a single-lane paved road into a valley bordered by hills covered with granite boulders, sagebrush and buckwheat, Joshua trees and junipers. Then the pavement gave way to graded, hard-packed dirt, and the flora became manzanita and piñon and bull pines, with a few scattered yuccas in early bloom.

The road had deteriorated to a rutted, rocky track by the time Suzanna stopped the jeep in the meager shade of a rock chimney, all that remained of a cabin that had vanished long ago. Dead gray branches of aged fruit trees still produced a few miraculous green leaves in the orchard nearby, and smooth, round stones still outlined a pathway to a nonexistent front door.

"Well," Suzanna said, just a bit breathlessly, flexing her fingers on the steering wheel. "Here it is. What do you think of it?"

They were sitting in a sunny glade looking out across the valley. It was a peaceful place; the breeze made a shushing sound in the bull pines, and from somewhere nearby came the tranquilizing sound of running water.

"What is this supposed to be—a picnic spot or a home for Henry?" Cam asked, teasing her.

"Both," she said lightly, watching him with a certain wariness.

"I think it's great," he said, laughing. "Can't speak for Henry, though." He opened the door and put a foot out.

"This was Papa's first homestead," Suzanna said, sitting still where she was and not looking at him. "He lived here before he married my grandmother. After they were married, they bought the place down there in the valley, but this still belongs to the family." She took a deep breath and turned to look at him. "This is where I want to put Angel's Walk."

He'd had an idea she was coming to that from the moment he'd seen that chimney and the fruit trees. But seeing it coming hadn't made it any easier; he still didn't know what to say to her.

"Well," she prompted in the face of his silence, "what do you think?"

"It's a beautiful spot," he hedged slowly, looking off across the valley.

"I *know* that," she said patiently. "I mean—can it be done? I know the road's bad."

"I don't know, Sue," he said, rubbing his neck doubtfully. "It's steep, rocky and rutted. It would have to be regraded, and even then..." He shook his head. Even without looking at her, he had no idea how much longer he was going to be able to keep up the charade. "It would take extra time," he managed bleakly.

"I know, but I've been thinking about that," Suzanna said, reaching out to touch his arm in her eagerness. "I think I have an idea. Couldn't I move the house in two stages? You know—get it out of the lake bottom first and put it somewhere temporary, like one of the stack yards on the ranch. And then, as soon as this site and the road are ready—I thought you'd know whether it's feasible. I know you mostly build dams and levees and things like that, but—" She stopped, faltering because he'd turned to stare at her. "There's plenty of money."

He was staring at her because he was tingling all over from the shock of an idea. It was the old adrenaline flow, the creative energy and excitement that had kept him continent-hopping for more than ten years. He didn't know for certain—there was a lot to look into, a lot to arrange—but he'd never had a brainstorm like this one fail him yet. *Suzanna, don't you cry!*

"Cam?" She was staring at him, wide-eyed and worried. Her fingers were pressing into the muscle of his forearm. "Is it a terrible idea? I mean—"

He laughed out loud with sheer exhilaration and leaned across the seat of the car to kiss her on the mouth. "No reason why it shouldn't work," he said, swinging himself out of the jeep. "No reason at all! Woman, I'm hungry. Don't just sit there. Let's get this picnic on the road!"

"Well, you scared me," Suzanna grumbled as she opened her door and reached for Henry's gunnysack. "You looked so fierce. I mean, I didn't think it was such a bad idea, or such a sensational one, either, for that matter, but you looked like you'd had a *house* fall on you."

She gave a breathless squeak as he swept her up into his arms and swung her around, Henry and all. "Cam—" she

gasped, hanging on to the sack and his neck for dear life
"—*now* who's crazy? Put me down!"

"I will," he responded, looking down into her flushed
face, "if you'll promise me, absolutely, that there will be
no mention whatsoever for the duration of this picnic of
Angel's Walk, house moving, dam building or lake waters. Agreed?"

"Agreed," she whispered demurely. "But what on earth
will we find to talk about—the weather?"

Cam winced. "*Hell*, no," he said roughly, and set both
her feet and his thinking back on solid ground. The
weather—he wasn't out of the woods yet. Even brilliant
ideas take time.

Henry's gunnysack had begun to wriggle furiously. Cam
took it from Suzanna and held it gingerly at arm's length.
Suzanna gazed at it in distress and murmured sympathetically, "Poor thing. We'd better turn him loose first thing.
Near the spring—he probably needs a drink."

The spring was just uphill from the cabin site. It bub-
bled up through sand and rock and trickled down into a
natural rock basin. Where the water overflowed, the face
of the rock was covered with thick brownish-green moss.
Below the rocks the water ran away in a little stream that
flowed through emerald grass and watercress, finding its
way into warm, stagnant pools before disappearing into
the thirsty ground. The pools were alive with bubbling al-
gae, insects and polliwogs—a snake's paradise.

Stepping cautiously on the spongy ground and alert to
the presence of indigenous—and unfriendly—wildlife,
Cam placed the bag on the grass and untied the twine that
secured it. As gently as he could, he tumbled the disgruntled king snake out onto the grass and stepped quickly
back to Suzanna's side.

With swift, coiling movements, the snake sorted himself out and then lay absolutely motionless except for the sensory forays of his tongue. Cam and Suzanna watched in suspense, their arms around each other, until Henry at last began to move, just his head at first, in short, uncertain explorations. And then, like a rippling shadow, he seemed to blend with the background, and in another blink of an eye he was gone.

Suzanna turned slowly into Cam's chest, and there was something about her stillness...

"Sweetheart," he said in wonder, "are you crying?"

She sniffed and stirred but didn't raise her head. After a moment, her voice came, muffled and low. "It's just—I think I'm just realizing that it's really going to happen. I know I promised—I'm sorry."

"It's all right," he said softly, stroking her hair.

"I mean—I know I can save the house, but even so, it won't be the same, will it? My life is never going to be the same again."

He couldn't think of a thing to say, so he just stood very still and held her.

THEY ATE LUNCH on a carpet of pine needles in the shade of a stand of medium-size bull pines, because, as Suzanna pointed out, while planting Henry here was a little like sending in an advance patrol to secure the area, at present the spring and its immediate surroundings were still entirely too attractive to rattlesnakes.

She was determined, after her brief emotional lapse, to keep the mood of the day light and carefree, for Cam's sake. He was looking so tired and tense; she knew he'd been under a terrible strain and that he had been working long hours besides. She didn't know what time he'd come home last night, but she'd waited up for him until long past midnight.

So while they ate, she told him a lively version of Lucy's encounter with Henry, and Henry's subsequent capture, and then compared the incident to Mrs. Hopewell's first meeting with the king snake. After several years it could still cause Suzanna to collapse with laughter to recall the day she'd come home to find Mrs. Hopewell's hat, gloves and purse on the front walk and the lady herself creeping through the currant bushes on all fours, hot on Henry's trail.

"You and Mrs. Hopewell are a lot alike," Cam said when the laughter had subsided. "That's why I can't figure out—"

"What?" Suzanna prompted when he stopped, looking perplexed.

"Why you have this ... fixation for the past."

"I do not have a fixation!"

"An affinity, then. Mrs. Hopewell was a misfit in her time, and you would have been, too." He leaned across the picnic spread and kissed her lingeringly. "You'd have made a lousy Victorian, sweetheart."

His mouth carried the cool moisture of wine. She felt herself melting, like ice cream in the sun, and put her hand on his waist to steady herself. He kissed her again, moving his mouth over hers, sliding his tongue across her lips and the inside of her mouth. Bubbles of laughter began in his belly and flowed into her fingers and through her body, erupting in breathy gusts of delight. Little eddies of love rippled through her, like raindrops disturbing the surface of a pond. Impulsively, she pushed him, bowling him over onto his back and landing full-length on top of him, wriggling to adjust her body to his bumps and hollows. He made a sound in his throat, a sound of pleased surprise, and altered the angle of his head, turning the teasing, maddening sallies of his tongue into full penetration. In contrast to the heart-stopping intensity of his kiss, his hands held her lightly, just where the swell of her breasts flattened against his chest. A sudden craving swept her, a desire to be immersed in him, enveloped by him. It frustrated her, and she moved restlessly, sinuously, pressing herself against him. In response, his knee slowly lifted, filling the space between her thighs. She drew a long, shuddering breath and turned her face into his neck.

"You see?" He touched the words like kisses onto the shell of her ear. "You're too sexy, too sensual, too *responsive* to be a Victorian...." With each whispered indictment, his knee rose higher, a hot, searing pressure. His hands moved upward over her shoulder blades, then slid down her back to tug her shirt from the waistband of her slacks.

"I...can't breathe," she gasped when he filled his hands with the curve of her bottom, giving her a giddy ride on the taut-flexed ridge of his thigh. Desire produced soft explosions inside her.

He offered a low sound of reassurance and lifted his head and torso, reaching for her mouth. His hands and legs guided and demanded, urging her thighs farther apart. In one swift motion he rolled her onto her back and pressed hard against her body's pliant and vulnerable softness. Clothing became a frustration, a source of resentment, even anger. It became a nuisance, then expendable.

She'd wanted to be immersed, enfolded; she wasn't prepared to be overwhelmed. Passions surged, boiled and erupted out of control. For a moment panic touched her; and then she realized that to fight what was happening would be like swimming against a flash flood. There was nothing to be done except to hold on to Cam and let the torrent take them both.

CAM WAS ASLEEP with his head in Suzanna's lap. She didn't mind. He needed the rest badly, and besides, seeing him like this, so vulnerable, with his high-voltage power switch off, always touched her with a soft sunshine glow of love. Seeing him like this—with a few diamond drops of sweat still clinging to his forehead; his thick, stubby lashes lying golden against the purple-brown shadows beneath his eyes; his mouth, relaxed and soft, his lips slightly parted; his breath coming in the sweet, childlike snores of complete oblivion—it was hard to believe the storm that had just swept them could really have happened.

She shifted slightly, wincing a little as she discovered lingering sorenesses, and smiled a secret, feminine smile. Oh, it had happened, no doubt about it. Passion that consuming couldn't help but leave its small remembrances.

The first words Cam had spoken in the aftermath had been an anguished question. "Did I hurt you?"

"No," she'd whispered fervently. "No, John, of course not." She felt dazed and exhilarated. She felt fulfilled, and she felt loved.

Extraordinary, she thought now, looking down at his sleeping face, watching her fingers comb idly through his hair. And impossible. He couldn't really love her; he'd certainly never *said* so, not even in extremes of passion. He'd warned her more than once, in fact, that he wasn't to be taken seriously. And yet still, she'd never felt so secure, so loved.

Funny—she'd been looking all her life for someone like Papa, someone solid and dependable, the security and foundation she needed. Someone like...Ron. And yet she'd always known that Ron wasn't what she wanted. She'd wanted someone dynamic and exciting, for Papa had been those things, too. She wanted someone to stir her blood and build fires in her soul. Someone like this man asleep in her arms—John Campbell Harris.

Oh, John, she thought, *why can't you be my rock as well as my . . . my skyrockets!*

A pine needle drifted down onto his chest. He was wearing only his pants, because she was wearing his shirt, loose and unbuttoned but covering her breasts. She brushed the needle away carefully, trying not to disturb him, but he stirred and turned toward her, seeking the soft skin of her stomach with his mouth. She held him close, discovering that she wasn't as sated as she'd thought she was. Her desire for him was already beginning to stir deep inside, like tiny sparks glowing in a bed of coals.

A grumbling of distant thunder startled her; she sat very still to listen, her fingers still laced through Cam's hair. She hadn't noticed that the day had grown heavy and sultry. There was no breeze, even in the topmost branches of the pine trees. Thunderstorm weather.

"What is it?" Cam mumbled, nuzzling the satin underside of her breast.

The sparks in her belly flared, spreading heat into her chest. Her breasts grew heavy. "Thunder," she murmured. "But it's a long way off, somewhere up in the mountains."

"Thunder." He lay back in her lap with his eyes closed.

"It's nowhere near us," Suzanna whispered, running her palm over the uneven ripples of his chest and ribs. "It won't rain."

He caught her hand and held it for a moment pressed against his stomach. "It's raining somewhere," he said cryptically and sat up.

Suzanna wasn't quite secure enough to tell him plainly that rain or no rain, she wanted to stay just a little longer.

Though he seemed to know without her saying a word. As she was helping to repack the remnants of his picnic lunch, Cam appeared from behind to hold her, wrapping his arms across her breasts and pressing his mouth, open and hungry, into the curve of her neck.

"We have to get back." His voice was husky with regret. "There are things I have to do."

"I know. It's all right." Her head had fallen forward like a wilted daisy. "I guess I'd better let you have your shirt back."

"Hmm." He pushed it over the rounds of her shoulders and let it drop to the ground, leaving her in nothing but panties. "I guess people might talk if you came home like this."

She laughed, shivering in the afternoon heat. "I sincerely hope I don't run into anyone I know on the way home. My own clothes are a disgrace."

"A disgrace," he solemnly agreed, turning her and pulling her slowly against his chest. For a few minutes they just stood there together among the pines, arms loosely holding each other, heads bowed and gently touching. Her breasts made soft, creamy pillows where they met the harder, darker contours of his chest. The contrast seemed to mesmerize them both.

"I wish we could stay like this," Suzanna said, shuddering. Suddenly, she felt almost frightened, beset for no reason by a vague and nameless dread. She gave an embarrassed little laugh. "I feel like Eve getting kicked out of the Garden."

His laughter was a short gust of irony. He kissed her, sliding his hands over her bottom and pulling her hard against him, and then sighed deeply and caught her in his arms in a great, enveloping, protective embrace. "Well, we've got a full cast of characters," he said dryly, "even the snake." He pressed his lips to her hair. His voice was muffled and gravelly, but she thought she heard him add, "I promise you, this story's gonna have a different ending."

THEY WERE ALMOST TO THE HIGHWAY when Suzanna heard the sirens. A deputy sheriff's car first, followed by an ambulance, both with red lights flashing.

"Why are you stopping?" Cam asked curiously when she pulled up to the intersection and sat, gripping the steering wheel and peering back up the highway after the disappearing lights. "They've already gone by."

She just looked at him, wondering how to explain to someone like him. She felt unimaginably sad. After their idyllic afternoon, nothing could have highlighted the differences between them more plainly.

"You know," she said slowly as she put the jeep in gear and nosed out onto the main road, "it isn't really the past I have an 'affinity' for. I'm not sure I can explain it; it's just something that's disappeared in a lot of places but that still exists here and in a few other communities." She glanced at him and managed a crooked smile. "I can't name it, but I can give you an example. That ambulance—the sirens. You know that line, 'Never send to ask for whom the bell tolls?' Well, here people really feel like that. What do you do when you hear a siren in the city? Chances are you don't even register it at all. Or if you're a very compassionate person, you might stop to think of the person in trouble. But in this place, when you hear a siren, you feel the cold chills of *fear*. You want to know where it's going. As soon as you can, you get to a phone, and you don't rest until you know. Because everyone in this valley is someone you know personally, and most of them are people you've known for years—all your life. You may not like them all—some of them might be royal pains a lot of the time. But they're your neighbors. And they aren't going to move away next month or next year, so you learn to get along with them. And in spite of yourself sometimes, you care about them. And they care about you. If you're in trouble, they'll rally around you. They come to help you out if they can." She turned to glance at him and found him staring at her. "In big cities, people talk about the loneliness, Cam," she said softly in a voice blurred with unanticipated emotion. "In a place like this, you're never alone. Do you understand?"

For a long moment he just stared at her, his eyes as sharp and intent as lasers. And then he rasped, "Yes...yes I do." His eyes darkened, and their focus turned inward, and he sat slightly forward, gazing through the windshield into a brassy sunset.

Back at Angel's Walk he showered, dressed, kissed her in the absentminded manner of a man with a job to do and then went out.

Only after his jeep had disappeared in a dust cloud did Suzanna remember that she hadn't reminded him about tomorrow—about Memorial Day and the picnic. She wondered whether, with all he had on his mind, he would even remember that he'd promised to go.

Chapter Thirteen

Memorial Day dawned brassy, hot and sultry. By seven o'clock in the morning, thunderheads were already hanging over the mountains like a gypsy's maledictions.

And Cam had forgotten the picnic. Or so Suzanna assumed. He hadn't come home at all last night, or if he had come home, he hadn't been to bed and had left again before daylight.

All the joy and excitement went out of Suzanna's morning, leaving her feeling as depressed and heavy as the weather. She lay between sheets that felt cloying and sticky, remembering her miserable little nightmare about the runaway balloon. In spite of all her vows and promises, she was trying to hold on to that string, and already she could feel it slipping from her grasp.

Serves you right, she reflected miserably as she padded barefoot down the stairs to put on the coffee. It was what came of falling in love with a rootless wanderer.

The kitchen door was open. From halfway down the hallway she could see a big white box tied with brown satin ribbon sitting in the middle of the table.

"What in the world...?" she said aloud, and advanced cautiously, circling the table and the box with the awed wariness of a pygmy investigating a sleeping elephant.

There was a three-by-five card propped against the box. In bold, blocky handwriting it said: "Sue, this reminds me of you. Thought you might like to wear it to the picnic. Kind of seems like the right day for it. See you later. Love, Cam."

How like him it was—sensitivity trying unsuccessfully to hide in a camouflage of masculine brusqueness. Suzanna read it through three times, telling herself each time that the word "love" in that context was as meaningless as the word "Dear" in a business letter. And then she reached with unsteady fingers to untie the brown satin bow.

Moments later, she was sitting in one of the kitchen chairs, laughing and crying and trying to brush away tears before they could fall on the material she was hugging to her chest. She kept saying, "I don't believe it. I don't believe he did this. Oh, John."

It was . . . well, it was a costume, actually, a wonderful Gay Nineties costume, but far from the imitation junk found in costume rental shops. It was more the sort of thing that might have been made for a big-budget period movie—beautifully tailored and accurate in design and detail.

It had a long skirt of brown lawn and a blouse of finest cambric with a tucked bodice and high, ruched neckline adorned with a cameo brooch. The jacket was of crisp brown-and-white-striped linen, with a tightly fitted waist-length bodice and leg-of-mutton sleeves. There were high-buttoned shoes, which looked too small, and there was a hat, a Gay Nineties number of brown straw topped with brown-and-pink roses and champagne-colored ostrich feathers. The only thing missing, Suzanna thought, still overcome with wonder and surprise, was a matching parasol.

And a *corset*, she added later, puffing and breathless from trying to button herself into those tight-fitting bodices. She just hoped she'd be able to breathe without popping a button on her blouse. A corset would have been a big help, though miraculously everything fit rather well. There were, she decided, advantages to being "average." The shoes were too small, but she didn't mind that—they'd looked uncomfortable, anyway.

She fixed her hair in a loose Gibson-girl style, with curled wisps on her neck and temples, and arranged the hat at a jaunty angle, with its largest feather curving around to just barely brush her cheek. It looked great but tickled; she kept thinking it was a fly and swiped at it with her hand. The hat was not secure. What she needed was an old-fashioned hat pin. Mrs. Hopewell had been notoriously careless with her hat pins—maybe she had overlooked one or two. Suzanna went down the stairs at a sedate pace, because it was hot and she didn't want to spoil the beautiful costume with perspiration. And sure enough, there was a hat pin lying on the rug under the windowsill in Mrs. Hopewell's room. It might just as well have been on the moon; Suzanna couldn't have bent over if her life depended on it. She was just standing there, forlornly contemplating the hat pin, when there came a firm rap on the front door.

It was Cam—in a stiff, high collar, a brown bow tie and a brown-and-white seersucker jacket. One hand was mysteriously hidden behind his back; in the other he held a walking stick and a white straw boater. His hair was dark and slicked back with moisture, and his face looked scrubbed and earnest and young.

"Good morning, Miss Day," he said solemnly, and then, unable to contain himself a moment longer, broke into a grin that was the Hardy Boys and Norman Rockwell and the Little Rascals all rolled into one. With an awkward flourish he drew his hand out from behind him and thrust a nosegay of violets at Suzanna. Dangling by a strap from his wrist was the missing item of her ensemble—the parasol.

Suzanna melted into a puddle. Tremulous with love and silent laughter, it was all she could do to pick up her cue and murmur, "Why, how very thoughtful. Thank you, Mr. Harris." She took the flowers and sniffed their delicate fragrance, and then, unable to maintain the little charade, let her arms fall to her sides as she whispered, "Oh, John."

He cleared his throat and touched his bow tie tentatively. "Sorry I'm late. Had to wait for the damn—excuse me—*darn* flower shop to open...." His voice trailed off as his eyes swept over her from head to toe. "Sue, you look—"

"The shoes didn't fit," she put in hurriedly, suddenly feeling nervous and self-conscious. Her dress *was* too tight; she couldn't seem to breathe.

"Beautiful."

"Do I?" she asked. *Definitely too tight.* "I think—do you think I need a corset?"

"Oh, no!" He reached for her, measuring her waist with his hands as he pulled her against him. "When I hold you, I want to feel *you*, not a suit of armor."

She leaned against him, tilting her head back and lifting a hand to steady her hat. "Why Mr. Harris! What will people say?" She knew her shining eyes were an open invitation, and he took it. When he lifted his head a few moments later, she said demurely, "I do believe I've been compromised."

"Then we'll have to do something about it, won't we?" He spoke lightly, matching her tone. But his eyes were dark and luminous, like pewter. She stared back at him, unable to think of a single thing to say that would be in character. The curiously intense moment stretched until his fingers, fanning over her back under her jacket, hesitated at a spot between her shoulder blades.

"What's this?" His voice was bumpy with gentle laughter.

"Buttons." Suzanna sighed, closing her eyes. "I couldn't reach them all. These clothes just weren't made to be gotten into and out of by yourself!"

"Hmm. I think," Cam said judiciously as he helped her out of the jacket and turned her, "that there may be aspects of Victorian life I approve of, after all." His fingers were dealing unhurriedly with the missed buttons.

"I was thinking of maids and valets," Suzanna murmured, though it was hard to think of anything at all as he bent to kiss the nape of her neck, carefully avoiding ostrich feathers.

"Mmm ... I like your hair like this. This is one job I'd definitely reserve for myself."

"You're not patient enough," Suzanna said, giggling, remembering the way he'd dealt with her clothes on other occasions, including yesterday under the pines. "There'd be buttons all over the place. And then I'd have to sew them back on."

"Uh-uh, what do you think maids and valets are for?" He turned her back to face him and gathered her close, knocking her hat hopelessly askew.

She clung to him, laughing, aching with the bittersweet agony of love, aching to tell him, to *say* it, just once. But the mood of the day was light, a fantasy; he'd set the mood, and she must play along. So she cleared her throat and stepped back, straightening her hat, and said coolly, "My dear, impetuous Mr. Harris, you forget yourself!"

With a sigh he clutched his hat to his chest. "Miss Day, please forgive me. I promise to behave like a gentleman." With a flourish, he placed the hat back on his head and offered her his arm. "Please allow me to escort you to the picnic."

Before she placed her hand in the crook of his elbow, Suzanna picked up a brown paper bag that was sitting at the foot of the stairs.

"What's this?" Cam asked as he took it from her, momentarily dropping his role.

"A change of clothes," Suzanna told him with a gleam in her eye. "You may recall that I did mention baseball."

"WHAT IS YOUR FAMILY going to make of all this?" Cam asked as he was helping Suzanna out of her car. They had arrived late; most of the clan were already gathered in the community park and were eating and talking in the shade of evergreen trees.

"Don't worry—they're pretty unflappable," Suzanna said with a smile of reassurance. "There isn't much that surprises them, or impresses them. Just don't expect them to make a fuss over you—you know, treat you like company. You'll just be sort of assimilated, like one of the family. It doesn't mean you're being ignored, just accepted."

"I'll try to remember that," Cam said dryly. Suzanna had already told him quite a bit about her family, but he still wasn't really prepared for their numbers and variety. The offspring of Harland and Sarah Day had married into a fascinating mix of racial and ethnic backgrounds and

varied life-styles. There were ruddy farmers in jeans and
crisp blue chambray and cattlemen in Stetsons and boots;
muscular young men in sleeveless T-shirts that revealed
more than one tattoo; men in sport shirts and slacks and
with the unmistakable pallor of the city. There were teen-
agers in the latest clothes and children who might have
stepped out of a Norman Rockwell painting—lots of children and babies. And the women... What Cam noticed
about the women was that, old or young, plump or ma-
tronly, bloomingly pregnant or professionally chic, they all
had that warmth and genuineness that he'd first noticed in
Suzanna.

In the middle of all the bustle and activity, Sarah Day sat
in the shade on a hard folding chair; a tiny woman, she was
a young and indomitable spirit trapped in an incredibly
fragile shell of a body. Her face wore the patient and se-
renely vacant gaze of extreme age, but when Suzanna took
her hand and kissed her cheek, she broke instantly into a
bright smile of delighted recognition and welcome. She
accepted Cam's hand and acknowledged Suzanna's intro-
duction without comment, nodding and beaming, and
then said abruptly in a voice that kept breaking, "You
know, my father used to wear collars like that. Of course
he only wore them to church—they were too uncomfortable to work in. And too much trouble!" And then, to
Suzanna, she said, "You look very nice. Very pretty. You
remind me of my mother when she was quite young." Her
gray eyes crinkled with humor, and she leaned forward
slightly to add in a rusty whisper, "But you must be aw-
fully *hot*!"

As he stood patiently listening to Suzanna and her
grandmother, Cam was thinking that Harland Day wasn't
the only one possessed of strength and spirit and an iron
will.

But the old lady was right; it was hot. A brassy, oppressive heat he'd seen too many times before. As hard as he tried to concentrate on Suzanna and her family and enjoy himself, he kept watching the darkening sky and listening to the sounds of distant thunder.

"Forget it," Tony O'Brian told him, coming quietly up behind him and handing him a plastic bowl filled with homemade ice cream. "There's nothing you can do about it, anyway."

"About what?" Cam said irritably.

"The weather. That's something farmers have to learn, you know. There's not a darn thing you can do about the weather except get old worrying about it."

"Yeah..." Cam sighed, "I know. How are things coming on your end? Everything set to go?"

"Tomorrow morning, bright and early," Tony promised, and added with an irrepressible twinkle, "Rain or shine."

"Yeah, well I just hope we have that long. Tomorrow's a long way off, and something sure as hell's happening up in those canyons right now."

"Like I said, you can't control it, so quit worrying about it," Tony said, giving him a long, steady look. "You've done all you can. Come on—drink that ice cream and let's go play baseball before we get rained out!"

"STRIKE TWO," the umpire said.

"Strike?" Cam repeated, his voice rising in indignation. "Come on, Tony!"

Tony pushed his thick glasses up onto the bridge of his nose and looked unperturbed.

"Time," Suzanna yelled, stepping off the folded gunnysack that was third base and beckoning to Cam. As they met halfway betwen third and home plate, there was a portentous rumble of thunder that made them both glance reflexively upward. Suzanna took off her cap and wiped her face with a dusty forearm. "How are you at bunting?"

"Bunting?" He'd been grinning at her, probably amused by her pigtails and smudges. When Suzanna played baseball, which she dearly loved, she did so with tomboyish abandon, and damn the torn pants and skinned elbows! Now, however, Cam's smile became a frown of disbelief. "With two strikes and two outs? You gotta be kidding!"

"I'm not talking sacrifice. I'm talking suicide squeeze."

"Suicide! That's cr—"

"Shh!" She moved close to him and spoke out of the side of her mouth. "The way I see it, we're about five minutes away from a deluge here, right? Score's tied—all we need is one run, the rains come down and we win."

"Sure, if it works."

"It'll work. Listen, that pitcher is Frankie Crosetti—he pitched for the high school varsity last year. He's going to come right down the middle with a fastball, I guarantee it. All you have to do is lay one down right up the first-base line and then get out of my way."

"Don't like it," Cam said, looking mulish. "You could get hurt."

"I hate to pull rank," Suzanna said sweetly, "but who's captain of this team?"

"Sue," Cam grumbled, looking wounded, "I hope you realize this is a very un-Victorian attitude. All right, I'll do it. But I don't like it."

Tony called time-in. Cam stepped up to the plate, and Suzanna took her lead at third. Frankie Crosetti stared down from the mound while thunder crashed and rolled all around them. Suzanna felt a large drop of rain on her nose and glanced up at the sky with satisfaction. Perfect.

Frankie went into his windup. Suzanna didn't see Cam square around to bunt; she already had her head down and was charging full tilt down the line. She heard shouts, alarm and outrage from the defense and encouragement from her own team. Above them all she heard Cam yelling, "Slide, slide!"

She hit the ground and the catcher—her cousin Edna's husband Rusty, who drove a truck—at the same time. As she lay in the dust, blinking and dazed, she heard Tony yell, "Safe!" Several drops of rain struck her in the face.

"Sue, Sue, are you okay?" Cam was bending over her, looking grave and concerned. "Geez, you guys play for keeps!"

She grinned up at him. "What did I tell you?"

"You're crazy! I missed the damn bunt. Your pitcher threw a curve that missed everything, including the catcher, or you'd have been hung out to dry! You're a lunatic—I always said so, didn't I?"

"Hush—it worked, didn't it?" Suzanna said smugly, and hooking an arm around his neck, pulled his head down and kissed him.

Around them the battle was raging. Frankie was yelling at Rusty, Rusty was yelling at Frankie, and both were yelling at Tony, who had just called the game on account of rain. The staccato patter of large drops in the dust had become a roar.

"Let's get out of this!" Cam said, pulling Suzanna to her feet. His hair was already streaming, and his T-shirt was plastered to his back. Looking down at herself, Suzanna nodded wordlessly and took his hand, and together they sprinted for the car.

THE SUDDEN VIOLENCE of the thunderstorm had given way
to a steady downpour. In the murky false twilight, Angel's
Walk looked lonely and forsaken. It seemed to huddle in
the rain like a lost animal, dormer windows like half-closed
eyes, patient and resigned to its misery.

In the car, Cam reached into the back seat to find the
plastic suit bag that held the Victorian costumes and gave
it to Suzanna.

"You aren't coming," she said in a flat voice, gathering
the bag into her arms. His hand came out to trace the curve
of her cheek, and then silently he pulled her into his arms.
For a few minutes they listened to the steady thumping of
the windshield wipers, and then Cam took her arms and
held her gently but firmly away from him.

"Sue," he said with gravel in his voice, "I want you to
do something for me." His face was grave, his eyes dusky
shadows without expression. Her heart began to keep time
with the windshield wipers. "You've got to get ready to
evacuate."

Her head moved in violent denial, but his fingers tightened on her arms, compelling her to silence. "*Please.*
Promise me. Just the necessities—mine and yours. And the
irreplaceables—your book notes, photographs. Papa's
tapes. If I can't—just be ready for me when I come for
you. Promise me. Please, Sue."

She nodded silently. He pulled her against him and gave
her a hard, almost-desperate kiss that made her think of
that night on the front porch. He'd been leaving her then,
too; leaving her to face disaster all alone.

Although it was only late afternoon, the house was dark.
Almost in defiance, Suzanna went from room to room,
upstairs and down, turning on all the lights.

She had only one suitcase, a small overnighter. She used
it for her precious notes and photographs and put her

clothes and personal things in a cardboard packing box. Cam's things were simpler—he was used to moving around. His gear fit nicely in his one suitcase, and his portable radio and Springsteen tapes could go in Cat's tote bag, since she wouldn't be needing it anymore. Poor Cat. Suzanna wondered what had become of her and whether she was safely out of the rain.

The telephone began to ring while she was finishing the packing, and for once in her life she ran to answer it.

"Wow," Meg shouted at her over the bad connection, "that has to be some kind of record! Four rings. And you're out of breath—is everything all right?"

"I thought it might be Cam. Oh, Meg, this rain—it's a disaster, isn't it? Cam's told me I have to get ready to evacuate."

"Oh, Suzanna—"

"How's everybody up that way?" Suzanna hastily interrupted, knowing that sympathy would probably give her the excuse she needed to give in to despair. "How's Grandmother?"

"Mom and Dad took her home with them when it started to rain. She fussed blue murder, of course—she just wants to go home—but everybody insisted, so for once she had to give in. If Kelso Creek floods, her place would be cut off, maybe for days."

Suzanna murmured agreement. "Has there been any flash flooding yet?"

"Dad drove up the canyon about an hour ago to see what the creek was doing. He couldn't get past the mouth of Short Canyon. Suzanna, you just wouldn't believe it. The water's cut a gully right across the road, and it's buried one house in the Calder tract up to its eaves in mud already! Several homes have been washed out there, and I've heard it's even worse down around the lake. Can you imagine what's going to happen if this keeps up? This high desert country just isn't made to take rain like this. They're calling it a hundred-year flood. Tony says it's a tropical storm in the Pacific and that all of Southern California is in the same boat— Oh, listen to me. We might all be needing boats by tomorrow. Hey—do you need any help? Maybe I'd better come down there and—''

"Don't worry about me. I'll be all right," Suzanna said staunchly, hoping it was true. "Cam said he'd come for me if I need to leave."

After hanging up, she went out to the back porch to look for more boxes. There was a little lull in the storm right then; the rain had almost stopped. In the relative quiet, Suzanna heard a soft clanking sound. Intrigued, she went to the screen door and looked out. And that was when she discovered that the backyard was under water.

The clanking noise was made by the skunk's feed pans, floating in several inches of muddy water and bumping gently against each other and the porch step.

Suzanna stood staring at the bobbing pans in numbed disbelief. It was happening, really happening. Help, and hope, had come too late. Angel's Walk was doomed.

Chapter Fourteen

She didn't know how long she stood there, looking at the murky water. Sounds and a flurry of movement in the kitchen finally brought her out of her daze, and she turned back into the house.

Mrs. Hopewell was standing in the kitchen, shaking water out of a rusty black umbrella. She wore a yellow slicker, red boots and a flowered plastic accordion-fold rain bonnet—the kind prepared people always seem to carry in their purses.

"Oh, there you are," she said briskly, thrusting the umbrella at Suzanna as she began to deal with the slicker's fastenings. "I think perhaps you'd better put these things out on the porch, Suzanna. They'll make a puddle. I didn't like to leave them dripping out in the hallway—they'll spoil that lovely runner your great-aunt Marsha put down."

Suzanna tried to stifle a high bark of half-hysterical laughter. "Mrs. Hopewell, I don't think a few drops of water will make much difference. In a little while—"

The indomitable old lady gave her a quelling glare. "Don't invite disaster before it comes, Suzanna. Until the water arrives, there is still hope. Now, put on the kettle, dear. I've brought you some tea."

"Mrs. Hopewell," Suzanna said, pressing a hand to her forehead in exasperation, "the water *is* here. It's out there, right now."

"Well, it isn't in here. Not yet. You must not give in to hysteria. The kettle, please, Suzanna. A cup of herb tea will do you good, dear. It will help to calm your nerves."

Suzanna didn't want her nerves calmed. She didn't want to be strong and adult about this; she wanted to rant and rage and scream at the fates and the elements that had done this to her. She wanted to have someone else be strong and hold her tightly and stroke her back while she sobbed out her grief and frustration. She didn't want Mrs. Hopewell's tea; she wanted *Cam*. And half the anger and pain she felt was directed at him, for abandoning her again, for leaving her alone to cope, just when she needed him most.

But, she told herself angrily, that was the thing about balloons. If you tried to lean on them they just popped, leaving you with nothing.

"Where on earth did you get these?"

Suzanna started and turned from the stove. Mrs. Hopewell was holding up the pair of high-buttoned shoes she had left on the table. "Cam brought them," she said with a reluctant smile, and went on to tell Mrs. Hopewell about Cam's wonderful Memorial Day surprise. How long ago this morning seemed—as long ago as Victorian times.

"Where is your young man this evening?" Mrs. Hopewell asked when Suzanna had finished, dropping the shoes onto the table.

Suzanna shrugged irritably. "I don't know. And why do you keep calling him 'my young man'? He isn't anybody's young man—least of all mine!" She sniffed, touched her nose and glowered at Mrs. Hopewell over her hand.

Mrs. Hopewell gazed shrewdly back at her. "Because," she said firmly, "you are very much in love with him." There was a pause, and then, with characteristic directness, she asked, "Have you told him?"

Suzanna stared at her in horror. "No! Of course not." Behind her, the teakettle began to whistle. She set it off the burner with an angry thud.

"Why not?" Mrs. Hopewell's strong, cool hands gently but firmly rescued the tea things and steered Suzanna to a chair.

"I just can't," she confessed, and then laughed painfully. "I think it would probably frighten him to death if he knew how I felt about him."

"I very much doubt that," Mrs. Hopewell said mildly, pouring tea. "What makes you say such a thing?"

Suzanna jumped up to pace restlessly. Mrs. Hopewell sat calmly waiting.

"He's a vagabond!" Suzanna cried suddenly, tired of holding in her emotions. "He's nothing but a wanderer. An adventurer. He just goes from place to place on these troubleshooting jobs of his and never forms any attachments or makes any commitments—nothing that might tie him down. No roots. No strings, that's his motto. And that's what I promised him—no strings!"

"Suzanna, calm yourself," Mrs. Hopewell commanded. "And when you have done so and are capable of thinking rationally, you might consider that one may run *to* as well as *from*."

The cryptic statement was so unlike Mrs. Hopewell that Suzanna stopped pacing to stare at her. "What do you mean?"

"My dear, I mean that while one may indeed wander to avoid commitment, one may also wander in search of it.

Has it ever occurred to you that Mr. Harris may be looking for those roots you think he is trying to avoid?''

Suzanna shook her head. And then, as the idea began to take on dimensions, she said, ''But how would I know? How can you tell the difference?''

''Quite simply,'' Mrs. Hopewell said briskly. ''Tell him how you feel about him and see what happens.''

''Oh, no,'' Suzanna murmured in horror, shaking her head. ''I couldn't. I mean, what if—''

''Suzanna, you are not a coward.'' Mrs. Hopewell sat very straight, and her eyes were fierce and direct. ''There comes a time in every relationship when you must place your cards on the table and declare yourself, no matter what the risk. Anything worth having is certainly worth taking that risk for, isn't it?'' Her face relaxed suddenly into a smile of unheralded gentleness. ''My dear, it might interest you to know that *I* proposed marriage to Mr. Hopewell. Had I not,'' she added with a return to her customary crispness, ''I am quite certain I would have gone to my grave as Miss Amelia Dill!''

The silence that followed was suddenly filled with the deafening rumble and crash of thunder. Mrs. Hopewell caught Suzanna's hand and gave it a hard squeeze.

''Tell him, Suzanna. What have you got to lose?''

Suzanna set her lips and nodded. She would tell him, if she ever got the chance. But where *was* he? The thunder was frightening—an almost-continuous, deafening roar that shook the house. Lightning flickered and stabbed at the windows as if trying to gain entry. *Cam,* she prayed in silent desperation, *please come....*

''Suzanna,'' Mrs. Hopewell said suddenly, ''that is not thunder.''

Suzanna stood frozen for several seconds, listening intently and staring at the lights that flickered beyond the rain-streaked windows. Then she bolted for the door. As she ran down the hallway, she heard Mrs. Hopewell call, "Suzanna—take my umbrella! You'll catch cold!"

But she got no farther than the front porch. Angel's Walk had become an island in a vast sea of confusion and turmoil. The early darkness was a seething tapestry of sound and motion rent by slashes and stabs of light. The rush of the wind and rain had become mere background for the harder, percussive roars of huge behemoths that prowled through the deluge beyond the yard. Earth movers; bulldozers; tractors of every kind and description; a generator truck with huge floodlights; men in slickers waving their arms in silent shouts, oblivious to the rain that ran in torrents down their faces; a voice on a bullhorn, shouting orders and directions. A familiar voice.

It was a scene from Dante. And the man who suddenly appeared at the foot of the steps could have crawled straight out of the pits of hell. He wore only mud-caked jeans and heavy rubber boots; the lights and the rain turned his body to polished bronze and glanced off his hard hat like sparks. His face was a mask of mud, and when he took off his hat, the rain made pale tracks down his cheeks. In that dark mask, his eyes were only darker smudges, and so it was almost a shock to have the mask split into an exultant grin.

"Cam…" Suzanna breathed, and felt her stomach twist and her knees buckle.

He made a futile swipe at his face with a hand that was even muddier. Suzanna's eyes were pulled from his face to the bullhorn that dangled by a strap from his wrist.

"Cam," she gasped, "what is this? What's going on?"

"What's going on? I'll tell you—" There was a wildness about him, an exuberance she hadn't seen in him before. She wondered for one brief moment if he could be drunk. "Sweetheart, we are building you a levee! Don't know why it took me so long to think of it—must be losing my touch. Fact is—you're the one who said it. 'You . . . build dams and levees.' And by God, that's what I'm doing. Took a while longer than I thought it would, and I've jumped the gun a little bit on the red tape, but—"

"Cam, where did all these people come from? Where did you get all this stuff? Who are all these people?"

"They're your neighbors!" Cam lifted his arms and burst into exultant laughter. "Your *neighbors*. And you said that, too, sweetheart. In a place like this, your neighbors come when you need help."

"My neighbors . . . but I don't have any—No one who knows how or has the equipment—"

"Well, a few of these guys are friends of mine, and some of the equipment is rented or borrowed. But—"

A huge shape lumbered out of the darkness, wearing a sodden sleeveless nylon vest and a once-white T-shirt. "Hey, Cam—what d'you want us to do about the trees in that orchard over there?"

"If they're in the way, mow 'em," Cam shouted. "All that matters is the house!"

The giant nodded and loped away across the lawn.

"That wasn't—" Suzanna said in a strangled croak. *"Elwood?"*

"Sure was, and Ron's out there on a Cat, too. Most of the guys in your family are here with their tractors. That's Tony in the light truck. Oh, and Lucy's here with her camera."

"You're building a levee," Suzanna said, shaking her head as if that might have any effect at all on the fog of shock and confusion that had settled upon her brain. "For me? I don't understand."

"Nothing fancy—" Cam made a sweeping gesture with his arm that encompassed the house. "Just a nice little wall of earth to keep the water out of Angel's Walk. Can't let a historical treasure like this get wet, can we?"

"Historical? Cam, did you—Angel's Walk isn't a historical landmark!"

He shrugged, looking unabashed. "Well, it will be, as soon as the bureaucrats get around to it. I may have speeded things up a little, but they'll thank me later."

"Cam, you could lose your job over this!"

He lifted his shoulders and grinned. He started toward her, then looked down at himself and stopped short of touching her. "Sue, sweetheart, go on back inside. Put on some coffee. I'll give you all the details later. I just wanted you to know—" He stopped, because Suzanna wasn't looking at him any longer. She was looking down at her feet. Something warm and furry was winding around her ankles.

"Cat!" Suzanna cried, dropping to her heels to gather the animal into her arms. "Oh, Cat." And she began to cry. She buried her face in the cat's damp fur and laughed and cried and babbled, "Oh, Cat, you rascal. Where have you been? Cam, look, she's back. And she's fine, just fine. Aren't you, you—"

She looked up then and caught a look on Cam's face that wrung her heart. As she watched, his face slowly turned to stone. She saw his throat move convulsively, and then in a cold, hard voice he snapped, "Told you she was an opportunist. She sure knows where to turn when she needs help. Damn cat . . ."

He jammed the hard hat back onto his head and turned abruptly away. Suzanna stared after him in stunned disbelief. He really was going to try to make himself—and her—believe he didn't care!

"John Harris," she screamed, "you come back here!" And she launched herself off the porch and down the steps into the deluge. Cat gave one yowl of outrage at being forced to abandon her refuge on the porch and then tried to bury her head under Suzanna's arm. "You stop right there, you—you fraud!" She grabbed at his arm, shouting at him with fury and joy while rain streamed into her eyes, blinding her. "You...love...this cat! I know you do. Admit it, damn you—admit it." And she thrust the squirming wet cat into his arms.

He stood blinking away raindrops and holding the cat, staring at Suzanna as if she'd just arrived from another planet. "Sue, for God's sake, I've got a job to do."

"Oh, yeah? Why? Why are you doing this, John? Tell me!"

"What do you mean, *why*! Dammit, it's your house, that's why! And it means more to you than anything in the whole world—right? So take this cat and let me save your house for you!"

"Wrong!" Suzanna screamed at him. "You're wrong, dead wrong!" Her hands gripped his arms, shaking him with all her strength. Her throat was raw with the strain of trying to make him hear her through the racket of the storm and machinery, of trying to break through the blockade that protected his emotions. For a few terrible moments she thought she'd failed. He was like a rock, unmoved and immovable. And then his fingers stirred in Cat's fur. With tears choking her, she watched the rough, strong hands try to smooth the rain-rumpled hair while the cat twisted her body in a frantic effort to rub her head against his arm.

"Wrong," she said again. The word was a sob. Her voice had broken and was almost inaudible in all the storm and fury. "*You* are the most important thing in the world to me, John Harris, not this house. It's just a house. I love you. I love you. I don't care about the house. I *don't*. Oh, John, I—"

The hard hat and bullhorn both hit the cement with a crack. Cat leaped from Cam's arms and went like a streak for the shelter of the porch. He hooked an arm around her waist and pulled her hard against him, holding her as if his world would disintegrate if he let her go, his arms wrapped around her and his face buried in her hair. He didn't say a word, but the violent tremors that coursed through his body told Suzanna all she needed to know.

"I love you, John Harris," she said fiercely, stroking his wet hair. "I don't care about the house. It's just a house. I'll build another one. I just want—"

"*I* care!" His hands tangled in her hair, pulling her head back so he could look into her face. "I care." His eyes closed, and when he drew her back against him, his voice sounded raw, as if it hurt him to talk. "I want to live in this house . . . with you. I want our children to grow up in this house. Sue, let me save Angel's Walk—for us."

Aching and trembling, she nodded and pulled away, touching her nose with the back of her hand. "All right . . . all right." She kept breaking into jerky, laughing sobs. "I suppose you have to go now."

"Yes," he said intently, "but I'll be back. You know I'll always be back."

Suzanna hesitated only a moment and then smiled and lifted her face fearlessly to his, and to the rain.

"JOHN," SUZANNA SAID, laughing with loving exasperation, "what do you think you're doing?"

"Hush," Cam replied, taking a deep breath. "I've waited six months for this."

"Most grooms," Suzanna said, addressing the high ceiling with resignation, "are content just to carry their brides across the threshold. But not you— Oh, help!" She hid her face in the hollow of his neck and hung on for dear life while he carried her up the stairs, two at a time.

He kicked open the door to the master bedroom and lowered her feet carefully to the floor. "Welcome home, Mrs. Harris."

"Welcome home, Mr. Harris." She leaned into his kiss with a sigh and then turned her back and bowed her head. "Would you care to do the honors?"

A curious void opened up in the pit of his stomach. He wondered if his fingers would be steady enough to manage all the buttons on the high-necked ivory lace antique gown.

As soon as the top few buttons were undone, he lowered his mouth to the first vulnerable bump in her spine. She swayed, and he put his hands on her waist to steady her.

"Mmm," she said thickly, "I told you these clothes were meant to be shared. John . . ."

"Hmm?"

"I never asked you—where did you get the clothes? The Memorial Day costumes and my wedding gown."

"In Sacramento," he murmured. "When I went to arrange for the spillway. They were in a department-store window display. I thought they looked like you."

"And they *sold* them to you?"

"Well, I had to promise them our firstborn."

"John," she said softly, sounding breathless, "did you really feel that way about me, even then? To buy a wedding gown?"

He'd made it to the last button, his lips following his fingers all the way to the base of her spine. Now he pushed the two halves of the dress forward, and she pulled her arms free. "I knew," he answered, and turning her, pressed his mouth to the petal-soft skin of her belly. "But there was Angel's Walk."

"Uh-huh, it did get between us a little." Her fingers were trying to dispose of his collar and tie. "John—" she gasped suddenly, "if you don't stop doing that, I'll never manage this—Oh, help."

MUCH, MUCH LATER, she remembered the subject. "John, I think she's going to be happy here, don't you?"

"Who, Cat?" he asked sleepily. His face was cradled between her breasts, and her fingers were combing idly through his hair.

"No, Angel's Walk."

"Oh." He lay still a moment, listening to the wind in the bull pines. It was autumn, and the wind had a lonely sound. "Well, I think she'll feel better when we get the lawns in."

"And the fence. Don't forget the white picket fence."

"I know, I know . . . with roses."

"Rambling roses. Red ones."

"Right."

"And an apple orchard. And currant bushes and Virginia creeper and—"

"But no bees," Cam put in, lifting his head.

"No bees," Suzanna agreed, lifting her head to meet his kiss.

Her mouth was so soft and sweet; under him her body stirred, molding to his as naturally as if she were a part of him. He couldn't believe how much he loved her. How much he needed her. With a sigh he moved his mouth to her throat and put his hand under her, to lift her more fully against him.

And something vibrated across his back; something no more tangible than a premonition or the feeling that he wasn't alone. It came again, and his spine contracted; he couldn't help it.

"Sue," he whispered hoarsely. "I don't believe this, but that isn't—It can't be—"

"Yes," she said, looking beyond him and shaking with silent laughter. "It is. It's Maggie."

Harlequin American Romance

COMING NEXT MONTH

#153 SHADOWS by Stella Cameron

Leah knew she was gambling her future on a man she'd met only once, but Guy had offered his help one lonely night. When she arrived on his doorstep, she understood that Guy was bound to help her. Leah saw, too, that the feelings she'd harbored for him would have to be forgotten. But how could that be, when those feelings were all she had left?

#154 MACKENZIE'S LADY by Dallas Schulze

It began so innocently, as a quest for a friend's stolen watch, but Holly was quickly subjected to the horrors of multiple propositions, a barroom brawl and a dubious rescue by an unsavory character named Mackenzie. She yearned for home— for safety—but with Mac still on her heels, she feared how the adventure would end.

#155 MINOR MIRACLES by Rebecca Flanders

Leslie watched the demonstration of supernatural strength as Michael Bradshaw melted iron chains, boiled water and caused disconnected phones to ring—using nothing more than the power of his mind. She was trained to seek rational explanations, but when his topaz eyes smiled at her through the two-way mirror, she could only wonder: exactly what was Michael Bradshaw?

#156 HEAVEN SHARED by Cathy Gillen Thacker

For years the Cavanaughs dreamed of having a baby, but it never happened. Then the fertility pills paid off. Ellie's pregnancy seemed to occur at the wrong time: her law career was taking off and Neil was busier than ever at the hospital. Could they expect a second miracle—could they expect the baby to sort out their tangled lives?

Take 4 books & a surprise gift FREE

SPECIAL LIMITED-TIME OFFER

Mail to **Harlequin Reader Service** ®

In the U.S.	In Canada
901 Fuhrmann Blvd.	P.O. Box 2800, Station "A"
P.O. Box 1394	5170 Yonge Street
Buffalo, N.Y. 14240-1394	Willowdale, Ontario M2N 6J3

YES! Please send me 4 free Harlequin American Romance ® novels and my free surprise gift. Then send me 4 brand-new novels as they come off the presses. Bill me at the low price of $2.25 each —a 11% saving off the retail price. There are no shipping, handling or other hidden costs. There is no minimum number of books I must purchase. I can always return a shipment and cancel at any time. Even if I never buy another book from Harlequin, the 4 free novels and the surprise gift are mine to keep forever.

154-BPA-BP6S

Name _____ (PLEASE PRINT)

Address _____ Apt. No. _____

City _____ State/Prov. _____ Zip/Postal Code _____

This offer is limited to one order per household and not valid to present subscribers. Price is subject to change.   DOAR-SUB-1R

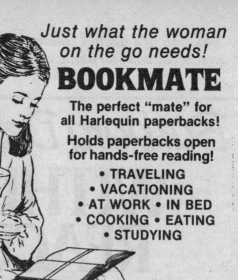
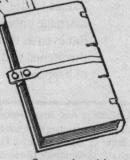